SOLVING

Sophronia

A Victorian Romance

OTHER BOOKS AND AUDIOBOOKS
BY JENNIFER MOORE

REGENCY ROMANCE
Becoming Lady Lockwood
Lady Emma's Campaign
Miss Burton Unmasks a Prince
Simply Anna
Lady Helen Finds Her Song
A Place for Miss Snow
Miss Whitaker Opens Her Heart
Miss Leslie's Secret

THE WAR OF 1812
My Dearest Enemy
The Shipbuilder's Wife
Charlotte's Promise

THE BLUE ORCHID SOCIETY
Solving Sophronia

STAND-ALONE NOVELLAS
"The Perfect Christmas" in *Christmas Treasures*
"Let Nothing You Dismay" in *Christmas Grace*
"Love and Joy Come to You" in *A Christmas Courting*

SOLVING
Sophronia

A Victorian Romance

JENNIFER MOORE

Covenant Communications, Inc.

Cover image: *Regency Woman on Grand Building Steps* © ILINA SIMEONOVA / Trevillion Images
Cover design by Natalie Brown

Cover design copyright © 2020 by Covenant Communications, Inc.

Published by Covenant Communications, Inc.
American Fork, Utah

Printed in the United States of America
First Printing: May 2020

27 26 25 24 23 22 21 20   10 9 8 7 6 5 4 3 2 1

ISBN: 978-1-52441-235-7

For Margot,
the Crabtree to my Higgins

PRAISE FOR
JENNIFER MOORE

"All the delightful characters, historical detail, and charm I expect from a Jennifer Moore novel, along with a new time period and a clever mystery that keeps those pages turning. I can't wait to see what the rest of this series holds!"

—Josi S. Kilpack, author *Rakes and Roses*

"Jennifer Moore's new series, The Blue Orchid Society, is off to a spectacular start with *Solving Sophronia*. We have all the hallmarks of the author's creative dialogue, beautiful prose, and impeccable research, set in atmospheric Victorian London. The reader is subtly and deftly drawn into the story, sinking into Sophie's mind and heart, which are timely representations of a young woman's desire to stretch beyond traditional boundaries and utilize her skills. Reading *Solving Sophronia* was an absolute pleasure; this author tells a darn good story."

—Nancy Campbell Allen, author *Brass Carriages and Glass Hearts*

"Moore . . . launches her vivid Victorian-era Blue Orchid Society series with this romantic murder mystery that sees a gutsy upper-class Londoner defying the rigid expectations of her time.

"The detailed descriptions and gentle push and pull between the couple will please readers looking for chaste historical romance. A plucky heroine and engrossing mystery make this a treat."

—*Publishers Weekly*

ACKNOWLEDGMENTS

TRYING SOMETHING NEW IS TRULY scary, and this story and series are like nothing I've ever done before. The genre and time period really made me stretch. And plotting out five books at a time was more complicated than I thought it would be. So I am enormously grateful to the people who helped turn my scattered thoughts and unsure ideas into a book.

First of all, so much thanks to my sister, Mandy Kimball. When I asked if she had any ideas of where to research Victorian-era crime solving, she brought me a stack of criminal justice and Jack the Ripper books. She's been an indispensable source of weird, interesting, and sometimes really creepy information as I tried to figure out how this mystery could play out.

Carla Kelly (*The Unlikely Spy Catchers*) was, as always, full of ideas for research sources—newsletters, movies, books, etc.—to give me a feel for the time period. That woman knows where to find anything—including yummy restaurants.

Jen Geigle Johnson (*A Lady's Maid*), thank you so much for your excellent information about women's suffrage in England. Your love of the subject radiates in your words and books.

Esther Hatch (*A Proper Scandal*) and Marion Jensen (*Searching for Super*), thank you for helping me figure out the Russian bit of the story.

And my dad, Ed (Starješina) Lunt, thank you for helping me with the Serbian names and history.

As always, thank you to my critique partners: Josi Kilpack (*Rakes and Roses*) and Nancy Campbell Allen (*The Lady in the Coppergate Tower*) for all the brainstorming and plotting and character help. There is so much of you two in this story, and at times, it felt like you understood what I was trying to do better than I did.

Margot Hovley (*Glimmering Light*), thank you for being my reader, for keeping me accountable every day, and for fully joining my obsession with *Murdoch Mysteries*.

Thank you to my publisher, Covenant Communications, for taking a chance on me and on this series. Kami Hancock, your editing goes above and beyond fixing punctuation, and I'm so grateful for your listening ear and marvelous ideas. Natalie Brown, this cover is splendid. You perfectly captured the feel I was looking for but couldn't quite explain.

And always, thanks to Frank and my boys: James, Ben, Andrew, and Joey. Having a mom who spends so much time in imaginary worlds gets old and, I'm sure, frustrating. Thanks for being patient and for understanding when I forget things because I'm writing. You five guys are my heart.

PROLOGUE

April 19, 1873

LADY SOPHRONIA BREMERTON GLANCED TOWARD the ballroom doors, calculating her chances of a discreet exit. Her Ladyship the Marchioness of Molyneaux's invitation to her annual ball held the Saturday after Easter was the most coveted of the Season; therefore, Sophie could hardly claim boredom as her reason for wishing to leave.

The Viscount of Kensington and Lord Hawthorne had already claimed a waltz, and three separate countesses had offered to accompany Sophie to A Private View at the Royal Academy. But Sophie didn't flatter herself that her charms or others' desire for her company were to be credited for the attention. Rather, her position as a society reporter for the *Illustrated London News* made the members of England's upper class either seek her out or deliberately avoid her.

The grand clock echoed through the ballroom, chiming eleven. She'd arrived just after nine. Two hours of dancing and socializing should sufficiently please her parents. She looked across the room, trying to catch a glimpse of the feathers in her mother's hair. Truth be told, her parents would likely not notice her absence—not when her sister had waltzed with the future Duke of Norwood.

Moving at a quick pace, Sophie made her escape. She hurried along the edge of the crowded ballroom toward the entrance, giving only polite nods and avoiding direct eye contact with anyone who might hope to bend her ear with a whisper of gossip.

Reporting rumors, scandals, and on-dits of the upper class was her occupation, but tonight she had no interest in discovering a story. She already knew what her next report would be, and it was hardly news. She smirked, certain the young lady involved would feign adequate surprise when the announcement was made, as would the other guests. London Society kept a secret as effectively as a wicker basket held water.

Tonight the Marquess of Molyneaux was to announce the engagement of his son and heir, Lord Ruben. The identity of the lucky young lady who would one day become the marchioness was, of course, taken for granted. Lord Ruben and Miss Dahlia Lancaster had carried on the most intentionally visible and highly gossiped-about courtship in decades. Sophie had written so many articles and created enough illustrations of the pair that she was relieved the nonsense would finally come to an end. She would, however, need to endure a conspicuous engagement . . . and then the wedding.

Sophie blew out a breath as she neared the doorway. How she longed to move away from the society columns and turn her skills to uncovering a real story—an important story about something that mattered, not just which member of high Society wore the most extravagant gown or had deliberately avoided a particular soiree to spite a rival. Unfortunately, Mr. Leonard, the editor of the broadsheet paper, valued Sophie's artistic ability and access to high-Society events above her investigative skills.

"Lady Sophronia?"

Drat. The voice was too near for Sophie to pretend she hadn't heard. She masked her irritation with a pleasant smile and turned.

Lord Everleigh stepped around a group of matrons. When he reached Sophie, he took her hand and bowed stiffly. "Good evening."

As usual, the man's clothing was impeccable. Slender and pale-skinned, he wore his fair hair short, parted smartly on the side. A waxed mustache graced his upper lip. Sophie inclined her head. "Lord Everleigh."

"I'd hoped to engage your sister for the next waltz." He released her hand and clasped his own behind his back, glancing toward the dancers. "Have you an idea where I might find her?"

Sophie should have guessed his reason for stopping her. She and the future Earl of Kirkham had only exchanged the briefest greetings in the past, and although they moved in the same social circles, she would hardly call the man more than a very remote acquaintance.

"I believe she is there, near the west windows." Sophie lifted her chin toward the far side of the ballroom, where a cluster of young ladies gossiped and preened. Her younger sister, Priscilla, was no doubt the very center of the group. "At least, that is where I last saw her."

"Very good. Thank you." He moved as if to leave but stopped, perhaps thinking it rude not to bestow a compliment or at least engage in some conversation.

For her part, Sophie was perfectly happy to forego niceties and hasten her departure.

"I, ah, enjoyed your latest article, my lady." Lord Everleigh ran a finger over his mustache and glanced across the ballroom again. "Something about spring fashions on the Brighton Palace Pier, wasn't it?" He looked down at her and nodded. "Very cute."

Sophie bowed her head so he couldn't see her nostrils flare. She was so tired of patronizing tones when it came to her work. *I am beyond ready to move on to something real.* "Thank you, my lord."

"If you'll excuse me." He straightened his neckcloth, making the large ruby of his tiepin gleam in the light of the gas lamps, gave another bow, and then strode away.

That ruby tiepin, given to him by Lord Ruben—who thought the gem a clever play on his name—identified Lord Everleigh as a member of an elite group: the West End Casanovas. Sophie had first used the appellation in an article, intending it as sarcasm, but the group had been delighted by the moniker and had adopted it as their own. The five Casanovas were extremely handsome and tremendously wealthy young men, each coming from old and established families and each an heir apparent to a high-ranking title. The men had attended school together at Eton and university at Oxford and were considered by all of London to be the most eligible bachelors in the kingdom. They were the future leaders of the country, and nearly every unattached young lady and her mother aspired to catch the attention of one of them.

Sophie suspected Lord Ruben, as self-appointed leader of the group, had delayed his engagement for just that reason. Though he had courted Dahlia Lancaster for two Seasons, his attentions had by no means been exclusively to her. He enjoyed the role of flirt, and Sophie thought he must be reluctant to give up the game and commit to matrimony.

Before anyone else could approach her, she quickly made her way through the entrance and down the wide passageway of the grand London home, passing sculptures and paintings but giving them hardly a look as she walked on the thick carpet of a side passage. Surely there was a quiet room where she could find respite from false smiles, petty gossip, and backhanded compliments.

Ahead a band of light glowed beneath a door. When she pulled it open and peeked inside, wooden shelves, heavy with leather books, glowed in the light of gas lamps. Before the lit hearth was a deep sofa and plush leather chairs that implored her to set herself at ease, forget her insecurities and frustrations, and pretend the ball was far away.

Stepping across the threshold, Sophie felt lighter already. She lowered herself into a soft armchair, rested her head back, and closed her eyes. Even before the newspaper had employed her, she'd dreaded situations in which she was expected to play the games of Society. Acting one way and thinking another was contrary to her nature, a trait that did little to win friends or the approval of her parents.

And the discomfort had only become greater when Priscilla was launched into Society last year at the age of eighteen. Sophie was only two-and-a-half years older, and sisters so close in age naturally invited comparison; next to Prissy, Sophie's shortcomings felt all the more obvious. She wasn't tall, blonde, and slender like her sister, but short with drab brown hair, and she struggled to keep her waist shapely, even with the strongest whalebone corset.

Hearing a sound, she started from her thoughts, rose quickly to her feet, and looked around the room.

On a chair in the darkened far corner, a young woman hunched over with her face in her hands, elbows on her knees.

Sophie cleared her throat, uncertain what to say. "I beg your pardon. I did not realize anyone was here." Now that Sophie saw her, she realized the woman's breath was coming in gasps, a sound she'd first assumed was made by the fire. Sophie walked nearer and crouched down as sympathy replaced her unease. "I didn't mean to intrude."

The woman raised her face, and Sophie recognized her as Miss Hazel Thornton. Though Sophie didn't know her personally, she had heard the young woman had recently come to live with relatives in London while her father, a general in Her Majesty's army, was stationed in Africa. Sophie had heard rumors that Miss Thornton had endured some trauma in India and was prone to attacks of panic. She presumed the poor woman was experiencing one at the moment.

Sophie raised her brows at the young lady's chalky complexion and damp forehead. "Are you all right?"

"No. I mean yes." Miss Thornton's hands shook, and she rubbed her eyes. "I'm sorry, Lady Sophronia. Yes, I am all right. I just needed a moment away from the crowd."

Sophie nodded. "I certainly understand that."

Miss Thornton closed her eyes and breathed deeply as if calming herself.

"Can I get you anything?" Sophie asked. "I could find a servant to bring tea, or . . ."

Miss Thornton shook her head. "No. Just a moment of quiet, and I will be well."

Sophie was not convinced. She pulled a chair closer and sat, hoping conversation would provide a welcome distraction from the young woman's distress. "I believe I've heard you attend nurse-training school. Is that right, Miss Thornton?"

"Yes." She looked down, and a flush covered her neck. "But I've had to suspend my attendance due to . . . panic episodes."

Sophie grimaced, thinking she'd brought up an issue too sensitive. "Oh, I'm sorry."

"Silly, isn't it?"

"Absolutely not." Sophie placed a hand on the arm of the young lady's chair. "If these episodes prevent you from being who you're meant to be, they are a completely legitimate concern." She gave an encouraging nod.

"And I believe you write for the society column."

"I do." Sophie pinched her lips together, feeling a resurgence of frustration. "But I intend to move on to something more . . . important."

"If that is your wish, I hope you do." Miss Thornton smiled.

Sophie noticed some of the color had returned to the young woman's face. Her trembling seemed to have lessened. "Thank you, Miss Thornton. And I hope you are able to return to nursing school."

The ladies continued in conversation, and Sophie was surprised when she glanced at the clock on the mantel and saw the hour was past midnight. She turned back to her companion and was about to comment on the passage of time when, across the room, the windowed door leading to the garden swung open. A young woman in a lavender gown stepped inside, looked back before closing the door, then leaned against it and exhaled heavily.

When she glanced across the room and saw Sophie and Miss Thornton, the woman's eyes went wide. "Hello, there."

Sophie knew the woman to be a Miss Elizabeth Miller, though she had not formed more than a polite acquaintance with her. Dahlia Lancaster, the young lady who was any moment to be engaged to Lord Ruben, was Miss Miller's cousin.

"I take it you are escaping the ball as well?" Sophie smiled wryly at the happy coincidence of the three meeting up in the library.

"Yes." Miss Miller flicked a strand of hair from her face. "Luckily I managed to get away before Lord Chatsworth asked for another dance. The nerve of that man . . . utterly pretentious." She stopped and closed her mouth, clasping her hands before her as if just now remembering her manners. "How do you do, Lady Sophronia? Miss Thornton?" She inclined her head to each of the women in turn.

Sophie smiled at the outspoken young lady and motioned her forward with a sweep of her arm. "Very well, and please, do join our little band of fugitives."

"How do you do, Miss Miller?" Miss Thornton's voice sounded much steadier than it had an hour earlier. "You look very pretty this evening. What a beautiful gown."

Miss Miller waved her hand in the air dismissively, then grimaced. "I thank you for the compliment, but if I could remove this infernal corset without completely disrobing, I'd throw the contraption into the fire." She pressed both hands at the sides of her waist and took a breath that Sophie knew from experience must only partially fill her lungs. "Honestly, whoever decided a woman was only fashionable if her breathing was restricted had a brain the size of . . ." She trailed off, her gaze moving around the room. "Oh my. What a marvelous library."

Sophie shared a smile with Miss Thornton as their new companion strolled around looking through the different books and periodicals.

Miss Miller dug through a stack of broadsheets on a side table. "I don't suppose the marquess keeps a copy of the *Women's Suffrage Journal*, do you?"

Sophie laughed at the idea. "I wouldn't imagine the most outspoken parliamentary member opposing women's voting rights keeps that periodical on hand."

The two shared a grin.

The library door opened, and Miss Vivian Kirby entered. Seeing the others, she stopped on the threshold, pulling back. "Oh, I was just—" Her gaze landed on the woman beside Sophie. "Miss Thornton, your uncle asked me to find you, to inquire as to whether you are recovered from your . . ." She looked at the others, perhaps wondering if she ought to mention the young lady's affliction in front of them. "Are you quite all right?"

"Much better," Miss Thornton said. "Thank you."

Miss Kirby rested her hand on the doorknob as if making ready to exit and close the door behind her, but she paused, looking at the shelves of books. "I apologize for the intrusion." She spoke without taking her gaze from the bookshelves. "It was not my intention to interrupt."

"There is nothing to interrupt," Sophie said. "Unless you are opposed to a respite from a crowded ballroom."

"Come in and make yourself welcome!" Miss Miller said with a wave.

Miss Kirby stepped inside, closing the library door. She gave a polite nod and greeted each of the women in turn.

She was tall, her movements extremely graceful, and surely one of the loveliest women Sophie knew. A few years older than Sophie, Miss Kirby was a studious person who seemed to keep to herself. From the comfortable way she moved along the shelves, Sophie decided that visiting a library during a ball was perhaps a regular occurrence for the woman. The few encounters they'd shared had given Sophie the impression of a socially awkward person who always wanted to discuss the latest scientific discovery.

Miss Kirby looked closer at a particular volume. "Sir Humphry Davy. I wonder if this includes his writings on electrochemistry," she muttered, lifting the heavy book.

As the women settled in, half of them chatting and half of them reading, Sophie considered the gathering—four women of a similar age and status, while well-connected, didn't quite fit the mold to which Society would have them conform. She felt a rush of warmth, a feeling of camaraderie with the group. Though they were all quite different in temperament and interests, these women were just like her.

"Oh, what have we here?" Miss Miller pushed aside the pile to pull out a broadsheet. "The *Illustrated London News*. And my cousin's face is right on the front page." She turned the paper toward Sophie. "Is this your artwork, Lady Sophronia?"

"It is." Sophie automatically tightened her shoulders, bracing for criticism.

"A very good likeness," Miss Thornton said, crossing the room for a closer look. "You have quite a talent."

Miss Kirby looked up from her book and tipped her head, studying the picture. "I agree. I've always considered your illustrations to be exceptional. Though, I admit, I rarely care for the content of the articles."

"Neither do I," Sophie said, not the least bit put off by the woman's direct comment. She'd take honesty over manners any day. "My hope is working for the society column will lead to a position as a news reporter."

"That is indeed a worthy cause," Miss Miller said. "You could report on the plight of the poor, the residents of the rookeries whose homes are being demolished to make way for the railroad, or the lack of women represented in local government." She shook the paper and tapped it with her finger. "This, this is all nonsense. In two months will anyone bother to recall which hat Dahlia wore to the Queen's garden reception, whether her underskirts were trimmed with French or English lace, or who accompanied her to the opera? Of course they won't. Society only cares about the latest scandal, not the true suffering directly beneath their noses." She scowled. "But I hope to change that, to do something more, just like you, Lady Sophronia. I intend to establish a finishing school for underprivileged young ladies. Poor children miss so many opportunities, as their entire purpose is survival. They have few chances of bettering their situations, especially the young girls."

"I hope for more as well," Miss Kirby said. "Unfortunately, the scientific and academic communities rarely acknowledge a woman's work. If I could—"

Her words cut off when the door opened and Dahlia Lancaster herself burst into the library.

The four ladies stared, and Miss Kirby fell silent.

Miss Lancaster's eyes were frantic as she looked from woman to woman and finally rested her gaze on her cousin. "Oh, Elizabeth, here you are." Her shoulders slumped, and her voice came out as a whine. "Oh, whatever am I to do?"

Miss Miller blinked and put the broadsheet behind her back. "Cousin, this is the *library*. Surely you've made a mistake. Your friends—"

"Friends!" Miss Lancaster's voice was dangerously close to a shriek. "How can you call them my friends?" She rushed across the room and dropped onto the sofa, burying her face against the arm and sobbing.

Sophie could guess what the others were thinking as they looked between one another and then at their weeping intruder: Why was the young lady alone? Sophie didn't think she'd ever seen her without Prissy and the rest of their group of close friends, the Darling Debs—Sophie had bestowed the nickname for the group in her articles, and just like the West End Casanovas, the name had been adopted happily by those it referred to—so where were the other ladies? And even more pressing and bewildering questions arose: Why wasn't Miss Lancaster in the ballroom for the announcement of her engagement? What had happened?

Miss Miller folded the broadsheet and set it on the side table, then sat beside her cousin, putting an arm around her shoulders, and voiced Sophie's thoughts. "Cousin, whatever is the matter? Where is Lord Ruben? Shouldn't you be—?"

"He's marrying Lorene." Miss Lancaster's voice was muffled as she spoke against the sofa arm.

"I don't . . ." Miss Miller glanced at the others. "What do you mean, dear?"

Miss Lancaster lifted her head and wiped tears from her cheeks. Her eyes were red. "Lord Ruben, *my* Lord Ruben, is engaged to Lady Lorene Stanhope. The marquess announced it just now."

Sophie and Miss Thornton gasped.

Miss Miller put a hand to her mouth.

Miss Kirby watched Miss Lancaster thoughtfully.

"Had you any idea?" Miss Miller said after a lengthy and rather uncomfortable pause.

Miss Lancaster shook her head. "None. He . . . we . . . I thought we . . . that I . . ." Her lip quivered and her face crumpled. She laid her head back on her arms and cried.

Though not titled, Dahlia Lancaster's family was old and wealthy, and all of Society considered her to be not only the most beautiful debutante but also the most accomplished. That she would be Lord Ruben's wife had been taken for granted. Sophie's heart sank. Even though Miss Lancaster certainly wasn't one of her favorite people, she couldn't imagine the humiliation the young lady must have endured standing in the ballroom while the engagement was announced.

"Those arrogant Casanovas." Miss Miller scowled.

"I am sorry, Miss Lancaster," Miss Kirby said.

Sophie sat in a leather wing chair on one side of the couch. Miss Thornton, from her matching chair on the other side, lifted a hand as if she might pat Miss Lancaster's head, but lowered it again. She bit her lip, and her expression mirrored the others' confusion at how to console the young lady.

Miss Lancaster spoke after a long bout of weeping. "I don't understand. What am I to do now?" She took Miss Miller's offered handkerchief and dabbed at her eyes, sniffling. "My heart is shattered, and I . . . I simply can't go on." She choked on a sob. "I just can't."

"You most certainly can." Miss Miller sat taller and spoke in a commanding voice. "The world will not end because you do not marry Lord Ruben."

Miss Lancaster twisted the handkerchief in her hands. "But how could he do this? He loves me."

"Men of his rank do not always have the privilege of marrying for love," Miss Thornton said in a gentle voice.

"Perhaps it is best that you found out now what sort of man he is, instead of once you were married," Miss Kirby offered.

Miss Lancaster glanced at her and then shook her head. "I shall never marry," she said in a small voice. "Not after this."

Sophie winced. The young lady's reputation should remain intact, but Dahlia Lancaster's name and humiliation would certainly be on everyone's lips. A scandal indeed.

The poor woman sighed. She looked down at the handkerchief she was twisting and, noticing a ruby bracelet on her wrist, she loosened it and slipped it over her hand. "He gave the very same bangle to Lorene. He has . . . *they've* kept their relationship secret. She was my dearest friend, and he . . ." Her lip quivered, but this time a spark of anger lit her eyes.

Sophie recognized the look. Frustration at knowing one was powerless to change her situation was all too familiar.

Miss Miller took the bracelet and studied it, shaking her head.

Sophie's stomach was heavy with discouragement. All of these women wanted something different from the hand they'd been dealt, and all felt powerless to do anything about it.

"Well"—Miss Miller handed back the bracelet—"this could be a good opportunity."

"Yes," Sophie agreed. "You have a chance to do something new, to focus on yourself and your own ambitions."

Miss Lancaster folded the wrinkled handkerchief in her lap and gave a delicate snort. "Ambitions? For the last two years my entire objective was to marry Ruben, and now . . ."

"Now you can stop worrying about him," Miss Miller said. "You can do whatever you wish. Set a new course, become a new person, if you'd like."

"I don't have . . . I've never . . ." Miss Lancaster's porcelain forehead wrinkled.

"Well, we shall do it with you, shan't we, ladies?" Sophie looked at the others, raising her brows meaningfully. She hoped they would catch on and join in to bolster Miss Lancaster's spirits. "I propose we each declare an objective we hope to accomplish."

"A marvelous idea." Miss Miller took her cousin's hand and gave a firm nod.

"I have an ambition," Miss Kirby said. "I, Vivian Kirby, should like to complete my steam-engine model and enter it for display in the International Exhibition of Industry and Science."

Sophie blinked, both surprised at the woman's words and the confidence behind them. She'd never heard of a woman entering the International Exhibition. An ambitious objective indeed.

"Excellent, Miss Kirby," Miss Miller said.

She gave a small smile and tipped her head. "Please, call me Vivian."

Miss Miller replied with a nod and took Vivian's hand. "I, Elizabeth Miller, wish to open a finishing school for young ladies of underprivileged upbringings."

Sophie's heart raced as she scooted off her chair to kneel in front of the sofa. She took Vivian's free hand in hers, looked at each of the women, and took a breath. A solemn feeling came over her, as if she were making a vow. They were really doing this. They were taking charge of their lives. What had begun as simply a gesture to console Miss Lancaster had become something real. She let her breath out slowly. "I, Sophie Bremerton, would like to report a real story—something important that must be uncovered, for which I must review sources and verify facts. I want to be an actual newsagent."

Vivian smiled in approval, and Elizabeth nodded.

The ladies turned to Miss Thornton.

"Have you a goal?" Elizabeth asked.

Miss Thornton came to kneel beside Sophie, taking her hand. She glanced at the others and took a breath, looking nervous. "I, Hazel Thornton, hope to finish nursing school, to achieve nurse probationer status."

Sophie squeezed Hazel's hand.

"Very good," Elizabeth said in a tone that reminded Sophie the young lady was a teacher. She turned to her cousin. "Now, Dahlia, it is your turn."

Dahlia looked down at her hands. "I really cannot think of anything."

"You are to inherit your father's company," Elizabeth said. "Your goal could be to understand the management of the business."

"That sounds very worthwhile," Hazel said.

"It certainly does," Vivian agreed.

Sophie nodded. As an only child, Dahlia Lancaster would be one of the first women of means to benefit from the recently passed Married Women's Property Act. Her inheritance would remain her own, even after she married.

Dahlia glanced at her cousin. "I suppose such learning could be advantageous."

"Do not merely suppose," Elizabeth said, giving an encouraging nod.

Dahlia frowned and, for a moment, looked as though she would argue. But as her gaze moved to each of the women, her lips pressed together and her expression cleared in determination. She sat up straight and took Hazel's hand, completing the circle. "I, Dahlia Lancaster, will work to understand the bookkeeping, operations, and management of the steamship company I am to inherit."

The air in the Marquess of Molyneaux's library seemed to thicken as the women sat in silence. Sophie felt her wish turn into something concrete, and a surge of confidence in her own abilities grew within her. She looked at the other women, feeling their hopes and strength join together. Her skin tingled. She could do this. They all could. And none would have to do it alone.

"It is settled, then." Elizabeth's voice sounded much quieter than before.

"When shall we meet to report our progress?" Vivian asked in her practical manner.

"The next ball?" Sophie suggested. "Lord Everston has a fine library."

Hazel smiled, and Vivian nodded.

Elizabeth looked at her cousin.

Dahlia hesitated, but after a moment, she nodded as well. The shadow of a smile pulled at her lips. "Shall we gather in the library at midnight?"

Once the time and place had been agreed on, Elizabeth clasped her hands together. "We shall do remarkable things this year, make ourselves into remarkable people, and none of us will need to rely on marriage to make it happen."

Dahlia's eyes went wide. "Elizabeth, be careful. Such talk is dangerous."

Elizabeth smirked. "I should hope so." She lifted her chin dramatically and pointed at the ceiling. "And we shall call ourselves the Dangerous Bluestocking Sisterhood. I like the sound of it. Positively scandalous."

Vivian patted Elizabeth's arm. "Perhaps it is a bit too . . . controversial."

Dahlia nodded. "To say the least."

Elizabeth looked as if she would argue with her cousin but stopped when Hazel cleared her throat.

The shy woman glanced at the others hesitantly. "In India the orchid represents femininity." She smiled at Elizabeth. "And there is a blue variety of the flower."

"I have never seen one; it must be very rare," Sophie added.

"To the ancient Greeks, deep blue symbolized strength and bravery," Vivian added. "A blue orchid, therefore . . ." She spread a hand in front of her, as if leaving the others to deduce the meaning for themselves.

"Blue orchid," Elizabeth said slowly, tapping her lip with her forefinger. "It's perfect." She grinned.

"I like it." Hazel smiled.

"I do as well," Dahlia said, glancing at the others and for the first time looking a bit excited.

Vivian and Elizabeth nodded.

"Then, ladies," Sophie said, "we shall officially be the Blue Orchid Society."

CHAPTER 1

DETECTIVE JONATHAN GRAHAM OF LONDON Metropolitan Police Force's Criminal Investigation Department stood in front of the bustling Paddington Railway terminal. He took a paper sack from his pocket and retrieved a peppermint, popped it into his mouth, and nodded to the constables accompanying the prisoners—the jewel thieves Alvin Marley and Boyd Wardle—as the wagon started east toward the H Division police headquarters in Whitechapel. Once they were well underway, he turned and strode to where Sergeant Gordon Lester waited, holding tightly with both hands to a leather satchel. Two blue-uniformed constables, Brunswick stars glinting on their helmets and collar numbers shining in the few rays of sunlight that pushed through the afternoon fog and smoky air, stood on either side of the sergeant.

The small amount of space the Duchess of Attenborough's jewels occupied inside the bag was at odds with their immeasurable value. One small gem was worth more money than any of these men would see in their lifetimes, and yet they'd not hesitated to risk their lives in returning the jewelry to the duchess. Jonathan felt a swell of pride as he looked at the men. Agents of law enforcement were, at best, offered grudging respect, typically disregarded or criticized, and more often than not, treated with contempt and outright hostility. Yet, there they were, walking their beats day after day, putting in long hours to return a lost child or apprehend a thief, and doing all within their power to protect the citizens of a rapidly swelling city.

As Jonathan approached, one of the constables caught his eye. Constable Ernest Merryweather looked dead on his feet. His uniform was rumpled, and his eyes were red. The man had been working since the day before, when they'd been called to the scene of the robbery. He'd proven himself to be tireless. And hadn't it been Constable Merryweather who'd discovered the broken latch on the cellar window?

The onlookers who had gathered to watch as the arrests were made had dispersed, but the street was still crowded.

Jonathan noticed Merryweather shift closer to the sergeant as a group of young lads darted past. The man's movements were subtle, his eyes alert. *Good instincts, that one.*

Sergeant Lester held out the bag of jewelry. "Still too early to knock off for the day." His smirk pulled at a scar that ran through the thick mutton-chops on his cheek. The sergeant's voice was gravelly and low, but he spoke loudly enough to be heard over the sounds of carriages and crowds.

Jonathan waved for the sergeant to retain the satchel. "Suppose so." He glanced at his pocket watch, then raised his brows and gave a small smirk of his own. "Pity we apprehended them so early. Left ourselves time to write up the reports."

"Congratulations, sir," Sergeant Lester said, and his mouth spread into a genuine smile. "Nice bit of detective work."

The praise made Jonathan uncomfortable, but he shrugged it off, look-ing away across the street and rubbing the pocket watch fob between his fingers. "It was a group effort, Sergeant. All of the men contributed." He motioned with his chin in the direction the prisoner wagon had gone. "Even Mr. Wardle and Mr. Marley contributed—unintentionally, of course. Only a matter of time before a criminal makes a mistake; that, you can count on."

Sergeant Lester laughed. "You're being modest, if you don't mind me saying so, sir. Poor blokes had no way o' knowing you'd investigate them so thoroughly. And I'll not soon be forgetting the look on their faces when we stormed the passenger carriage."

"Their disguises really were terrible, weren't they?" Jonathan grinned.

Beside them, Constable Merryweather snorted.

Jonathan watched the street traffic for a moment longer, then gave a sharp nod. "Right, then." He motioned to another of the constables. "Constable Hutchings, we'll be needing two hackney cabs, if you please. Direct them to wait. You others, be on your guard." He motioned to the satchel in the sergeant's hands. "I'm not interested in hunting down this bag a second time."

Seeing the men's acknowledging nods, Jonathan crossed Praed Street to a vendor and purchased a bag of tarts. The small gesture was by no means adequate compensation for his comrades' work on this case, but he wished to express his gratitude all the same. One solved theft hardly made a dent in London's crime situation, but it was still commendable, and he wanted the men to have a moment of celebration.

An hour later Jonathan stepped through the door of the H Division station and removed his hat.

Bert Abner, the desk sergeant, glanced up. "Detective Graham, I've some mail for you." He pulled a pile of envelopes from a compartment and reached forward to hand the bundle over the tall desk.

"Thank you, Sergeant."

Sergeant Abner grinned, showing missing teeth beneath an enormous red mustache. "Been an exciting day, sir." He chuckled. "Appreciated the package ye sent."

Jonathan smiled at the reference to the jewel thieves in their ridiculous disguises. Sergeant Abner had no doubt signed them in only moments earlier. "Thought you'd enjoy that." He leaned an arm on the tall desk beside the sergeant's penny-dreadful novel.

"The wig . . ." Abner chuckled again, the sound growing into a full belly laugh that had the man holding his sides. "And the lady's gown with the"—he waved his hands in front of his chest—"the cotton padding. Wish we'd a photography camera here at the station." He wiped his eyes. "There's a photograph I'd keep framed on me mantel."

The constables in the main room of the station laughed at this.

As Jonathan glanced through the letters, he chuckled as well, but he couldn't help thinking how beneficial photographs of criminals would actually be. There were often repeat offenders, and to easily identify them . . .

Seeing Constable Merryweather walk past, Jonathan was pulled from his thoughts. "Constable, I do hope you're headed for home."

The young man clasped his hands behind his back. "I'm on duty in an hour, sir."

"Nonsense," Jonathan said. "You haven't had a wink of sleep in a day and a half."

Merryweather shrugged. "If I might be so bold, sir, you've not slept either."

"That is entirely different," Jonathan said. "I don't have to walk a four-mile beat for the next—"

The station door opened, and a boy ran inside. "Come quick! There's been a murder!"

"What's all this?" Sergeant Abner scowled and leaned over the tall counter, pointing. "You, there. Boy! I will tolerate no yelling in the station house."

The boy breathed heavily, and his cheeks were flushed. He'd no doubt been running. "But sir—"

Jonathan set the letters back on the reception desk and approached the boy. "Now then, calm yourself. What's your name, lad?"

"Freddy Payne, sir. Constable Hutchings sent me. Said to fetch Detective Graham right away."

"I'm Detective Graham." He clasped his hands behind his back. "What's this about a murder?"

"A woman, sir, in a blue dress. She's dead in an alley off Wentworth. Behind the Porky Pie."

Spitalfields, of course. Jonathan glanced through the station's window; the summer evening was still light—at least for the next hour. Extreme poverty, disease, overcrowding, and crime made Spitalfields one of the most dangerous slums in the city. An ideal place for criminals to disappear, Spitalfields was a complicated warren of dark alleys and crumbling buildings. Pubs, bawdy houses, and opium dens were the primary businesses of the rookery, and in the interest of safety, police walked the street in pairs. Not that any of these concerns gave him a moment's hesitation. He was an officer of the law, after all. "Well, then." Jonathan put on his hat. "Off we go."

He motioned with a flick of his head for Sergeant Lester to follow.

"If I might accompany you as well, Detective"—Merryweather hurried toward them, bucket hat underneath his arm—"the Porky Pie is on my beat."

Jonathan nodded. He glanced up again when the group stepped outside. The fog was thickening into dark clouds. They would need to hurry before rain washed away evidence or the night became too dark to investigate properly. Poorly maintained streets and late-afternoon traffic would make the journey much quicker on foot.

"Lead the way, Freddy."

The boy planted his feet, fists on his hips. He scowled, lifting his chin defiantly. "I was sent to find one copper. Escortin' the three of ye'll raise the price."

Sergeant Lester opened his mouth to argue, but Jonathan tossed the boy a penny. "You'll get another when we reach the Porky Pie."

"Yes, sir!" Freddy grinned and tucked the coin into a pocket, then set off at a quick pace.

The men followed.

Jonathan smirked at the boy. Creative, he'd give him that. And cheeky. The Porky Pie was easy enough to find, with or without Freddy's help, but Jonathan would not begrudge the lad. Based on where the boy'd come from and the way his clothes hung loosely on his small frame, he knew a penny meant one less day with an empty stomach. Jonathan had felt childhood hunger pains firsthand.

As they all walked, Merryweather caught up to the boy, his long strides keeping time with Freddy's short ones. "You look familiar, Freddy. Payne, did you say?"

"Yes, sir."

"I've come across a Martha Payne a time or two on my beat. Works as a laundress. You know her?"

Freddy's small shoulders stiffened. "My mum never committed any crime."

"No, I apologize. That's not what I meant. Try to learn the names of all the people on my beat, I do. You've a good mum."

Jonathan wondered what it was about the woman that made Merryweather remember her. He hoped the circumstance was as innocent as the man had said, but he feared the odds of that were low. Hunger drove the most honest of people to breaking the law, and the woman had a child to feed.

A crowd had gathered outside the alley beside the Porky Pie, with constables holding the curious gawkers back from the crime scene.

As promised, Jonathan gave Freddy another penny.

Constable Hutchings met them at the edge of the gathering, falling into step beside Jonathan. "A young woman, sir. No blood. Best guest is she was strangled."

"We won't know for certain until Dr. Peabody inspects the remains," Jonathan said. "You've preserved the scene?"

"She's not been touched since we arrived, other than to check for a pulse," Hutchings said. "But there's no telling who might have been here before we were called."

"Keep an eye on the people, Merryweather," Jonathan said. "Watch for anyone acting unusual."

"Yes, sir." The constable broke off from the others and began making his way among the gathered citizens.

Jonathan and Sergeant Lester followed Hutchings to the mouth of the alley, the other constables making a path through the crowd. Jonathan glanced around for Freddy, wanting to ask the lad a few questions, but as soon as he'd gotten the coin in his hand, the boy had made himself scarce. Jonathan didn't blame him. It wouldn't improve Freddy's reputation to be the one bringing the police into his neighborhood.

Nightfall was approaching quickly, and the narrow alley was already cast in shadow. The nearest gas lamp was half a block away. Jonathan blinked, waiting for his eyesight to adjust. Even if it hadn't been evening, this area of the city was always dim beneath a layer of smoke. "Fetch some lanterns, Hutchings."

"Yes, sir."

Jonathan took another peppermint from his pocket and sucked on it as he surveyed the scene. Placing his feet carefully, he studied the ground as he stepped toward the body in the blue dress. The paving stones were uneven, and quite a few were broken or missing. Searching for footprints would be pointless.

The victim lay on her front, head turned to the side. One arm was beneath her body, and the other was outstretched above her head. Her hair had come partially unfastened and spread on the ground in a mess of blonde curls.

Jonathan tugged up on the pleats of his trousers and crouched down to examine the body closer. "What do you see, Sergeant?"

"Appears to be in her twenties, sir." Sergeant Lester moved the woman's collar. Even in the dim light, bruising was visible on her neck. "I'd say Hutchings is right. Looks like she was throttled."

Whether or not that was the cause of death was still to be seen. When the lanterns arrived, he could possibly discern more clues from the body. Jonathan stood and took note of the alleyway—one entrance from the street and, at the other end, a brick wall too high to climb. When he kicked aside a broken bottle, a cat dodged past, no doubt in pursuit of vermin of some kind. Pieces of crates and other rubbish littered the space, giving the air a foul odor and contributing to the rodent problem. A door on his left led into the Porky Pie, and above, on either side, were windows of upper stories from which lines of drying clothes were strung over the alley. He wondered vaguely if their owners would pull them inside before the rain started.

He tried the door handle. *Locked.*

Circles of light spread through the alley as Hutchings returned with two lanterns.

Sergeant Lester took one, and Jonathan the other. "Ask around inside the pub, Constable," Jonathan said to Hutchings. "Learn who has a key to this door and whether anyone noted anything suspicious."

"Yes, sir." The constable started away.

"Do you think the killer escaped through the pub?" Sergeant Lester asked. He tried the door handle as well, with the same result.

"If so, he either had a key or was assisted by someone inside."

Raised voices came from the crowd, Merryweather's among them. Jonathan shared a look with the sergeant, and they strode to the mouth of the alley to investigate.

"Let me through, sir." A young woman was attempting to push past the constable. "I insist you move aside directly."

Jonathan brought the lantern light closer. The woman was short with light-brown hair pulled up beneath a flower-embellished hat. Her skirt was striped, and she wore a matching fitted jacket over a blouse with a lace collar. A brooch with some sort of blue flower was pinned to her lapel. But the most conspicuous characteristic was the woman's cleanliness. Her clothing was laundered and her shoes unblemished. It was obvious the garments were costly, even to a person with no knowledge of fashion. Her appearance stood out like a beacon in the grimy street.

"I'll handle this, Constable," Jonathan said. He turned to the woman and tugged on his hat brim. "Detective Jonathan Graham, at your service, miss."

"Sophie Bremerton." She inclined her head.

"How might I be of assistance, Miss Bremerton?"

"Thank you, Detective." She darted a sharp look at the constable. "This man refuses to let me past."

Jonathan glanced at Merryweather, then back at her. "With good reason, miss. This is an active crime scene."

"Yes, I realize that, Detective. It is the very reason I'm here."

In just that moment Jonathan took her measure. She was confident and well-spoken, with an aristocratic accent. The woman was no doubt slumming—a favorite pastime of the privileged and bored. Curious wealthy tourists visited impoverished neighborhoods for amusement. The idea of these people seeking a thrill from witnessing the hardships of their fellow man made Jonathan's blood boil.

Very well, he'd teach this Sophie Bremerton a lesson. Show her the people he protected were not simply here for her entertainment.

"Stand aside, Merryweather." He took Miss Bremerton's elbow and pulled her into the alley with long strides, holding up the lantern so the body on the ground was completely illuminated.

Miss Bremerton cringed back. "Oh my. Do you know her name?"

"No."

"She's so young."

"*Was* young," Jonathan said, satisfied that the interloper had gotten more than she'd asked for. "So tell me, Miss Bremerton, is this what you hoped to see? Is it tragic enough for . . ." His words trailed off when he realized she was not listening but had stepped away and begun to speak with Sergeant Lester. Jonathan scowled and followed her.

"A pleasure to meet you, Sergeant," she was saying. "What do you suppose happened to this poor woman?"

Sergeant Lester knelt, set down his lantern, and pulled back the dead woman's collar.

Miss Bremerton knelt on the other side of the body, arranging her skirts around her and then leaning close to study the woman's neck. "She was strangled," she said.

"That's our guess, miss," Sergeant Lester said. "The doctor will know for certain."

"How terrible." Miss Bremerton's voice was much softer. It seemed she finally understood this was not simply a carnival show but a life cut short in a violent manner.

"Yes," Jonathan said, coming to stand behind her, glad the exercise had had its intended effect. "It is, as I told you, a crime scene—a *murder* scene. Of course it is not pleasant. Now, if you're quite done . . ." He reached out a hand to assist her to rise.

Sophie Bremerton apparently suffered from convenient hearing loss. She didn't even glance up as Jonathan spoke, but tipped her head to the side, looking at the body. "She didn't intend to go out of doors, I think. She wears no hat nor gloves."

"They may have been stolen," Sergeant Lester said.

"But not her ring?" Miss Bremerton pointed to the silver band on the woman's finger. "I do not think it is very valuable, but it is surely more so than a pair of gloves."

"Perhaps the thief did not see it in the dim light," Jonathan said. "At this point, we can't rule out any possibilities. Now, if you please . . ." He held out his hand again, but as before, she ignored him.

"The gown is very distinctive," she said. "Custom-made raw silk with Brussels lace." She sat back on her heels. "But it was not sewn for this woman."

"How do you know that?" Jonathan asked, curious in spite of his irritation.

"The sleeves are too short." Miss Bremerton pointed to the woman's wrists. "And of course the tournure is all wrong for this skirt."

Sergeant Lester looked up at the detective with a confused expression that Jonathan was certain matched his own.

"Tournure, miss?" the sergeant asked.

"The bustle," Miss Bremerton said.

Sergeant Lester furrowed his brows. "You mean the contraption that makes a hump on a lady's bum?"

Miss Bremerton nodded. "I suppose that's as good a description as any." Her voice trembled the slightest bit, and Jonathan thought she might be holding back a laugh.

"And how can you tell she was wearing the wrong bustle?" Jonathan asked, wanting to return the conversation to the business of solving the murder.

"You see, here." She pointed to the bottom ruffle of the woman's dress. "The rear of her skirts have been dragging. The proper tournure would have lifted the hem off the ground."

"So we can assume the woman purchased the gown secondhand, without the proper underclothing," Jonathan said. "While it is interesting, it is not unusual."

"I agree, Detective," Miss Bremerton said. "But a dress such as this . . . its value is very dear. I believe it was made for last year's Season. The collar design and color were the very height of fashion, and the basque-style overskirt had not yet been replaced by a polonaise."

The men shared another bewildered look.

Miss Bremerton continued. "If we can discern where the dress is from or how she came to be wearing it, perhaps it would lead to her identity."

Jonathan didn't like the woman's use of the word *we* or the way she was taking charge of the investigation. "Obviously, that is—what are you doing now?"

Miss Bremerton had pulled a notebook from her bag and started sketching. "It will be dark soon, Detective. And it looks like rain. I intend to document as much of the scene as possible. Would you move your lantern closer?"

Jonathan plunked down his lantern beside Sergeant Lester's in front of the lady. His irritation was evolving into something much more like anger. He'd had quite enough of this woman's presumptions and uninvited observations and intended to tell her. But before he had the chance, Sergeant Lester called to him. "Sir, have a look at this." He motioned him toward the victim's feet. "The backs of her heels are scraped."

"She was dragged here," Jonathan said. He noticed the young woman's boots were old and worn. They were nowhere near the quality of the gown she wore. Perhaps Miss Bremerton's observations about the woman's clothing would be useful after all. But the idea that she'd offered helpful insight grated at him.

Dr. Peabody entered the alley, his cane making a clicking sound where it hit the paving stones. He nodded to the men and knelt next to Miss Bremerton, showing no surprise at her presence, as was his way. Dr. Peabody was rarely rattled. "How do you do, miss? Dr. Phinneas Peabody. I don't believe I've had the pleasure."

"Sophie Bremerton. And the pleasure is mine, Doctor."

"Delighted." The older bowed awkwardly from his kneeling position, then looked down at the dead woman. "Now, what have we here?"

"We believe the victim was strangled." Miss Bremerton spoke before Jonathan could respond.

Sergeant Lester returned to kneel across from the others. He held his lantern closer. "Bruises on her neck, Doctor."

"Skin's cold," Dr. Peabody said, touching the woman's cheek with the back of his fingers. He lifted her arm and bent the elbow, checking for rigor mortis. "Hasn't been dead long." He pulled down her collar.

Jonathan crouched beside the sergeant, leaning forward for a better view, though so many people gathered around the body made it difficult.

"Definitely could indicate asphyxia," Dr. Peabody said. "Have you finished your initial examination of the scene, Detective? Might we turn her over?"

"Yes." Jonathan and Sergeant Lester turned the woman onto her back.

"Hold a lantern, if you please, Miss Bremerton." The doctor examined the deceased woman's neck, then pulled up her eyelids. "Ah, look here."

The three leaned closer, the flowers of Miss Bremerton's hat effectively blocking Jonathan's view.

"Petechial hemorrhaging," Dr. Peabody said. "Another sign of asphyxia." He lifted the victim's outstretched hand, studied it, laid it beside her, and then reached across the body to lift the other. "No defensive wounds."

"You think she did not resist her attacker?" Miss Bremerton asked.

"Impossible to say," Dr. Peabody replied. "I'll know more once I can examine her in the morgue." He looked closer at the hand he held, turning it over to study the nails. "Soft hands. A gentlewoman, perhaps?"

Jonathan spoke quickly before Miss Bremerton had the chance. "I'd considered it, but her clothing and jewelry would indicate otherwise."

"Well, that is your area of expertise, not mine, Detective." The doctor set the hand back.

"How long has she been dead?" Jonathan asked.

"Two hours, perhaps three." He moved to stand.

Miss Bremerton jumped up and helped the doctor to his feet, retrieving his cane.

"Thank you, my dear."

Jonathan and Sergeant Lester stood as well.

"I'll let you know my findings," Dr. Peabody said.

"Thank you, Doctor." Jonathan and Miss Bremerton spoke at the same moment.

The lady took the doctor's offered arm and accompanied him to the mouth of the alleyway, where he directed the waiting students from the medical college to retrieve the body and deliver it to the morgue.

Sergeant Lester picked up his lantern and Miss Bremerton's notebook and bag and followed.

Jonathan clasped his hands behind his back and took one last look at the scene, wishing for daylight or a photographer. He had very few clues as to the dead woman's identity and knew finding witnesses willing to talk would be difficult, if not impossible. As he walked to the mouth of the alley, he ground his teeth, frustrated that this would very likely be another unidentified woman in an unsolved case file.

"What is the next course of action, Sergeant Lester?" Miss Bremerton asked.

"We'll interview potential witnesses, look into the lady's identity, and hope the doctor is able to find anything on the body to give us direction."

She nodded, writing something in her notebook. "Very good. As far as the gown—"

"That's enough." Jonathan had reached the end of his patience. "Listen, Miss Bremerton. I've had quite enough of your thrill seeking. This is a police matter. It is not your place to advise my sergeant on police procedure, nor for that matter, should you travel in this part of the city alone."

"But I am not alone, sir. My carriage driver waits just—"

"Go home, Miss Bremerton." He took her arm and led her from the alley. "Make yourself a nice cup of tea. You've had sufficient adventure in the rookery to earn the envy of your friends."

"Detective Graham, I resent your implication. I—"

"Constable, see that Miss Bremerton gets home safely." Jonathan motioned to Merryweather, who took the lantern from the lady and moved to assist her. He felt no guilt ignoring her protests. He turned and strode away without even waiting for an acknowledgment. He could hear Miss Bremerton arguing behind him, but he was not worried. Merryweather would see his assignment completed. The woman would be sent away whether she wished to be or not.

Jonathan stopped in the light of a gas lamp outside the Porky Pie and checked the time, unconsciously rubbing the uneven edges of the fob hanging from his pocket watch chain as he considered the case. He had no real leads aside from an expensive dress and ill-fitting bustle. He doubted Hutchings would gather much from interviews. People tended to their own business in this part of the city. Perhaps the doctor would discover more, or perhaps the ring might reveal something upon closer examination.

When Sergeant Lester joined him, the two started back toward H Division.

With so many factors unknown, two things he was certain of: a young lady belonged nowhere near a murder investigation, and Miss Sophie Bremerton belonged nowhere near him.

CHAPTER 2

SOPHIE THANKED HER DRIVER, JASPER, as he helped her from the carriage on Park Lane. When she stepped inside the house, a maid took her gloves and hat. A wave of fatigue moved over her as she climbed the stairs, but instead of continuing on to her bedchamber for a nap, she followed the upstairs passageway toward the first-floor sitting room, where Mimi, her grandmother, would be at her writing table.

After returning from Spitalfields the night before, Sophie had stayed up into the early hours of the morning, sketching images of the murder scene and making notes when she should have been finishing the illustration she'd promised to deliver to the newspaper editor by tomorrow morning. Then, after only a few hours of sleep, she'd left early for Bond Street to call on various dressmakers in hopes of discovering who had made—and purchased—the gown the dead woman had worn. But lack of sleep was not the full cause of her exhaustion. Sophie couldn't avoid her mother forever, and anticipating the inevitable confrontation left her weary.

Last night Sophie had missed the Hamptons' ball—her third conspicuous absence from an event this week as she'd gone in search of a story. Her mother, Lady Mather, took personal offense to unconventionality of any kind. As it was, a daughter working for the newspaper was nearly more than the countess could endure.

But, in truth, pleasing her mother was not something Sophie imagined she'd ever be capable of. Not when she'd been presented four Seasons earlier and still remained unmarried—a failure of the highest degree in her mother's eyes, and one Lady Mather did not neglect to remind her daughter of on a daily basis.

When Sophie entered the drawing room, the dowager countess set aside her fountain pen, stood from her desk, and smiled. "Good morning, dearest."

From the floor beside the window, Dorrit, Mimi's beloved pug, jumped up and barked.

Warmth relaxed the tension inside Sophie as she took her grandmother's outstretched hands and allowed her to kiss both cheeks. "Good morning, Mimi."

In spite of her age, Sophie's grandmother was extremely active, both socially and physically. She was a member of various societies, a champion of causes, and a chairwoman of fundraisers. She also served on school and hospital boards and participated in a ladies' badminton league.

Her grandmother picked up the dog's leash from the desk. "Dorrit and I are just headed to the dining room, my dear. Have you eaten?"

"I had some toast earlier."

"Well, that is hardly enough to sustain you. The hour is nearly noon." Mimi shook her head, making her gray curls bounce around her face. "Come along."

"I'd love to."

"Time to eat, Dorrit." Mimi spoke in a cooing voice, then gave a whistle.

The dog ran to her mistress and allowed the leash to be attached to her collar.

Sophie linked arms with her grandmother as they walked down the stairs. "How was your ride?" Sophie could hardly hold back her grin at Mimi's most recent infatuation. She and a group of her friends had all purchased penny-farthing bicycles and met regularly to ride through Hyde Park in the mornings before the paths became too crowded. Six elderly women pedaling along the paths on the high-wheeled contraptions was certainly a sight to behold.

"It was lovely." Mimi waved her hand as she spoke. "The morning hours are spectacular. The air is crisp, birds sing, and a feeling of hopefulness prevails as the city wakes."

"I'm glad you enjoyed it," Sophie said. "And no falls today?"

"Oh, there are always a few." Mimi shrugged "But we don't let that stop us. Physical activity and fresh air are good for the body and soul, though the hard ground is not always good for my elbows and knees."

Sophie chuckled. She loved her grandmother's eccentricities. And while the rest of her family simply tolerated the foibles with a roll of their eyes, she felt jealous of them. At what age did it become socially acceptable to . . . not act socially acceptable?

They reached the dining room, and a footman took the leash from Mimi and led the dog away to eat in the kitchen.

Sophie took her place beside her grandmother at the dining table. The meal was served, and she poured the tea.

Mimi took a bite of fish. "You returned very late last night. Did you find your story?"

"Yes." The excitement of the investigation returned, making Sophie's stomach flutter. She dabbed pastry crumbs from her lips and leaned toward her grandmother. "I stumbled upon a murder in Spitalfields."

Her grandmother stopped with her teacup partway to her mouth. She opened her eyes wide. "Gracious, my dear. Jumped right in with both feet, didn't you?"

Mimi's reaction was exactly what Sophie had expected. Her grandmother never fussed or lectured but gave constant encouragement. Though she didn't know for sure, Sophie was almost certain Mimi had been the one who'd convinced her parents to allow her to take the position with the newspaper in the first place.

Sophie scooped fruit onto her plate. "The circumstance was extremely lucky." Seeing her grandmother's raised brows over her teacup, she shook her head. "No, not lucky for the victim, of course, but for me to have arrived right as the police did. I was able to assist with the examination of the scene. Watching the investigators at work, seeing what they noticed and what they were able to deduce—it was all fascinating."

"Do you know the victim's identity?" Mimi asked.

"No," Sophie said. "She was a young woman, and her dress . . ." She pulled her bag from beneath the table and slipped out the drawings she'd made the night before, leafing through until she found the one she wanted—a picture of the victim's clothing. "I hope the dress will lead to her identity." She set the paper between their plates.

Mimi looked through a quizzing glass, studying the drawing. "Not a gown one would expect to see in Spitalfields, is it?"

"Exactly what I thought," Sophie said. "Madame Delacourt, the modiste, recognized the pattern but was not certain whom this particular dress was made for, as the specific embellishments and alterations were done by various seamstresses in her shop, some no longer in her employ. Her records did indicate three gowns in this periwinkle-blue color were sold last year, and she gave me the names of the women: Julia Westerfield, Charlotte Grey, and Abigail Scott. I am acquainted with all of them, to some degree."

"But you did not recognize the victim. She was not one of the young ladies to whom the dresses were sold?"

"No. Someone wearing one of their dresses, I believe." Sophie explained to her grandmother about the gown's too-short sleeves and the tournure.

"How very intriguing." Mimi dabbed her lips with a napkin. "You truly have a gift for observation and deduction, Sophronia."

Sophie's chest warmed at the praise. She bit into another pastry, set it down, and then wiped the crumbs from her fingers before returning the drawing to her bag. She debated showing the others to her grandmother but decided pictures of a murder scene were hardly appropriate at the breakfast table.

"Do you believe the gown was stolen?" Mimi asked.

"I do not know. The doctor pointed out that the woman's hands were very soft, so she must have enjoyed some level of comfort."

Mimi nodded. "But if so, why was her dress not altered to fit properly?"

"Why indeed," Sophie said. "I intend to pay a visit to Misses Westerfield, Grey, and Scott this afternoon." She winced, glancing at the clock. The young women were very likely not taking visitors this early, and if she was to attend Mrs. Jeffries's garden party this evening, she needed the entirety of the afternoon to prepare her article and drawing that were due tomorrow morning. She blew out a frustrated breath. "Or perhaps tomorrow."

"Since when are you friends with any of those young ladies?" Priscilla's voice came from the doorway.

Sophie and Mimi turned in their chairs.

"Good morning, dear," Mimi said.

"It would be a good morning if I hadn't awoken so early." Prissy flounced into the dining room and sat in a chair on the other side of the table. She reached for the basket of pastries.

"And what are you doing today, Prissy?" Sophie turned the subject away from her investigation and onto her sister's favorite topic—herself.

"Paying visits with mother this morning." Prissy rolled her eyes, but then she tipped her head, giving a superior smile. "Everleigh has invited me to a picnic at Kensington Gardens tomorrow." She sighed, clasping her hands. "He is so handsome, and he quite prefers me, you know."

"And why wouldn't he, Priscilla?" Mimi said. "A gentleman would be foolish not to take notice of my lovely granddaughter."

Prissy smiled. "Thank you, Mimi." She blinked as if an idea had just occurred to her. "You should come as well, Sophie. Really, you must. All the Casanovas and Darling Debs will be there."

Sophie was surprised her sister would make such a suggestion. Prissy had certainly never sought her company socially—let alone acknowledged in public at all the fact that they were related.

"Thank you for the invitation, but I'm afraid I have plans tomorrow."

Prissy pouted, setting down her teacup with a clatter and folding her arms. "But Everleigh's dull railroad friend *Hans*, from Germany, is invited." She spoke the name with a groan and rolled her eyes. "If you came, you could keep him occupied, discussing . . . whatever it is tedious people discuss."

Ah, this explanation makes sense. Sophie did not take offense. Her sister seldom thought before speaking, nor realized how her words would be received.

"That does sound very tempting, but I'm afraid I will be busy," Sophie said.

"What could you possibly need to do that is more important than picnicking with the most prominent members of high Society?" Prissy wrinkled her nose. "Drawing pictures, no doubt?"

"Illustrations for the newspaper are hardly more frivolous than—" Sophie bit off her witty rebuke when Lady Mather entered the dining room, and at the sight of her mother, the muscles in Sophie's neck tightened.

Lady Mather sat beside Prissy and nodded in acknowledgment as the others bid her good morning. She slid her teacup closer and stirred its contents. "I heard the carriage earlier." She glanced at Sophie. "You've been out already?"

"Yes." Sophie pushed the bag with her drawings farther beneath her skirts. "To the dressmakers'."

"I take it your waist has expanded beyond your corset's capacity to contain it." Her mother sighed. She shook her head, glancing at Sophie's plate. "You are not taking your reducing diet seriously, Sophronia. How many times have I told you to limit your pastries? And now your gowns must be altered . . ."

Mimi snorted. "Honestly, Maxine. Sophronia's waist is perfectly suitable for its purpose of housing her vital organs, and the idea that she must conform to Society's ideal of—"

Mimi's words stopped as Sophie clasped her hand beneath the table, giving it a squeeze. She knew Mimi would understand that as grateful as she was for her grandmother's defense, the argument was unnecessary, as her mother's mind would not be changed by a lecture on the abstract criterion of feminine beauty.

"The dressmakers'!" Prissy obviously took the pause in the conversation as an invitation to speak—or, more accurately, to complain. "I have need of new gowns as well. I've seen two other young ladies in the very color I'd intended to wear to the opera tomorrow. Could you imagine my humiliation if we were all attired similarly?"

Prissy continued speaking, but years of living with the young woman had given Sophie the ability to ignore her sister's prattle. She caught her grandmother's eye, giving a grateful smile. What would Sophie ever do without her staunch support? She thought how Elizabeth Miller adored Mimi and imagined her grandmother must have been very much like her new friend when she was young.

". . . I am being courted by Lord Everleigh, and I cannot afford to look anything less than spectacular," Prissy continued to her mother. "The gown I wore last night was so ordinary—Everleigh hardly noticed me at all. He spent most of the evening in private conversation with that dull German. I've half a mind to give the dress to my lady's maid and be done with it."

Sophie stared at her sister, and her mind spun with what the younger woman said. She'd not considered that the dead woman's gown might have been a gift from her mistress. Could its method of coming into her possession be so simple? A lady's maid was often the recipient of the gowns the woman she served no longer wanted, and that would explain perfectly why it did not fit her.

She considered what she knew of the three women whose names the modiste had given her. Which of them might be inclined to give away a costly gown after wearing it for only one Season? The answer was immediately clear. Charlotte Grey was one of the Darling Debs, and if Sophie had to choose a young lady who was nearly identical in temperament and behavior to Prissy, Miss Grey would be at the very top of the list.

"Sophronia." Lady Mather's voice was sharp, cutting into her thoughts. "You will do me the courtesy of listening when I speak to you."

Sophie shook herself from her thoughts. "I apologize, Mother. My mind was wandering."

Her mother sighed, and her jaw tightened. "I was reminding you about Mrs. Jeffries's garden reception this evening."

Sophie forced her shoulders to remain down instead of hunching. "I plan to attend, but I have quite a few obligations this afternoon that might interfere."

Her mother's right brow ticked upward, and though it was a miniscule movement, Sophie winced. Lady Mather's anger was never displayed in fits of yelling but with carefully worded attacks. And her sharpest weapon was guilt.

"We made apologies for your absences last night and the night previous," Lady Mather said.

"Not to mention Mrs. Rothschild's luncheon," Prissy added helpfully.

"The position this puts me in"—Lady Mather's voice grew softer, which was far more frightening than if she'd screamed—"coming up with excuses day after . . ." She sighed. "Finding a husband for you has been difficult enough with your"—she motioned with a wave of her hand—"ordinariness. And after *four* Seasons—"

"I have not asked you to apologize for me." Sophie could sense Mimi preparing to interject. She knew better than to interrupt her mother, but she didn't wish for the argument to grow or for her grandmother to have to defend her again. Sophie shifted, feeling heat rise to her cheeks. "I will do my best to attend, but I am very busy today."

"She'll probably arrive with Dahlia Lancaster and her bluestocking cousin." Prissy spoke her former friend's name with a contemptible curl of the lip.

Anger flashed through Sophie.

"Priscilla." Mimi's voice held a reprimand. "That is unkind. You used to be dear friends with Dahlia."

"Well, of course, that was before Lord Ruben rejected her," Priscilla said. Her expression did not show one bit of remorse. "It makes one wonder what is wrong with her if he'd not have her."

"Quite so," Lady Mather agreed. "And it appears he was wise to escape when he did. I hear Miss Lancaster has since taken to the company of suffragettes and misfits."

"Such an embarrassment. He is very lucky to be rid of her." Prissy shook her head.

Sophie could typically ignore her family's insults, but today she was tired, and the affronts to herself and her friends were more than she could overlook. She set her napkin on the table and stood. "I'm afraid I am in complete disagreement with both of you." She lifted her bag over her shoulder. "If anyone is to be congratulated, it is Dahlia Lancaster for escaping not only an unfaithful man but spiteful friends as well."

"Well, I never," Prissy sputtered. "Mother, did you hear?"

"Sophronia, that was quite uncalled for," Lady Mather began.

Sophie ignored the outburst from the other side of the table. "Have a lovely day, Mimi." She kissed her grandmother's cheek, received a private wink and a smile in return, then left the room without a backward glance.

CHAPTER 3

JONATHAN RUBBED HIS EYES AS he and Sergeant Lester walked toward H Division station house after another long day. The two had been called back to Spitalfields in the early hours of the morning with the discovery of another victim—a young man this time. By the time they'd investigated the scene and Dr. Peabody had taken away the body, daylight had come, and they'd spent hours interviewing potential witnesses and following weak leads, with no luck. Two unidentified victims in fewer than ten hours.

Jonathan sucked on a peppermint and scowled at the frustration of an entire day of dead ends. How was it possible that not one single person saw anything in either case? He shook his head. Of course that wasn't true. The rookery was overpopulated to the extreme. People lived thirty to a room in the crumbling tenements. There were eyes on every inch of Spitalfields. The reality was people were afraid. And Jonathan knew that fear firsthand. Though they were no guarantee of survival in the dangerous city, remaining silent, minding one's own business, increased the odds.

Sergeant Lester stopped in his tracks. He crouched down, leaning close to study something in the gutter. "Will you look at that?" he muttered. "The poor dear." He shook out the folds from his handkerchief, then used it to gently lift a dead bird. He brought the carcass close to his face to examine it. "And her feathers are pristine."

"Delightful," Jonathan said. He'd been hopeful for a moment that the sergeant had discovered a clue that pertained to the case, or at least something of interest. He opened his pocket watch, glancing at the time. The hour was nearly five thirty—much later than he'd thought. He closed the timepiece, slipping it back into his waistcoat, and watched with growing impatience as Sergeant Lester extended the bird's wings one at a time. The sergeant's obsession with small-animal taxidermy was something he'd never understand. But Jonathan knew better than to rush him.

"Know just the place for this one." The sergeant wrapped the bird carefully and slipped it into his coat pocket. "I've an avian choir in need of a soprano." He stood, wiping his hands on his trousers.

The two had walked only another block when the smell of jellied eel reached Jonathan, and he realized he'd not eaten anything but sweets since the evening before. "Hungry?"

"Famished," Sergeant Lester answered, looking toward the eel cart.

The men turned their steps in that direction, paid the street vendor, and waited as the man dipped cups into his bucket, scooping out servings of the gelatinous mixture.

Jonathan splashed a bit of vinegar into his cup, then slurped up a bite of cold meat. The sour taste made his tongue recoil for a sharp instant.

"The only lead we've not followed is the gown," Sergeant Lester said, pouring in his own splash of vinegar.

Jonathan grunted and chewed on the rubbery eel.

"What was her name again?" Sergeant Lester wiped jelly from his mustache with a swipe of his thumb. "The lady in the fancy clothes? Miss Bremerton, wasn't it? If she could help us discover where the dress was purchased . . ."

Jonathan grunted again. He shook his cup to loosen another chunk of eel. The thought of asking that woman for help rankled him. "We'll call on the dressmakers tomorrow."

"Call on the dressmakers?" Sergeant Lester stared, disbelief pushing up his brows and creasing his forehead. "Have you any idea how many dressmakers there are in London? And what would we ask? 'Pardon me, madam, do you happen to know who purchased a blue gown with frilly bits here and here and a backside that only fits with the correct bum contraption?'"

Jonathan gave him a flat stare. "We'll think of something."

"Why not just ask Miss Bremerton?" The sergeant tipped back his head, shaking the rest of the jelly into his mouth.

"Because this doesn't concern her."

"She would know which dressmakers to speak to. If we—"

Jonathan held up a hand, cutting him off. "Involving a civilian in a criminal case is a bad idea." *Especially* that *civilian.* "I'll not consider it." He ran a finger around the inside of his cup to scrape up the last bits of jelly, then handed the cup back to the seller. His pride was the motivating factor in the decision, but asking that woman for help—though she'd probably be thrilled at the chance of further adventure—felt like a failure. And he didn't care to give her the satisfaction of knowing the Whitechapel Police Force could not solve the case without her.

As they drew near the station house, the streets became more crowded with workers headed toward their homes at the end of the day. The feeling of exhaustion as well as relief at the few hours of respite gave the journey a more satisfactory feel, rather than the resigned feeling that came with the morning travel.

Jonathan kept an eye on the crowds, watching for any disturbance or thievery. Pickpockets didn't only prey on the wealthy.

Upon reaching the station house, Sergeant Lester opened the door.

But as Jonathan entered, he heard his name called from behind. When he turned, he found a group of three children on the street and smiled, knowing exactly what they were after. The urchins of Whitechapel often sought him out, and he recognized two of the boys he'd met before. He nodded a farewell to the sergeant and stepped closer to the children. "How can I help you lads this evening?"

"Have you a sweet for us, Detective Graham?" the oldest of the boys asked.

The other children watched with hopeful faces.

Jonathan put his hands in his pockets and pulled together his brows thoughtfully. "You're after a sweet, are you? Well, that depends, of course. Have you done a good deed today?"

"I helped my da sharpen knives at his cart," the boy said.

"Well done." Jonathan nodded. He reached into the sack in his pocket and drew out a piece of peppermint, tossing it to the boy.

The boy caught it with a grin. "Thank you, Detective."

"I tended to my sister while my ma fetched the mending," another of the boys said. "And I only got cross with her once."

"Very commendable." Jonathan held back a smile as he gave the boy a sweet.

He turned to the last boy, a small lad he'd not seen before. The child was almost sickly thin, and the way he hung back behind the others gave the impression of a boy who constantly expected to be either abused or ignored. Jonathan felt a pang of sympathy. Life in the rookery was difficult enough for those with strong constitutions.

"And what's your name, young man?" He spoke in a softer voice, not wishing to frighten the child.

"Archie." He glanced up, then cringed back. The boy's eyes were enormous and appeared even more so in his gaunt face.

"Hello, Archie."

"I've not done anything good today," Archie said in a voice nearly too quiet to hear.

Jonathan crouched down to the boy's height, resting on his haunches. "Nothing at all? That's hard to believe. Did you help your mother?"

Archie shook his head, and Jonathan wondered if the boy was an orphan. It would not surprise him.

"Perhaps you offered someone a kind word?"

Archie shook his head again but paused and glanced up. He pursed his lips as if considering. "I helped a kitten out of a gutter drain," he whispered after a moment.

"That was very kind, Archie. I could tell right away that you are a good lad." Jonathan gave the boy a piece of peppermint.

Archie snatched it from his hand and stuck it into his mouth. Jonathan recognized the action. The boy was used to eating quickly before his food was taken. Very likely a skill developed in an orphanage. He wondered why the boy had left the institution. Had he been abused? Neglected?

Jonathan rose, knowing he needed to earn the boy's trust further before inquiring about his situation. Doing so now would only cause the boy to be wary. "You may come to the station anytime, Archie." He looked at the other boys. "And all of you. The police are your friends. Our duty is to protect you."

The children thanked him and hurried away.

Jonathan watched them go with a mixture of affection and extreme sadness. He couldn't save every poor, hungry, or neglected child. There were simply too many. But he'd decided when he became a constable that the one thing he could do was make them feel safe around the police. Let them know that he would help them when needed. Whether or not it made a difference, he didn't know. But it gave him hope. The course of his own life had been changed by a police officer who had genuinely cared about a penniless orphan.

When Jonathan entered the station house, he greeted the desk sergeant with a wave. Constables at the end of their shifts sat in any unoccupied chair and wrote hasty reports, anxious to go home. Most of the detectives were finishing their work for the day. Some had already left. The door to Sir Peter Dennington's office was closed, and no light shone beneath. The chief inspector did not work extended hours but expected his subordinates to do so. Though many of the detectives and constables complained, Jonathan didn't begrudge the man wishing to spend time with his family.

Jonathan removed his coat, hanging it and his hat on a coatrack, and settled in at his desk, eyeing the stacks of papers and folders—many of which hadn't been there when he'd left the evening before. He pushed a pile to the side, clearing a space, and opened a fresh folder to document the murder discovered this morning. He'd have the coroner's report and the photographs when they were ready, but aside from a few paragraphs documenting his own observations at the scene, the file was nearly empty. He closed it and set it atop a stack, hoping as he always did, that it would grow, filling up with evidence, and the case would be solved. But he feared it would end up in a dusty cabinet somewhere, and the victim would be yet another unidentified body in a pauper's grave.

He sighed and opened another folder, popped a piece of peppermint into his mouth, and set to work.

Four hours later he was barely able to keep his eyes open. His stomach rumbled, the noise loud in the nearly empty station house. Mrs. Simpson, his landlady, would have served supper hours ago. He put on his coat and hat and turned off the desk lamp but stopped in the doorway. He returned for the file on the woman from the alley outside the Porky Pie and then started for home.

When at last he arrived, he stepped quietly up the narrow steps until he reached the second floor and then unlocked the door to the small room that made up his lodgings. A tray with a covered bowl and a hunk of bread sat on the round table beside his one chair. Tossing his coat and hat onto the bed, he peeked beneath the cloth. Beef stew. *Bless you, Mrs. Simpson.*

He settled back and enjoyed the stew, not caring that it was cold and the bread stale. As he ate, he looked through the file. Over the course of the night he'd come back to this case time and again. Who was the poor woman? And what events had led to her body being discovered in a Spitalfields alley? There must be some clue they'd missed. But even Doctor Peabody's report had given no new information.

Jonathan had originally thought his interest in this particular case stemmed from the victim's singularity. She was most obviously out of place, a genteel woman in a dirty slum's alley, but as the night drew on and Jonathan became more tired and less guarded, memories intruded into his thoughts.

He had lived the majority of his life without knowledge of what had become of his parents. He had never known his father, and aside from their shared name, he knew nothing about the man. He remembered his mother only through impressions. Her hair had been blonde, he was certain, and she'd been beautiful. In his mind, she wore a shawl and a necklace with a cross. But as hard as he tried to focus on the memories, they were slippery and wouldn't form into a complete image. Sometimes he caught a fragrance or heard a voice that reminded him of her, but only as a vague feeling. He knew her name was Maggie, and as a child, he had whispered it again and again, loving the sound of it and fearing he'd forget the word if he didn't say it.

His mother had disappeared when he was four. One night, she'd simply never returned home, and despite searching every police record he could get his hands on, he'd never discovered what had happened to her. Had she been buried in a common grave in Highgate or Abney Park? Had she ended up a victim with nobody to identify her? She'd never have deserted him; of that, Jonathan was certain.

He set aside the file and undressed for bed, setting his hat carefully over the preserved toad with tiny spectacles that sat in a miniature easy chair with one webbed foot resting on his knee and holding a copy of the *Times*. The taxidermic amphibian had been a Christmas gift from Sergeant Lester, and though it made Jonathan's skin crawl, he kept it, partly because it had undoubtedly taken the sergeant hours to create and partly because Christmas gifts had been a rare thing in his life.

As he laid his head on the pillow, his thoughts returned to the mystery woman in the alley. Who was she? She must be missed by someone, somewhere. And as his thoughts slid into dreams, they became images from a little child's memories, of having a hungry belly and shivering beneath a threadbare blanket in a crowded Wapping tenement room waiting for the woman to come home.

CHAPTER 4

WHEN SOPHIE OPENED THE DOOR of the *Illustrated London News* office, she was met with the smell of printers' ink and machine oil, the hum of news presses, and the general chaotic energy of deadlines and headlines. She felt a rush of excitement at the activity. Journalism felt like a living thing, something changing and vital, pulsing with life. Newspapers were important, and she longed to be a more important component, to provide meaningful information rather than merely trivial gossip.

A clerk rushed past with a stack of newsprint, and another hurried in the opposite direction, papers flying out of his overloaded arms. The main office in front of the larger press room was a small space with high windows that gave far too little light. Men and women worked in a crowded maze of desks, dipping quills and scribbling quickly beneath a cloud of cigarette smoke. In a far corner the engraving artists sat, hunched over a table lit by desk lamps.

Upon completion of her first story and illustration, Sophie had been fascinated at the process of wood engraving. She'd watched, mesmerized as her drawing was transferred to a boxwood surface by a series of intricate carvings, and considered the carvers much more talented than she was. When she'd said as much to the editor, Mr. Leonard, he'd discounted her observation with a shake of his head. "They merely copy, my lady," he'd said, blowing out a cloud of smoke. "The artists and reporters—they do the real work."

She didn't think the engravers had been pleased by his commentary. One man in particular, a Mr. Potts, had appeared especially insulted. His scowl had made Sophie wince, and each time she'd come to the newspaper, she'd made a particular effort to notice and mention something praiseworthy about his carving.

Sophie made her way through the room to the larger desk in the corner opposite the engravers, pausing to greet Mrs. Ingram, the editor's research assistant. According to Mr. Leonard, Mrs. Ingram knew the newspaper archives better than anyone in London and could find any story, no matter how obscure. The notion of the woman managing a complicated cataloguing system surprised Sophie. Mrs. Ingram's curls were always falling out of her pins, her clothing was wrinkled, and she seemed generally disheveled. Perhaps her organizational skills didn't extend to her outward appearance.

Mr. Leonard rose when he saw Sophie approach, cigarette hanging from his lips. Sophie had been shocked, on her first visit to the office, that he would smoke in front of her, a lady. Such a thing was unthinkably rude. But now she was used to seeing it and thought she would be startled to see him without the accessory.

"Miss Propriety, there you are." He smiled and bowed. "Lady Sophronia, I should have never doubted your story would arrive on time."

Mr. Leonard's belly was round, the buttons straining to hold his waist-coat in place. He had a thick dark mustache and thin dark hair, his scalp shining between the greased rows combed across the top of his head. His eyes bulged slightly, and he smiled with yellow teeth between jowls that hung from his jaws. The man's appearance gave an impression of a walrus.

"Good morning to you, Mr. Leonard." Sophie would have taken a seat, but there was not an empty chair to be had. And she was pleased not to be coddled or fussed over. In the newspaper office she was treated like any other employee. She took her notebook from her bag and drew out the story she'd written about the Royal Academy's Private View.

Mr. Leonard took the paper. He sat back in his chair, making notes with a pen as he read. "Yes, yes. Very nice." He crossed out a few words, then an entire paragraph, made another note, and put the article into a basket on his desk.

Sophie had been offended the first time he'd marked up her story, especially since she'd spent hours composing it, but Mr. Leonard had explained that he was simply "tightening the prose." The paper had a limited amount of space. Each word needed to be important, and some sentences were unnecessary. Once she'd gotten past the initial affront to her pride, Sophie had to admit the story was better for his improvements, and in the months since, she'd come to trust his judgment fully.

"And your illustration?" he asked.

Sophie opened her notebook, fishing through the pictures until she found the one she was looking for. The drawing was extremely detailed, showing a crush of people: men in top hats and tails, women in gowns with trains, and even children—admonished to be on their best behavior. The crowd was surrounded on all sides by the works of the masters in thick frames, brought in specifically for this year's summer exhibition. The drawing did little justice to the beauty of the art on display, but Sophie had purposely paid tribute to works she thought readers would recognize and appreciate.

She handed the paper across the desk, but Mr. Leonard's gaze was upon her notebook.

Sophie closed the notebook, not wanting to make the crime scene drawing available until she was certain she'd be allowed to write a story to go with it.

Mr. Leonard took the illustration, studying it closely. "Very nice, my dear. You captured the showcase exquisitely."

Perhaps he'd not noticed the other picture.

The editor gave back the drawing. "Thank you, my lady. Deliver the illustration to the engravers right away. Your story will run in tomorrow's edition." He turned back to his work.

Sophie recognized the dismissal but remained where she stood. "Sir, I wonder if perhaps I might write a different type of story."

Mr. Leonard glanced up. He blinked as if not understanding what she'd said. "What's that?"

"I hoped to write a different type of article. To report on an actual news story."

He set down his pen and leaned back in his chair, clasping his hands together over his tight waistcoat. "Such as?"

"The plight of orphans in the rookery or the expanding railroad's threat to city tenement buildings. Or perhaps the growing tension between France and Prussia . . ." Her words trailed off as he shook his head.

Mr. Leonard waved his hand, his brows pulling down as he frowned. "I see no need for that."

"Or suppose I was to report on a murder." She spoke carefully, not wanting to give any indication that such a story was already in the works.

Mr. Leonard chuckled, making his jowls wiggle. "My dear, Miss Propriety would never concern herself with something so unpleasant." He leaned forward, picking up his pen. "Focus your energy on ball gown sleeve length and ladies' face creams or something of the sort. Know your strengths. That's a lesson every good journalist should remember." He held up a finger. "Let the real reporters deal with the more complex stories."

Real reporters. His words stung, though she knew he didn't intend them to. Was he right? Was she being silly, hoping to venture beyond her world? Discouragement settled heavily on Sophie's shoulders as she bid Mr. Leonard farewell and crossed the room to the engravers.

Not wishing to startle Mr. Potts and cause him to make an error in his carving, she stood next to his table and cleared her throat quietly. "What a beautiful landscape, sir. You've captured the clouds quite perfectly."

"You've another drawing for me, my lady?" the carver muttered without looking up.

She set it on the table next to the block of wood he was carving.

He glanced at it and grunted. "More lace. Told you to simplify those details."

"I did."

He poked a finger at the image of a woman's gown. "This will take extra time."

"I apologize." Sophie winced at his sharp tone. "I didn't intend—"

"Lady Sophronia," Mr. Leonard called to her.

She was glad for the interruption. She left the overly detailed picture with Mr. Potts and returned to the editor's desk.

"The Hyde Park balloon launch tomorrow—you'll be there?"

"I planned on it."

"Good." Looking pleased, he nodded. "There's a real story for you, my lady."

As she left the office, the bit of self-doubt dissipated and was replaced by resolution. She was capable of so much more than sharing gossip about beauty regimens, fashion, and social blunders, and she'd prove it.

Instead of returning directly home, Sophie opened her notebook and gave the driver the list of names from the modiste, directing him to take her to the ladies' houses. She had a murder to investigate.

⚜

Two hours later Sophie returned home, surprised to see a functional-looking carriage in front of her house—surely it must be for a delivery, but it was strange that the unsightly conveyance was not parked more discreetly in the lane near the servant's entrance.

She removed her gloves and hat, feeling extremely satisfied by her outing. Fortunately she'd not had to speak with Charlotte Grey at all. Apparently the young woman's lady's maid had gone missing, and Charlotte was not receiving guests until she could find someone to arrange her hair before the picnic in Hyde Park.

The Grey's housekeeper had identified the young woman in Sophie's drawing as Jane Duffin, the missing lady's maid, but could give no further information about the young woman's whereabouts two evenings before.

Sophie considered which avenue to pursue next. She might call on Dr. Peabody to see whether examination of the body had provided any new clues. Or perhaps she would return to the neighborhood around the Porky Pie and question potential witnesses, but either way, she ought to change her clothing. The dress she'd worn before had stood out far too blatantly in the rookery. And, of course, she could use a cup of tea and perhaps a croissant.

The butler, Holloway, met her in the front hall. "Lady Sophronia, you have visitors."

Sophie smiled at the idea of her friends paying her a call. It was new to have women as friends. She'd been taught by her mother to consider other ladies as competitors or rivals. But Elizabeth, Hazel, Vivian, and Dahlia's support and friendship felt like an unexpected gift. Over the past weeks she'd grown surprisingly close to the four Orchids, as they called themselves. They were more like sisters to her than Prissy had ever been.

Sophie touched the brooch on her lapel. Dahlia had presented one to each of the young ladies a few weeks earlier as they'd congregated in yet another library. "If the Casanovas can have their silly tiepins, then the Blue Orchid Society shall have our own emblem," she'd declared.

It was no surprise that an article of jewelry chosen by Dahlia Lancaster would be exquisite. Surrounded by filigreed silver and hand-painted on a mother-of-pearl background, the deep-blue flower was stunning.

A clearing throat pulled her from her train of thought, and she realized the butler was still awaiting an answer. "Thank you, Holloway. Who are the visitors?"

"A Detective Graham and Sergeant Lester, my lady. They are with your grandmother in the drawing room."

She blinked, and a wiggle of apprehension moved through her middle as Sophie remembered Detective Graham's dismissive attitude at the murder scene. What could the man want? Had he learned she'd continued her investigation and had arrived to reprimand her? The thought of the man's disapproving frown made her hesitate.

But Sophie intended to be a news reporter, and of course, such a profession required perseverance. Detective Graham was not the first person to resent her investigating—nor, she feared, would he be the last. Besides, Mimi would be there, and Sergeant Lester was friendly enough.

As she climbed the stairs, Sophie lifted her chin and took a deep breath, blew it out slowly, and adopted an expression of calm confidence.

When she entered the drawing room, the men rose from their seats on the sofa, and Dorrit lifted her head from her napping-pillow in the sun and barked.

Mimi smiled widely as if it were the most natural thing in the world to entertain two policemen. "There she is now. Come and join us, my dear. I've already sent for tea."

Detective Graham inclined his head. "Good afternoon, Lady Sophronia." He spoke her name with a hint of exasperation, and she wondered if he was bothered she'd not told him her title before.

Well, that was entirely her prerogative. She'd decided even before meeting the men that her investigative work would go much smoother without the extra attention her title garnered. "Detective. Sergeant." She nodded at the men and sat on a chair beside her grandmother.

"Pleasure to see you again, miss . . . I mean, my lady," Sergeant Lester said.

She smiled at the man, noticing in the light of day that he had a thick scar on his cheek, cutting through his reddish side-whiskers. "And you as well, Sergeant."

Mimi clasped her hands. "And what a merry coincidence, don't you know. The detective here is the very same constable who arrested me at the suffragette demonstration in front of Westminster Palace all those years ago." She smiled at the detective. "How long has it been, Detective? Eight, nine years at least, I believe."

Detective Graham cleared his throat, looking decidedly uncomfortable at the revelation. "Yes, your ladyship. And as I said earlier, I apologize for the wrist shackles, but it is a policy of the constabulary."

"Oh, I bear you no ill will," Mimi said, waving it off. "None at all. I understand you were only doing your job. And it is not every day a woman is taken into custody by such a handsome man."

Sergeant Lester cleared his throat, his hand covering a grin as his gaze met Sophie's.

She let a smirk pull at her lips but didn't permit the detective or her grandmother to see.

Mrs. Fredrickson entered with a tea tray, and Sophie could sense the detective's relief at the distraction.

Mimi thanked the housekeeper and motioned toward the table. "Sophronia, will you pour out?"

As she served the tea, Sophie took the opportunity to study the detective through glances. Her grandmother's assessment was not wrong. Detective Graham's hair was dark and his jaw strong, and if Sophie was a romantic person, she'd say his eyes were the deep blue of a clear sky on a late summer evening. But she was definitely not a romantic person, and the color of a man's eyes did not compensate for his patronizing manner. And she'd had enough of that for one day.

Once they all had their tea, Sophie stirred milk and sugar into her cup, then sat back in her chair and took a sip. "Now, gentlemen, to what do I owe the pleasure of your visit?"

Detective Graham set his cup on his saucer. "My lady, we've come for your help." He frowned, looking as if he didn't like what he was saying. "Your observations about the dead woman's gown Monday evening were very astute, and of course, you would know better than we where to inquire about its origins. If . . ." The detective cleared his throat and glanced at Sergeant Lester.

The sergeant nodded.

Detective Graham pursed his lips. "As you suggested, my lady"—he scowled, looking as if the words tasted sour in his mouth—"we might discover where the gown was purchased, perhaps we can learn the identity of the victim."

A very self-satisfied feeling came over Sophie, and she took another sip of tea to keep smugness from showing in her expression. "I see." She set the teacup on the saucer and placed it on the table in front of her. "Yes, I can certainly help with that." Reaching down, she opened her bag and took out the drawings and notebook, holding them in her lap. She glanced at her grandmother and saw Mimi's encouraging nod. "Or, to save time, I could just tell you the murdered woman's name."

CHAPTER 5

JONATHAN STARED, DUMBFOUNDED AT LADY Sophronia as his mind processed her statement. He turned to the sergeant, who looked every bit as confused, and then back to the young woman. "I'm sorry, my lady; did you say you know the victim's identity?"

"I do." Lady Sophronia glanced between the men, looking very pleased with herself.

Her demeanor chafed at Jonathan, as did her claim. That she, a snooping noblewoman, should, on a whim, make headway in the investigation when seasoned police officers had come up short was frustrating, to say the least.

"Well done, my lady." Sergeant Lester leaned forward, clasping his hands together and apparently feeling none of the irritation that made Jonathan's jaw tight. "How did you work it out? Was it the dress?"

Lady Sophronia nodded. She fingered through the papers and pulled one out, glanced at it, and then extended it across the low table to Jonathan.

He took it and studied the illustration, recognizing it immediately as a drawing of the dead woman's gown. The depiction was remarkably detailed, with layers of ruffles and lace. It was even colored with a light-blue chalk.

Sergeant Lester moved closer to examine the picture. "My lady, this is very impressive."

"Of course it is." The dowager countess leaned forward to see the paper as well, then sat back in her carved chair and shrugged. "Did you expect anything less?" She whistled, and the pug jumped up and ran to her, allowing the woman to settle the dog onto her lap.

"Thank you," Lady Sophronia said. She lifted her chin toward the paper. "I showed this picture to the dressmakers I considered likely to have sewn the gown, and Madame Delacourt—a modiste on Bond Street—recognized it. She gave me the names of women who'd purchased gowns in this style and color, and after more inquiries, I discovered to which young lady it belonged." She stopped herself, apparently before giving away the lady's name. "The victim worked as her lady's maid."

"That's why the gown didn't fit." Sergeant Lester snapped his fingers. "Brilliant, my lady."

The dowager countess scratched behind her dog's ears and nodded at her granddaughter, pride evident in her smile.

"A good bit of detective work," Jonathan admitted, trying to keep the grudging tone out of his voice.

"Thank you." The smallest smile pulled at Sophronia's mouth, and her cheeks went pink.

The effect was charming, and one Jonathan supposed had enchanted quite a few gentlemen of the *ton*. The thought further irritated him, and he shook it away, leaning back into the plush sofa. "So who is she?"

Lady Sophronia set the remaining papers on her lap atop a notebook and folded her hands over them. She paused before speaking, her brows pinched together as if considering her answer. After a moment, she looked directly at Jonathan. "Before I tell you, I wish for you to understand that I am not simply engaging in this investigation for a diversion or out of boredom. I work as a society columnist for the *Illustrated London News*, and I—"

"'Miss Propriety's People and Prattle'?" Sergeant Lester interrupted with a gasp, setting down his biscuit. "My lady, *you're* Miss Propriety?"

Lady Sophronia's cheeks went even darker. "Yes, I—well, you see, the name was my editor's idea."

"My mother reads your column religiously—quotes Miss Propriety on a regular basis." He grinned like a child in a confectionary shop. "Your story about the Queen's talking parrot was very diverting."

"Wasn't it?" The dowager countess laughed, breaking off a piece of biscuit to feed to her dog. "A bird that begs for money, if you can believe it."

"And just last week Mother insisted I take her to purchase a round-brimmed hat, per your recommendation," the sergeant continued.

"A round-brimmed hat is very fashionable this year," the older woman agreed.

"And wouldn't you know, while we were out, I found a cerulean blue necktie that quite brought out the color of my eyes—"

Jonathan cleared his throat, interrupting the sergeant. He had no desire to discover where this conversation might lead. He shot a look at Sergeant

Lester, telling him silently to hold his tongue and keep to the topic at hand. *We are trying to solve a murder here.* "Lady Sophronia? Please continue."

The young woman nodded. "I hoped that by discovering and reporting a story—a real story, not simply a commentary about fashion or gossip—the editor would take my writing more seriously. I wish to work as a news reporter."

She glanced at her grandmother, and the dowager countess smiled and nodded.

"So in return for providing me with the name of the victim, you want the exclusive story on this murder," Jonathan said.

"Not only on the murder. I hope to see firsthand the solving of the crime and the arrest of the person responsible. I wish to assist in the investigation."

Jonathan shook his head. *Absolutely not.* A murder investigation was often dangerous. The very idea was ridiculous, and he would not entertain it for a moment. They had wasted enough time drinking tea and chatting about hats and parrots as it was.

Lady Sophronia's eyes tightened, as did her lips.

Stubborn.

Compelling her to give the victim's name would not be difficult. Withholding information in a criminal investigation was in itself a punishable offense. If she refused to reveal it, Lady Sophronia would, at the very least, be taken into custody. Perhaps a bit of time in the cells at H Division would loosen her lips. And if it came down to it, he and Sergeant Lester could find the information themselves. She'd given them enough to go on.

Jonathan steeled himself for her reaction and opened his mouth to refuse her proposal, but something in her expression made him pause. Beneath the self-assuredness and defiance, she held herself tightly, as if bracing against a rejection she was certain would come. A flicker of doubt moved in her eyes, and something else Jonathan knew she hadn't intended to show. He recognized the glimmer of hope that if she was just given a chance . . . A memory surfaced in his mind of a young man, an orphan from Wapping, submitting his application to join the police force. Out of habit, he rubbed the fob on his pocket watch chain.

Lifting the picture of the dress, he studied it as he contemplated. Truth be told, Lady Sophronia had done a fine job pursuing her lead, and her knowledge on the subject of ladies' fashion had saved him hours of footwork and interviews—in dress shops, of all places. And she was intuitive. She'd pointed out things he did not think a typical civilian would have noticed.

If he refused Lady Sophronia, she would most likely make inquiries on her own, and a young noblewoman investigating a murder in Spitalfields was hardly an ideal situation.

He set the picture back on the low table in front of him and glanced at the others.

Lady Sophronia, the dowager countess, the dog, and Sergeant Lester watched him silently, awaiting his answer.

"My lady," he began slowly. "As you are no doubt aware, law enforcement and the press are often at odds. A reporter seeks a compelling story in order to sell newspapers, while the police, on the other hand, are working to apprehend a criminal. You understand my reluctance to reveal the progress of the investigation to a person who intends to make it public."

Lady Sophronia nodded. "Yes, I understand. I won't write the story until the case is solved and the criminal apprehended. I wouldn't want to tip off a murderer to any specifics of your hunt for him."

Jonathan nodded. "I have your word on that?"

"You do."

"In that case, my lady, you have a deal. Information about this case will be given to you alone."

Lady Sophronia extended her hand but stopped before taking his. She pulled back. "And I will be allowed to help with the investigation?"

She wasn't to be easily dissuaded, that was for certain. "Insofar as I determine it to be safe. We search for a murderer, a person who has killed and may kill again. You are not a police officer, my lady, and I will not allow you to expose yourself to potential harm. Nor will I put the investigation at risk. If I feel you are in danger, I will forbid you to continue, and you must comply. Do you understand?"

"Yes, I understand." She shook his hand, looking very serious, even as excitement sparked in her eyes.

Jonathan studied her expression for any sign of deception. "And you'll not go off investigating on your own?"

"I will defer to your expertise, Detective." She gave a nod.

"Very well, then." He released her hand and sat back, satisfied. Now that he'd made the decision, he considered how to best use the young lady's talents.

Lady Sophronia handed the other two papers across the table.

Jonathan took them, angling them so Sergeant Lester could see as well. The first drawing was a rendering of the dead woman's face, and the second . . .

"Good heavens." Sergeant Lester blew out a breath. "This is marvelous."

Jonathan could not argue. The depiction of the crime scene was incredible. The murdered woman was drawn in detail, as was the entirety of the alleyway, even down to the bottle Jonathan had kicked and the clothes on the lines overhead.

"Look here." Sergeant Lester pointed. "You can see the scuffs on her boots. And I remember this stack of crates. The entire alleyway looks exactly as it was."

"This is exceedingly accurate, my lady." Jonathan said. "How did you—there was not time for you to have drawn this level of detail in the alley on Monday. Did you return to the scene?"

Lady Sophronia's cheeks were pink again.

"My granddaughter possesses a remarkable memory, the ability to recall details and record them in pictures," the older woman said.

"The specifics of the memories do not last for long," Lady Sophronia said. "So I must draw them quickly. That is why I made the initial sketches at the scene."

"Your grandmother is correct; this is remarkable. And helpful to the investigation," Jonathan said. The combination of artistic talent and an exceptional memory was an impressive tool. "I'd have sent for a photographer to document the scene, but as you know, it grew dark too quickly. And rain surely washed away any remaining evidence." He held up the picture. "Can I keep this?"

"Of course. I have another."

He set the drawing on the pile. "And now, my lady, would you tell me the victim's name?"

Lady Sophronia opened her notebook, glancing at the page. "Her name is Jane Duffin, lady's maid to Miss Charlotte Grey on Arlington Street."

How fortuitous; they were only a few streets away. "And did you speak to the family?"

"No, only the housekeeper. I didn't wish to disturb them earlier than was appropriate for visiting."

Interesting that the same woman who unapologetically barged onto the crime scene should now hesitate to offend. "My lady, this is a criminal investigation. Time is of the essence. We need not wait until it is convenient to speak to a person of interest." Jonathan glanced at an ornate gold clock on the mantel. The hour was past noon. He'd already invested a day and a half into this case and finally had a lead worth pursuing. Rising, he took the drawings from the table and inclined his head to the women. "Thank you for the tea."

"You are welcome anytime, Detective Graham," the dowager countess said. "And you as well, Sergeant Lester."

"A pleasure, ladies." The sergeant set his cup and saucer on the table, picked up a few extra biscuits, bowed, and started from the room.

Jonathan followed. When he reached the door, he turned back. "Lady Sophronia, are you coming?"

The young woman's face lit in a smile as she jumped up, kissed her grandmother, patted the dog, and hurried toward him.

Jonathan inclined his head, allowing her to precede him from the drawing room. As he followed, he realized this was the first true smile he'd seen on Lady Sophronia. Her round cheeks held the most fascinating dimples, and her bright-eyed enthusiasm was something Jonathan did not encounter often in a murder investigation. And surprisingly, the sight alleviated quite a lot of the irritation of her company.

CHAPTER 6

THE THREE RETRIEVED THEIR GLOVES and hats, and Sergeant Lester handed Sophie into the carriage beside Detective Graham. Since there was room for only two in the police carriage, the sergeant climbed up to sit by the driver.

Sophie fingered her notebook through the velvet fabric of her bag. Despite giving every indication that he did not want her assistance, the detective had acquiesced, and Sophie could neither explain his apparent change of heart nor contain her anticipation. She crossed her ankles to keep her feet from tapping. As they drove, she considered the case, and her mind turned with scenarios. Had Jane Duffin been killed in a lovers' quarrel? Or perhaps she'd stumbled upon a plot and was murdered for the killer to maintain secrecy. Had she been involved in something illegal?

"You're nervous," Detective Graham said.

Sophie glanced to the side and saw that he was watching her. "I'm not," she began, but following the detective's gaze to her hands, she realized she was twisting her fingers and gave a sheepish smile. "Well, perhaps I am a bit. I wonder what we shall find. Why was Jane Duffin murdered? And who did it?"

He shrugged. "Don't expect the answers to be spectacular. Most murders are committed over money or passion." He held up a finger for each word. "Anger, pride, and of course, some are crimes of opportunity; but usually we find the killer is at the very least an acquaintance."

"Have you investigated many murders, then, Detective?"

He snorted. "I work at H Division stationhouse in Whitechapel. Yes, you could say I've investigated my share of murders. And most are never solved."

"Why is that?" The information surprised her.

"No one reports the person missing, no family comes forward . . ." Detective Graham shrugged. "We do our best to identify the deceased and search for the next of kin or, if possible, a friend or employer. But more often than not, the victim remains unnamed and is interred in a pauper's grave."

"It is tragic, isn't it?" Sophie said quietly. "That a person should leave the earth without anyone to mourn him or even to notice."

"It is indeed, my lady," Detective Graham said. He swallowed.

His face didn't show any emotion, but she could hear a touch of bitterness in his voice. "What you have—a beautiful home, food, a loving family—it should not be taken for granted."

She didn't appreciate his appraisal after spending only a short amount of time with her, but she agreed with his words all the same. She *was* very fortunate. Life in the rookery with poverty, hunger, and danger a factor of everyday existence was completely the reverse of her privileged upbringing. She shifted at the twist of guilt she felt and found it difficult to meet the detective's gaze.

Instead she looked out the window. "I'm glad at least Jane Duffin has a name."

"Let us hope we can give her justice as well," he said.

When the carriage stopped, Sergeant Lester jumped down and assisted Sophie to alight.

The Greys' housekeeper, Mrs. Trenton, opened the door and raised her brows in surprise when she saw Sophie on the doorstep for the second time that day. "You've returned, my lady." She gave a curtsy and glanced behind at the two men accompanying her.

"Yes," Sophie said. "I'd hoped to speak to the family. Are they at home?"

"I'm afraid Mr. and Mrs. Grey are out, and as I told you earlier, Miss Grey isn't taking visitors. Good day, my lady." The housekeeper moved as if to close the door.

With a quick motion, Detective Graham stepped forward and pushed against the door, blocking it from closing. He cleared his throat. "Good afternoon. Detective Graham, of the Metropolitan Police." He opened his jacket to display the silver badge on his waistcoat. "Please notify your mistress that I will speak to her at once."

Mrs. Trenton tightened her hand on the door, looking as if she would argue.

"We are investigating the murder of a member of this household," the detective said. "If Miss Grey cannot receive us here, perhaps she would prefer to conduct an interview at the station in Whitechapel."

Mrs. Trenton's lips pressed together. "Of course, sir. Please come in."

Sophie exchanged a gratified look with the sergeant at the detective's handling of the situation.

She quite liked the idea of Charlotte Grey being taken to a police station in London's East End, and she almost wished the housekeeper had continued her protest so she could witness it.

She and the men removed their hats and gloves, giving them to a downstairs maid before following Mrs. Trenton up the staircase to a sitting room.

"Would you care for tea?" the housekeeper asked in a tone at odds with the politeness of her inquiry.

Sergeant Lester's face lit up. He glanced at the detective.

"That will not be necessary," Detective Graham said. "This is not a social call. Please fetch Miss Grey."

"Very well." Mrs. Trenton departed.

Disappointment creased the sergeant's forehead, but he covered it quickly. "I say, this is a splendid room." He took a step forward and tilted up his head to study the crystal chandelier. "A man could get used to investigating in Mayfair. The tea alone . . ."

Detective Graham strode to the window, moving aside the lace curtains with a sweep of his arm to peer out at the street below.

Sophie had just sat in an armchair when Charlotte Grey entered. "Lady Sophronia." She gave a small curtsy. "I was sure Mrs. Trenton was mistaken and it was your sister who'd come."

"Thank you for seeing us." Sophie took the notebook from her bag, opened it on her lap, and removed the pencil from between the pages.

"Prissy and I are to go picnicking today with the Casanovas, but of course you know that." Charlotte fluffed her overskirts and glanced into the gold-framed mirror above the mantel, fixing a blonde curl into place. "You heard, no doubt, that I danced with Lord Meredith twice at the Hamptons' ball two evenings ago. I expect that is what you wished to ask me about." She sat in the chair opposite Sophie, lifting her chin to elongate her neck.

Of course the young woman assumed Sophie had come to interview her for a story, that she'd opened her notebook to sketch a picture. "Miss Grey, I am actually here regarding another matter." She set her pencil back in the crease of the notebook and turned deliberately toward the men. "This is Detective Graham and Sergeant Lester, of the Metropolitan Police."

Charlotte looked at the police officers as if just realizing they were in the room as well. "Oh yes." She sniffed and looked away as if the sight bored her.

Sophie cringed at the woman's rudeness.

Detective Graham did not seem to notice the ungracious behavior, nor did he wait for Sophie to finish her introductions. He removed a notebook from his breast pocket, flipping open the leather cover with a practiced move. "Miss Grey, you are aware that your lady's maid is dead, are you not?"

She sighed. "I heard."

"When is the last time you saw Jane Duffin?"

"Monday evening. Jane arranged my hair for dinner."

"At what time?"

She tipped her head, squinting. "I suppose it was around five o'clock. I attended dinner at Helen Rothschild's."

"And Miss Rothschild can confirm this?"

"Of course. As can Lady Lorene and Lady Priscilla. We always take dinner together before a ball."

The detective made a note. "And you did not see Miss Duffin after dinner?"

"No. My friends and I dressed at the Rothschilds' and went directly to the Hamptons' ball."

Sophie was certain Charlotte's account was true. The Darling Debs always arrived at a ball en masse.

"What time did you leave the ball?" Detective Graham asked, taking a seat across from Miss Grey.

"Two thirty yesterday morning, I believe. And Jane was not here when I returned. I was quite put out at having a chambermaid help me undress."

"I imagine it was very difficult," Detective Graham muttered as he wrote in his notebook. He looked up. "And you returned directly home from the Hamptons'?"

Charlotte studied her fingernails. "Yes."

Sophie followed the detective's example, writing down the times in her notebook. A record of the chronology was a very intelligent idea. She wished she'd thought of it herself.

"Can anyone verify your presence at the ball, Miss Grey?" Detective Graham asked.

"Everyone. I wore a very fashion-forward gown and danced the waltz twice with Lord Meredith." She gave a shrug and a pleased smile. "I'm certain it is all anyone is talking about."

"And did you not wonder what had become of your lady's maid?" the detective asked. "Did you make no inquiries?"

"I assumed she ran off." Charlotte shook her head. "You know how unreliable servants can be."

Sergeant Lester's good-natured face seemed to darken as he watched Charlotte.

A hot wave of shame swept over Sophie as she listened to the conversation and watched the men's reactions. Did they assume Sophie possessed the same self-important prejudices just because she and Charlotte had both been born into high Society? *I am not like this.* She kept her face turned down toward her notebook as her cheeks burned. *Am I?* She was different; she knew she was. Sophie glanced up at the two men, willing them to see she was more than the Earl of Mather's spoiled daughter.

Detective Graham continued writing in his notebook. "And your parents?"

"They ate dinner at home, I presume. They were already at the Hamptons' when I arrived. Surely you do not think *they* know anything about Jane's death?"

Detective Graham looked up but didn't respond to Charlotte's question. His expression did not reveal his thoughts. "Sergeant, you will verify Miss Grey's alibi, won't you? And those of her parents?"

Sergeant Lester nodded, writing in his own notebook. "Yes, sir."

"Alibi?" Charlotte gave an offended scowl. "Certainly I am not under suspicion."

"Did you notice anything different about Miss Duffin recently?" Detective Graham asked. "Was she acting peculiar in any way?"

"I didn't notice."

"Can you think of anyone who might have wished her harm?"

"I'm sure I don't know. The servants' private lives are their own." She rose. "Now, if you'll excuse me, Detective. I have an outing to prepare for and no lady's maid to assist with my presentation."

Detective Graham stood and inclined his head. "Thank you, Miss Grey."

Charlotte started toward the door. "Always a pleasure, Lady Sophronia." She spoke the words over her shoulder.

Detective Graham sat in Charlotte's vacated seat.

"My lady, do you know the location of the Hamptons' ball?"

"Grosvenor Square, just a few streets away." Sophie was glad he continued on with the investigation without commenting on Charlotte Grey's dismissive attitude. "And I could ask my family if the Greys attended. They were all there."

"While you were in the rookery investigating a murder." The detective smirked, but he didn't appear to be mocking her. His behavior felt more like a friendly tease.

Sergeant Lester sat on a sofa on the other side of the detective. "Imagine I'd rather be studying a corpse than mingling in that company too." He rolled his eyes toward the doorway.

"Not everyone's so . . ." Sophie grimaced. "She's definitely one of the worst."

"Well, that's a relief, ain't it?" The sergeant winked.

Sergeant Lester's simple action gave Sophie a warm swell of gratitude.

"My lady, how long did it take you to get to Spitalfields from Mayfair two nights ago?" Detective Graham asked, recapturing her attention.

"Well, I didn't go directly there," Sophie said. "I drove around for quite some time before arriving at the Porky Pie." She thought for a moment. "I'd estimate a straight trip would take forty-five minutes, maybe more. The roads were very crowded."

"Don't suppose the Greys could have left Mayfair, traveled to Wentworth Street, dumped the body, and returned in less than an hour and a half at minimum," Sergeant Lester said.

"Surely not," Sophie agreed.

Detective Graham frowned as he considered. "Even with lighter traffic, the absence would have been noticed." He tapped his pencil on his lips. "So what transpired between when Miss Duffin arranged Miss Grey's hair at five o'clock and when her body was discovered just after eight?"

"What indeed?" Sergeant Lester said.

Detective Graham looked down at Sophie's notebook, appearing as if he'd comment on her timeline, but stopped and stood when Mrs. Trenton entered the room. "If you please, madam, gather the staff."

The housekeeper looked irritated at being ordered around by someone who was not her employer, but she left to do as he asked.

"Sergeant, interview every member of this household. Discover their whereabouts Monday night, and verify alibis."

"Yes, sir," Sergeant Lester said.

Detective Graham leaned closer to the sergeant, lowering his voice. "Pay attention to inconsistencies."

After a few minutes, members of the staff began filling the room.

"I should like to see Miss Duffin's quarters now," the detective said when Mrs. Trenton returned.

She nodded. "Come along, then."

"My lady." Detective Graham stood aside, motioning for Sophie to precede him.

As the housekeeper led them from the common areas of the house, Sophie's confidence shrank, and her discomfort increased with every step. She walked as softly as possible on the carpet of the corridor leading through the family's private rooms and winced at the sound of Detective Graham's steady footsteps behind her as they ascended to the upper stories. He apparently didn't share her unease at intruding on the Greys' personal space.

They continued up a narrow staircase to the attic and started down the passageway. The top floor of the house was very warm, nearly stifling, and Sophie imagined it was uncomfortable at night. Unlit candle sconces were set at intervals along the walls. The upper story must not be equipped with gas lighting, and she wondered if her own household's servants' quarters were similar.

"Here we are." Mrs. Trenton opened a door to reveal a small chamber. "Jane's bed is on the left side."

Inside the room were two wooden frame beds separated by a narrow bureau beneath a window. A wardrobe and washstand stood on the wall beside the door. *So few possessions.* A surge of emotion welled up in Sophie's throat. Seeing the space where Jane Duffin had lived made the tragedy of her death feel very real. She swallowed, forcing back the tears threatening to spill over. The surprise emotions frustrated her. Weeping on an investigation was hardly befitting of an investigative reporter.

Detective Graham strode through the door, not seeming shaken at all. "Who shared this room with the deceased?"

"Miss Primm," the housekeeper said. "I'll send her up directly." She departed, her shoes clacking on the steps.

Sophie hesitated at the doorway, then entered the room. She studied the pattern of the worn quilt on the woman's bed, keeping her face averted from the detective until she could master her emotions.

He opened the wardrobe, looking over the hanging gowns. "I imagine some of these are castoffs from her mistress as well?"

Sophie wiped her eyes and joined him. Most of the dresses were practical-looking, as she'd expect for a servant, but among them hung gowns of a much higher quality. She tugged the skirt of a rose-colored dress, feeling the fine silk between her fingers. "This one, certainly."

He nodded and began inspecting the pockets of the coats and dresses.

Sophie wasn't certain what he was looking for, but the idea of searching through a person's belongings without their consent troubled her.

She glanced at the doorway, thinking this may be her only opportunity to speak to the man alone. "Detective Graham, I feel I should apologize for Miss Grey."

He pulled his head from the wardrobe, confusion creasing his features. "Why?"

"Well, she was very rude, and—"

"And how is that your fault, Lady Sophronia?"

She grimaced, feeling foolish at mentioning it in the first place. "I don't know. I just wanted you to know I disapprove of her behavior."

He studied her face and after a moment gave a nod, then returned to looking in the wardrobe. "Do you think she's the murderer?"

Sophie wasn't certain if the nod was a dismissal of her sentiment or an acknowledgment. But she was relieved to focus once more on the case. "No."

"Neither do I. She has no motive that I can discern." The detective took a hatbox from the shelf and peered inside.

"She didn't act guilty, rather bothered by the whole business, it seemed," Sophie said. "Besides, she didn't have time to remove the body to Spitalfields and return for the ball."

"The murderer and the person who delivered the body to the alley behind the Porky Pie are not necessarily one and the same." He closed the wardrobe and opened a bureau drawer.

"I had not considered that," Sophie said, realizing she'd jumped to a conclusion without sufficient evidence. The murderer could have had a partner. Or could have imposed on someone else to dispose of the body.

"Hello." A slender woman in a simple dress stood in the doorway. By the threads of gray beneath her white cap and the wrinkles around her eyes, Sophie judged her age to be close to forty.

"You must be Miss Primm." Detective Graham did not appear the least chagrined at being caught pawing through the woman's clothing.

"I am."

"Detective Graham, of the Metropolitan Police." He showed his badge. "And this is Lady Sophronia Bremerton."

"How do you do?" Miss Primm curtsied and swallowed hard.

Sophie recognized her red eyes and the trembling of her lip as indicators that the woman was near to breaking into tears. She offered her handkerchief and led Miss Primm to sit on one of the beds, then sat on the other, facing her. The space between them was so narrow that their knees were nearly touching. It occurred to Sophie that the women must have been close friends—it would be difficult not to be, sharing such a room. Perhaps they sat this way in the evenings and confided in one another. "We have only a few questions." Sophie tried to speak in a soothing voice and glanced at the detective, grimacing. She hoped he would not upset the woman further with his interrogation.

Detective Graham lifted his chin toward the woman, tipping his head. He wanted Sophie to conduct the interview.

She took a calming breath, considering how to go about questioning a person who was very much distressed. "I am very sorry about your roommate, Miss Primm. I take it the two of you were friends?"

"Yes." Miss Primm's voice was a sob. She cleared her throat and wiped her eyes. "I beg your pardon."

"Take your time," Sophie said, feeling her own tears returning. She gave a sympathetic smile and glanced at Detective Graham.

He watched her, brows drawn together.

At the scrutiny, Sophie felt heat rise in her cheeks. Of course he was pondering the case, not her. What a silly thought.

"Jane and I have worked together for the past five years," Miss Primm said finally.

"And when did you last see her?"

"Monday, late afternoon—I am not sure of the precise time."

Sophie hesitated, unsure how to proceed. She glanced at the detective, and seeing his nod, she took a deep breath. "When Miss Duffin . . . when she was discovered, she was dressed very elegantly. I expect she was going somewhere special? Perhaps to meet a man?"

Miss Primm looked down at the handkerchief in her lap, creasing the folds between her fingers. "I don't know . . ." She glanced up, then to the side.

Sophie recognized her look of guilt. If it were known that Jane Duffin had had a beau, her position would likely have been terminated. She reached forward, placing a hand over Miss Primm's. "I know you want to keep her secret, and that is admirable, but if we are to discover what happened to Jane, we need to know the truth. She is beyond reprimand now."

Miss Primm spoke after a long pause. "George Lewis." She didn't look up. "He works as a footman at the Belcourt Assembly Hall."

"Thank you," Sophie said.

"Did Jane have any family?" Detective Graham asked. His voice had softened, sounding more gentle.

Miss Primm shook her head. "Her parents died, and her brother."

"Did either Miss Duffin or Mr. Lewis have any enemies?" Detective Graham asked.

"Jane was well-liked. I can't imagine anyone wishing her harm." Miss Primm creased the handkerchief some more. "But George—Jane told me he was in a fistfight last week with her old sweetheart, Nick Sloan. Nearly got the pair of them sacked."

"And does Mr. Sloan work at the Belcourt as well?" Sophie asked.

She nodded. "In the stables."

"Is this George Lewis?" Detective Graham lifted a frame from the bureau and turned it toward the women. The photograph inside was not of good quality and was very small. It appeared to have been taken at a fair or exposition. But the woman was clearly recognizable as Jane Duffin. The man standing beside her was young and had a trimmed mustache and long sideburns.

"Yes, that is him."

"I've seen this man," Detective Graham said. "And I can be fairly certain he is not Jane Duffin's murderer."

"How could you possibly know that?" Sophie asked.

"George Lewis's body lies at this moment in the city morgue."

Miss Primm gasped.

"He was found Monday night just a few streets away from Miss Duffin," Detective Graham said. He tapped his finger on his lips as he studied the picture. "Dr. Peabody estimated the time of his death to be between six and seven that evening as well."

"Another murder?" Sophie rose and took the photograph from him. "Why did you not tell me?" She had assumed they were sharing their information, but he had deliberately kept this from her.

"Murder victims being discovered in the rookery are not so uncommon that I even considered the two might be related."

"Well, they clearly are." Sophie still felt indignant at being taken by surprise.

"I think we're done here," Detective Graham said. "Thank you, Miss Primm. Make certain you also speak to the sergeant."

"Yes, sir, Detective." She stood, curtsied, and held out the handkerchief to Sophie. "My lady."

"Keep it." Sophie clasped a hand over the woman's and patted her shoulder. "And again, I am so very sorry for your loss."

"Thank you." Miss Primm hurried from the room.

Sophie gave the photograph to the detective and started to exit as well.

Detective Graham caught her elbow, stopping her. "Well done, my lady." He glanced toward where the maid had gone. "You conducted a fine interview."

CHAPTER 7

AFTER MAKING CERTAIN SERGEANT LESTER had the remaining interviews of the household well in hand, Jonathan sent for constables to meet them at the Belcourt Assembly Hall, and he and Lady Sophronia left the Greys' house for Chelsea.

While the carriage made its way through the quiet streets of Belgravia, Jonathan glanced to the side, considering the young woman who sat next to him. Lady Sophronia Bremerton was very much an enigma. And while Jonathan considered himself to be an exceptional judge of human nature, this young lady was a puzzle he had yet to solve. In less than a day she'd repeatedly surprised him, and each time he thought he'd reached an assessment of her nature, she proved him wrong yet again. Was Lady Sophronia the impertinent snoop he'd encountered at the murder scene, the smug aristocrat who'd withheld the victim's identity, the hopeful journalist who wished only for a chance to further her career, the hesitant trespasser in a high-Society house, or the gentle woman who'd comforted a servant with kind words? Were all of these attributes the facets of a complicated woman? Or was each a mask exhibited deliberately to manipulate a situation and achieve a desired result?

He was, both by nature and as a result of his occupation, a distrustful person. But in spite of Lady Sophronia's contradictions of character, she had, at moments, seemed very genuine. Her emotional reaction to entering the dead woman's room had surprised him, as well as her kind treatment of Miss Primm. Neither response had felt contrived.

Jonathan would certainly not have been as patient with the weeping servant. And he didn't flatter himself thinking he'd have done a better job questioning her. Lady Sophronia's understanding had produced more information from the woman than he could have collected with his tried-and-true tactics.

He grudgingly admitted to himself a feminine perspective, in some situations, was perhaps not the worst idea.

"Is that a bullet?" Lady Sophronia asked.

Her words shook him from his musings, and he shifted in his seat to better speak to his companion. "Pardon me, my lady?"

"If you don't mind, Detective, while we are working, I would prefer you call me Miss Bremerton. And introduce me as such."

"I hardly think that is appropriate."

She wrinkled her nose, her expression thoughtful. "Being referred to as *lady* might put people off. I don't wish to jeopardize our investigation because someone is intimidated by the title."

She was probably right. People were likely to be on their guard speaking to the daughter of a nobleman. Getting information from witnesses was difficult enough without the added layer of caution. And here was yet another of the woman's surprising attributes. He didn't imagine many would so readily obscure something as powerful as a title in order to put others at ease. But he also didn't imagine many peers or their families participated in murder investigations.

"Very well, Miss Bremerton," he said.

"Thank you."

He felt the cold of his watch fob and realized the ornament was the object of Miss Bremerton's earlier inquiry. "It *is* a bullet. It . . . ended the life of a friend of mine." A lump constricted his throat, and he was surprised he could still be so affected after all these years.

She leaned closer, squinting to study it. "Rather macabre. I wonder that you keep it."

The question in her tone didn't seem to be criticizing, only curious. "It is a reminder," he said.

"Of your friend?" She glanced up from her scrutiny, her gaze meeting his.

Saying yes would be easy enough, and it would end the conversation, but he owed Tom more than that. The bullet was a reminder of so much more than the man who'd given him a chance when the world would just as soon have been rid of another orphan pauper. He felt the bumps and ridges of the lump of metal with his thumbnail. The fob represented not only the loss of his mentor but also his own failure that day.

"It reminds me to take nothing for granted." He held up the bullet between two fingers, reinforcing the small size of the deformed lump of lead. "That something small and seemingly insignificant can change everything."

His voice was raspy, and he cleared his throat as he let the chain drop back against his waistcoat.

"I'm sorry," she said. "He must have been important to you."

"Yes."

"What was your friend's name?"

"Tom Stackhouse." Jonathan hadn't spoken the name aloud since the funeral three years earlier. Hearing it made his heart ache. But at the same time, it was of some comfort that a new person would hear it and know Tom had lived. "He was the best man I ever knew."

"High praise indeed." Miss Bremerton gave a soft smile. She turned to look out the window, leaning back to get a better view of the road ahead. "We are nearly there."

Jonathan was grateful for the change of topic. Breaking into tears on the way to apprehend a murderer would seriously undermine his competence as a representative of the Crown.

When they reached the assembly hall, a woman led them to the administrative wing of the building. They passed through a waiting room and were shown into the manager's office. Upon their entering, a slender man with wire spectacles and a thin mustache rose to greet them.

"Edgar Smudgely." He motioned to the seats in front of his extremely tidy desk, and once Miss Bremerton and Jonathan were seated, he sat behind it and clasped his hands together on the desktop. "How may I be of assistance?" Mr. Smudgely's dark hair was parted quite precisely and appeared to be plastered to his head.

"Detective Jonathan Graham, and this is my associate, Miss Bremerton." Jonathan set his hat on his knee and pulled aside his jacket to reveal his badge. "Mr. Smudgely, are you aware that one of your employees was murdered two nights ago?"

"Oh my." He opened his eyes wide, the effect magnified by his spectacles. "Who?"

"George Lewis," Jonathan said.

"He was a footman, I believe," Miss Bremerton added.

Mr. Smudgely crossed to a cabinet and slid open a drawer. "I'm afraid I do not know every employee by name," he said, fingering through the files. "Our full staff consists of more than one hundred, you see. Though, how many are present at one time varies depending on the needs of the particular event." He slid out a file. "George Lewis. Here we are."

"Was Mr. Lewis working Monday evening?" Jonathan asked.

Mr. Smudgely sat back at his desk. He opened the file and ran his finger down one of the pages inside. "He was."

"At what time would he have arrived?" Jonathan watched the man closely.

"Three p.m. at the very latest." Mr. Smudgely closed the file and handed it across the desk to Jonathan. "I have no patience for tardiness. The event that evening required quite a lot of preparation—arranging furniture, hauling displays, that sort of thing—and footmen, of course, did the brunt of it."

Jonathan copied down the address of Mr. Lewis's boardinghouse, but aside from the report of the man's fistfight, he saw nothing else of interest in the folder. He started to hand it back to Mr. Smudgely but stopped and offered it to Miss Bremerton instead. "May I also see the file of a Nick Sloan?"

"Certainly." Mr. Smudgely returned to the cabinet. "And I can personally attest to Mr. Sloan's presence Monday night. He is the stable manager's assistant and tended to my carriage himself when I arrived."

Jonathan accepted Nick Sloan's file, looked through it, and wrote down the man's address. "Is he here today?" He handed the file to Miss Bremerton.

The young lady paused writing in her notebook to take it from him.

"No, only the stablemaster, Mr. Parker."

As Miss Bremerton read through the files, Jonathan studied Mr. Smudgely. The man was twitchy and nervous, but the temperament appeared to be his natural disposition, not a result of any guilt.

"Thank you." Miss Bremerton returned the files to Mr. Smudgely's desk.

The man immediately reached forward and straightened them, squaring the edges with the desktop's corner. "Shall I show you the assembly rooms?" Mr. Smudgely asked.

"Yes, thank you," Jonathan said. "And one more thing, sir, if you don't mind. May I have a list of your employees, their addresses, and a report of which were working Monday evening?"

The man nodded. "Of course." He straightened a row of fountain pens with his fingertips. "As I said, the list is extensive. My secretary will be able to provide the most accurate account."

Mr. Smudgely spoke for a moment to the woman sitting at a desk in the outer room of his office and then led the pair of investigators back to the main lobby.

Jonathan had never had occasion to visit the Bellacourt Assembly Hall, and he tried not to gawk at the enormous globe chandelier suspended over the entryway. Thick oriental-style rugs covered dark wooden floors, and the same dark wood was used in carved panels on the walls. Leading from the lobby were sets of doors that opened into different entertaining areas. Directly across from the main entrance, in a place of honor, were large double doors, one of which was open, revealing a grand ballroom beyond.

A maid in her white apron and cap was dusting a table in the entrance hall. When she saw them, she curtsied and withdrew into another room.

Jonathan glanced at Miss Bremerton and saw she was again writing in her notebook.

Mr. Smudgely stepped to the left and opened the doors on that side of the lobby. "Here is our dining room."

Tables and chairs were pushed to the walls, and maids were sweeping the floors. At the far end of the room, more doors led to what Jonathan assumed was the kitchen area.

"The arrangement for Monday evening's event was rather a casual one, as you see," Mr. Smudgely continued. "We do have the option of one long table in this room that seats as many as fifty."

"What exactly was Monday evening's event?" Miss Bremerton asked.

"Oh, you would hardly be interested, miss." Mr. Smudgely gave a dismissive smile and directed his attention to Jonathan. "William Charles Baldwin, a big-game hunter, presented a lecture on his recent safari to the dark continent. It was fascinating." Mr. Smudgely gave what appeared to be a shiver of excitement.

"Oh," Miss Bremerton said. "I believe I did hear about the event."

Mr. Smudgely smiled again as if he were indulging her fancy and gave Jonathan a knowing look. If he only knew who she was, Jonathan imagined the assembly hall's manager would be falling over himself with flattery instead of rudely dismissing her.

He glanced at Miss Bremerton, but she did not appear to be offended by the man's condescension. She watched him with a flat stare, and Jonathan wondered if she was accustomed to her questions being disregarded. The idea gave him a twinge of guilt, and inside he cringed. He'd been guilty of the same.

"Mr. Baldwin brought an elephant's skull and tusks of ivory and the most amazing photographs," Mr. Smudgely continued. "The presentation was in the drawing room, through here." He led them into another room that was arranged with a stage at one end and rows of chairs for an audience facing it. "This space serves very well as a lecture hall, you see." He gave Miss Bremerton another patronizing smile before returning his attention to Jonathan, as though he were expecting some sort of praise.

They both ignored him, and Miss Bremerton spoke directly to Jonathan. "My father mentioned it. I believe he may have been here."

"It was very well attended by exceptionally prominent people." Mr. Smudgely put a finger in front of his mouth and leaned closer to Jonathan, facing away from Miss Bremerton. "I really should not say, but there was a member of the royal family in attendance." He glanced around as if he might be overheard. "Prince Alfred," he whispered.

Behind Mr. Smudgely, Miss Bremerton rolled her eyes.

Jonathan coughed, and using the excuse to turn quickly away from Mr. Smudgely, he widened his eyes at Miss Bremerton, sharing a look of amazement with her at the foolishness of their host. He turned back, adopting a thoughtful expression. "Do you have a list of attendees, Mr. Smudgely?"

"The Kingsclere Hunting Club hosted the event. They are the ones to whom you should speak about a guest list." He shook his head as if success in acquiring such a list was not to be expected.

Jonathan opened his notebook. "What time was the event, sir?"

"An early dinner was served at six. But as I told you, it was very informal, as is often required during the Season. Men come and go as they are able with family and social commitments. Some arrive late; others leave early." He shrugged. "The lecture began promptly at seven thirty."

"How long did it last?" Jonathan asked as he noted the start time.

"An hour. But many of the men remained to speak with Mr. Baldwin after the formal lecture ended."

"And are you hosting an event tonight?"

"No."

Miss Bremerton moved away from Jonathan and Mr. Smudgely. She walked around the edges of the room, writing in her notebook. Or perhaps she was drawing. Jonathan was eager to hear her opinion on the interview as well as discuss theories.

"So tonight the hall will be minimally staffed." Jonathan muttered the words, not expecting an answer. He walked through the lecture hall, tapping his hat against his thigh and picturing the room as it must have been on Monday night, filled with men listening to William Charles Baldwin speak about his African hunting tour.

"Where are these chairs stored when they're not being used?" Jonathan asked.

"The cellar," Mr. Smudgely said. "The lower level is for storage, the scullery, and the laundry."

They would need to search that area as well as the kitchen and stables.

As Jonathan contemplated where to begin, a knock sounded at the assembly hall door, and a moment later Mr. Smudgely's secretary entered the lecture hall, followed by four constables from H Division. Jonathan was pleased to see Merryweather among them.

The secretary gave a paper to Mr. Smudgely and left.

"If that is all," Mr. Smudgely said, glancing at the paper, then handing it to Jonathan, "I am very busy."

"One moment, if you please, sir." Jonathan raised his voice as he tucked the secretary's list into his notebook. "Miss Bremerton?"

She looked up from her notebook and crossed the room to join them.

"Have you any questions for Mr. Smudgely?"

The assembly hall's manager pulled back, hardly hiding his surprise.

Miss Bremerton raised a brow, turning from Jonathan to the manager. "I do, as a matter of fact." She held her pencil over the notebook page. "Mr. Smudgely, would you care to know how Mr. Lewis died?"

If Mr. Smudgely had appeared surprised earlier, that was nothing to the way he looked now. He opened and closed his mouth, staring at Jonathan as if hoping he might rein in his renegade assistant, who was clearly unaware of what things young ladies should speak of.

Jonathan ignored the man's distressed look and crossed his arms, delighted to observe the interaction.

"You did not ask," Miss Bremerton continued in a conversational tone. "I find it curious that you should learn of an employee's murder, possibly in this very building, and not wonder at it." She watched him, awaiting his reply.

Mr. Smudgely glanced at the constables near the door. "In this very building, you say?" His voice was hardly more than a whisper.

"That has yet to be determined." Miss Bremerton shrugged. "You said yourself he was here Monday evening." She wrote something in her notebook. "And you claim to have been here as well."

"Claim?" Mr. Smudgely sputtered. "Miss, it would have been impossible for me to leave during such an event. Any number of people can vouch for my—"

"So you and Mr. Lewis were both here two evenings ago," she cut in. "He is dead, and you did not seem at all curious about the manner in which he was killed."

"Miss, your accusation is highly offensive. I have a mind to report this." He looked again to Jonathan for assistance, but the detective had no intention of stopping the interrogation, nor did he know to whom the man might report Miss Bremerton. He clasped his hands behind his back, quite enjoying Mr. Smudgely's squirming under the lady's questioning.

She lifted her chin, appearing completely unconcerned by his threat. "Sir, I made no accusation. Simply an observation." She scribbled something in her notebook, pulling it against her chest when Mr. Smudgely leaned to see what she'd written.

Jonathan considered her action a particularly nice touch.

"Mr. Smudgely, this is a murder investigation." Miss Bremerton fixed him with a flat stare. "I do apologize if it is uncomfortable. I can, however, say without a doubt, your discomfort is much less than that endured by Mr. Lewis."

"Well, I never." He straightened his coat lapels and spun. "Further questions can be directed to my secretary." The assembly hall manager stomped from the room.

Jonathan could hardly keep back a grin. "Well, miss, your interrogation was certainly aggressive."

She folded her arms, glaring toward the doorway. "That man is intolerable."

"I concur," Jonathan said. "Do you think he is our murderer?"

"No." She sighed. "I don't see how it is possible. He would have been tending to guests and arrangements during the event. But I should still like to see him chastened somehow, if only to teach him a lesson in manners."

"We don't incarcerate people for being arrogant prigs," Jonathan said, holding in a laugh.

"A pity," she muttered.

The constables joined them, and Jonathan reassumed his professional demeanor.

He instructed them for a moment, and then the men left to search the property and question the few employees present. Jonathan ordered Merryweather to specifically search the stables and speak to the stablemaster. Nick Sloan was their top suspect, and if anything was to be learned, Jonathan trusted Merryweather was the man to do it.

The constables departed, leaving Jonathan alone with Miss Bremerton. "What task do you have for me, Detective?" she asked.

He smiled at her eagerness to assist. "I wonder if you might contact the hunting club for their guest list from Monday evening's event." He imagined, out of all of them, Miss Bremerton would have the most luck getting that information.

"Of course." She wrote in her notebook, and a side of her mouth pulled into a partial smile. "They'll probably assume I'm writing a story about the lecture."

Jonathan nodded. Even better. "And if you have the opportunity, you might also speak to your father. He may have seen something last evening, even without realizing at the time that it was significant."

"I will talk to him." She wrote that down as well. "Anything else?"

"Now for the detective work." He gave a solemn nod and spread an arm toward the doorway. "Come along, Miss Bremerton. Let us see what we can discover."

CHAPTER 8

SOPHIE ACCOMPANIED DETECTIVE GRAHAM BACK into the entry hall, glad Mr. Smudgely was gone and they could at last get to the business of solving the case. She was already considering how to organize her story; she thought showing the police investigation rather than sensationalizing the details of the murder would be an interesting angle.

The detective set his brown hat on a side table of the entry hall, then opened the door to a coat closet and stepped inside.

"What exactly are we looking for?" Sophie asked from the closet's doorway.

He pushed aside a few coats, which had apparently been forgotten by partygoers, and took a pair of gloves from a shelf, turning them over and then returning them. "Anything that appears suspicious. Evidence, hopefully. A murder weapon would be nice."

"But surely you don't believe the murders were committed here. The entire place was filled with people Monday evening."

He furrowed his brows, sliding a top hat to the side and peering behind it. "You were the one who suggested the idea."

Sophie shrugged. "I was just hoping to make Mr. Smudgley uncomfortable."

"I see." The detective left the coat closet, his lips twitching as he brushed past her and leaned on the doorframe.

She didn't let herself think about how close he stood. Did Detective Graham smell like a sweet shop?

"Well, it is indeed a possibility," he said. "This was George Lewis's last known location. And we know Jane Duffin told Miss Primm she was going to meet him. Whether she did, and whether their meeting was intended for the assembly hall or somewhere else, is still to be determined." He pushed wide the double doors and stepped into the ballroom, his footsteps echoing through the cavernous space.

Sophie walked beside him, having no idea what they were meant to find in an empty room. She didn't imagine the murderer would have left a signed confession tucked behind a painting. The large windows on the far side gave the ballroom light, but the space still felt cold and empty without the chandeliers glowing and music playing. The pair walked around the edge of the room. "How exactly did George Lewis die?" She winced at the loudness of her voice and spoke softer. "Was he strangled like . . . ?"

Detective Graham took a small paper sack from his jacket pocket. He offered Sophie a peppermint, then put one into his own mouth.

"Blow to the head," Detective Graham replied. "Dr. Peabody said the object used was heavy with a straight, sharp edge. Smashed in half of his skull, which is another reason I don't believe Mr. Smudgely could have done it." He checked a window latch. "A strike like that would have taken exceptional force."

"By someone very strong," Sophie said around the piece of candy. She hoped her face didn't reveal the shock at hearing the detective speak so bluntly about the violent act and the grisly results. If he took her to be squeamish, he may not entrust her with further case details.

He nodded. "And possibly very angry."

"Nick Sloan?"

"So far, he is the only suspect we've come across with a motive. The jilted lover."

They completed the circuit of the ballroom and returned to the entry hall. Sophie's stomach felt ill as she considered the violent nature of the murders. Solving them, stopping the monster who was capable of something so gruesome, became even more vital.

Detective Graham looked between the different doors and rubbed his knuckle against his lip, apparently lost in thought. After a moment, he looked up. "Let us consider. Jane Duffin had a few rare hours to herself two nights ago, and what did she decide to do?"

"According to Miss Primm, she left to meet George Lewis."

Detective Graham nodded. "She dressed in her loveliest gown and set off for a romantic visit with her paramour."

"Did she arrange to meet him somewhere? Perhaps in Spitalfields?" Sophie shook her head as soon as she said it. "No, that doesn't make sense.

According to Mr. Smudgely, George Lewis was working Monday night." Sophie held out a hand, palm down. "Here."

"I imagine he wasn't eager to lose his position," Detective Graham said. "So the encounter likely took place here, at the assembly hall, where he could steal away for a short time." He opened his notebook, writing something inside. "I'll send officers to speak to cabdrivers, see if any remember her."

"But that night this place was filled with men, aside from the staff. As a woman, she'd have drawn attention."

The detective glanced toward the kitchen. "Not if she came by way of the delivery entrance."

"I suppose that is possible," Sophie said. "But she'd surely have been noticed by someone."

"I agree," the detective said. He removed a paper from his notebook and handed it to Sophie. "If Jane Duffin was here, someone assuredly saw her."

"But who?" Sophie took the paper and saw that it was the employee list from Mr. Smudgely's secretary. "How can we possibly interview all of these people?" She moved a finger down the list and counted in her head. "There are more than fifty on this list alone, not to mention the guests." A pity the full staff wasn't working today. Would they need to call on each of the employees at their residences? The people lived all over the city. And what of the men who had attended the dinner and lecture? Finding and interviewing each of them would take . . . perhaps weeks. "Oh," Sophie said as an idea occurred to her.

"What is it?" Detective Graham asked.

It was so simple. She considered for a moment, then turned to face him directly. "Detective, I have a thought." Seeing his nod, she continued. "In three days, there is to be a ball here at the Belcourt—the engagement ball for Lord Ruben and Lady Lorene Stanhope. It promises to be a very grand affair, and I am certain it will be largely attended."

"I'm not certain how that pertains—"

"With such an extensive guest list, the hall is sure to be fully staffed," she interrupted. Now that the idea was developed, she was certain it was a good one. "And most, if not all of the Kingsclere Hunting Club will be in attendance. Lord Ruben is a very prominent member of the club."

Detective Graham's puzzled expression indicated that he still didn't understand her point.

"*All* of the suspects and witnesses will be in attendance." She shook the paper for emphasis. "The employees and last night's guests."

"I see," Detective Graham said. "And I assume you will be a guest as well. You intend to interview each of them over the course of the night?"

"Indeed not." She put the paper in her notebook, closing it with a snap. For a detective, his powers of deduction were at times very poor. She folded her arms. "I thought *you* would accompany me." The moment the words were out of her mouth, she realized how very forward they sounded. A tingling blush spread up from her neck and over her cheeks. She looked away and attempted to keep her expression from showing embarrassment.

"I? Attend the ball . . . with you?"

"It was a silly idea." Sophie's voice came out softer than she'd intended, and the heat spread down into her chest. She opened her notebook again, took out the pencil, and cleared her throat. "Forget I mentioned it. Now, let us return to our storyline. Jane Duffin entered the assembly hall through a back entrance to meet George Lewis."

Though she didn't look up, she could feel Detective Graham studying her. "Yes," he said at last, and she released her breath. "And we must ask ourselves, what would a young couple with only a short time together wish for?"

"Somewhere to be together," Sophie said. "Privacy." *Curse this blush.* If the conversation continued on this course, the heat in her cheeks would never have a chance to disperse. She peeked up at him.

"Exactly," he said. A small smirk was the only indication that he'd noticed her discomfort. "They'd find a place to be alone. Somewhere close so George's absence wouldn't be noticed."

"But where—" Sophie began.

But she was interrupted when two constables entered through the main door. Seeing Detective Graham, the men hurried over, removing their bucket hats as they walked.

"Sir." The shorter of the two spoke. "We found something."

"Very well. Lead on, Constable." Detective Graham snatched his hat from the side table and motioned for Sophie to precede him.

As they followed the constables outside, Sophie was glad for the interruption. Their interaction had become strained, and her insecurities were the cause. Of course inviting the detective to a ball was improper. While she'd merely intended for the suggestion to be a means of continuing the investigation, he'd not understood it that way and clearly had not wished to hurt her feelings by declining the invitation. She should have predicted he would perceive it as a flirtation. And consider it an unwelcome one from a young woman with a plain face and a waist that no corset could restrain. Her chest burned in shame. How pathetic she must look to him.

The constables led them down the steps and around to the side of the building, along a narrow lane used for deliveries and maintenance. Other lanes branched off at intervals, leading to nearby businesses. The stables and the field for carriage parking were on the other side of the building, and manicured walking gardens in the rear, were accessible from a patio behind the ballroom. The group passed the kitchen door and a hatchway with a lock that most likely led to a root cellar. Barrels, crates, and rubbish bins were arranged tidily against the outer wall, save for one crate that appeared to have been dragged beneath a window.

"Look there, sir." The taller of the constables pointed. "On the sill."

Detective Graham stepped up onto the crate and studied the windowsill, then cupped his hands against the glass to look through. "Good eyes, men." He stepped down and motioned for Sophie to step up.

She took his offered hand, keeping her gaze from meeting his, held on to her skirts, and climbed up onto the crate. Standing on tiptoe, she could see the white paint of the sill was marked with a rust-colored smear a bit wider than her hand. The sight turned her stomach, and the reaction frustrated her. Sophie stepped quickly back down, pressing her hand to the side of the building and landing rather awkwardly—she hadn't wanted to reach for the detective's hand again. "Is it blood?"

"Looks like it," the detective said. "Do you know to which room this window belongs?"

Sophie shook her head, glancing back up at the blemish and calculating which rooms were on this side of the building. "It appears to be on the far side of the ballroom, opposite the dining hall." They hadn't even looked in that area. "If I remember correctly, there is a cardroom and a small parlor."

The detective pushed aside the crate and crouched down, studying the ground beneath the window and speaking with the constables.

Sophie crossed the lane to where she could get the best view of the side of the assembly hall. She sketched the window and the blood smear until Detective Graham joined her.

Together they returned to the front of the building, ascended the stairs once again, and reentered, this time crossing to the doors on the other side of the entry hall. It took only a moment to find the room they were looking for.

Detective Graham tossed his hat onto a table. He pushed aside the curtains that hung at the far wall of the small parlor, revealing that the smear they'd seen on the outside of the windowsill was also on the inside. He checked the window latch and opened the window. Nodding to the constables below, he turned, glanced around the parlor, and opened a closet.

Sophie still stood near the window. Outside, in the lane, the constables searched through rubbish bins. Sophie stared at the smear. Seeing Jane Duffin's body last evening had been shocking, but there had been no blood. Aside from her scratched shoes and disheveled hair, there had been no immediate sign of violence. She'd appeared peaceful, eyes closed as if she were sleeping. Sophie had been so determined to find a story and to prove that she was up to the task of investigating that she'd hardly considered exactly what she was seeing. But *this* . . . this was different.

"Miss Bremerton, look here."

Detective Graham's voice was muffled, coming from inside the closet. Sophie opened the door wide, finding it to be a small storage space. A broom, a bucket, two chairs, and a feather duster were the only things inside, aside from one detective who was crouched down, studying the wooden floor. He ran a finger over a crack between the floorboards, then looked at it closely. He leaned until his face was mere centimeters from the floor and sniffed.

He sat back on his heels and glanced up at Sophie. "Might I trouble you for a piece of drawing paper?"

"Of course." Sophie knelt down beside him. She tore a page from her notebook and handed it to him.

Detective Graham folded the paper, then slid it down, deep between two floor boards. When he brought it out, a brown stripe ran along the edge.

"More blood," Sophie whispered.

He nodded, his mouth pulling into a grim line.

Sophie took the paper, holding it up to see it in the light. Her hand shook the smallest bit. "Is there a way to determine whose blood it is?"

"I'm afraid not. However, Dr. Peabody will be able to tell if it is from a human."

Sophie gave back the paper and rose to her feet. She checked her skirts, making certain she hadn't knelt in blood, and sat on a settee as her thoughts spun. "You think George Lewis was killed here? It's impossible, isn't it?" The dinner was right across the hall. "Nick Sloan couldn't have come in here unseen." Someone would have certainly noticed a murder merely feet away from the party. The thought chilled her. She opened her notebook and began a sketch of the parlor and closet. Concentrating on the drawing kept her from feeling ill.

"Peppermint?" Detective Graham offered her a sweet, and she happily took it, hoping it would settle her stomach.

He popped another into his own mouth and moved back to crouch down and study the closet floor.

A knock sounded from the doorway.

"Sir?" Constable Merryweather stood in the doorway.

"Come in, Merryweather." Detective Graham stood again, motioning with his hand. "What have you found?"

Constable Merryweather inclined his head toward Sophie. "My lady." He turned back to the detective, pulling a battered notebook from his belt and shuffling through the pages. "According to a Liza Miller in the kitchen, George Lewis did indeed receive a visit from a young lady in a blue dress Monday evening."

"And did Liza Miller see what became of them?" Detective Graham asked.

The constable shook his head. "Said the pair of them left the kitchen, holding hands and giggling and figured they were headed off to . . ." He winced, glancing at Sophie. "Ah . . . talk privately."

"And that's the last she saw of them?" Detective Graham said.

"Yes, sir." Constable Merryweather turned a page in his notebook. "I also spoke to the stablemaster, a Mr. Parker. He confirmed that Nick Sloan was indeed working Monday. Said he was here all night, from three in the afternoon until past midnight, cleaning the stalls."

"Do you believe him?"

The constable straightened his tunic and nodded, tucking the notebook back into his belt. "He appeared to be answering honestly, sir. And as far as I could discern, he had no reason to—"

"Sir!" The pair of constables from outside entered the room. The smaller man rushed forward, holding out a wad of white cloth with rust-colored splotches. "We found this in a bin."

Detective Graham took it from him. The cloth made a thudding sound when he set it on the low table in front of Sophie.

She leaned forward, recognizing the wad was comprised of cloth napkins wrapped around something about the size of a short boot. And the cloths were most obviously covered in dried blood.

The detective pulled apart the stiff napkins, revealing a brass statue of a rearing horse.

He and Sophie looked at one another, then to the side table, where an identical statue stood beside a vase of flowers.

The detective gripped the horse around the middle and hefted it in one hand as if preparing to strike something with it, then turned the statue upside down and looked closely at the base.

"Oh my," Sophie gasped, nearly choking on the peppermint. *A heavy object with a straight, sharp edge.* "The murder weapon." Now that she looked at the side table, it seemed obvious the matching horse was missing from the arrangement. She turned a page in her notebook and started a new sketch, trying to push away the light-headed feeling that came over her.

"I believe you're right, Miss Bremerton." Detective Graham set the statue down. "Good work, lads." He sent the men away to speak to cabbies between Mayfair and Chelsea.

"But how did nobody notice anything?" Sophie said, not caring that she spoke with the sweet still in her mouth. "Surely a murder is noisy. And there is the matter of a body—or bodies. How did the victims end up in Spitalfields?"

"It's true," Constable Merryweather said. "With the river so close, why not dump them there? Why take the time and effort to transport the bodies through the city when the risk of being caught was so much greater?"

"I don't know," the detective said.

"Perhaps to divert police attention from the assembly hall, hoping the murder would not be traced back here?" Sophie offered.

"It's possible," Detective Graham said. "There are still a good many unanswered questions."

Merryweather looked through the window. "Do you suppose the blood on the sill is from pushing the body out of the window?"

The idea was preposterous. "Surely not," Sophie said. "It would have certainly been seen. And people don't just drop bodies from windows. It's . . . barbaric."

"Murder is always barbaric, miss." Detective Graham's voice was tight.

Sophie suspected he was holding back a laugh at her outburst. Well, let him laugh. She was not the one with the ridiculous theories. She kept her gaze purposely away from Merryweather, lest she see him laughing as well. This whole business was becoming more confusing and more horrifying with each discovery. It frustrated her, and she did not care to be mocked on top of everything else. "Certainly the blood is from the murderer escaping," Sophie said.

"Could be both," Detective Graham said. He joined Merryweather at the window, looking down. "If a carriage was waiting in the lane, it would be easy enough to escape quickly."

"With the bodies." Merryweather nodded. "Do you think he had an accomplice, then?"

"At this point, I'll not rule anything out." Detective Graham clasped his hands behind his back and stared toward the closet. "I still believe Nick Sloan is our best suspect. Did Mr. Parker say where to find him?"

"Sloan frequents a pub on the South Bank," the constable said.

Sophie stood, glad for a reason to leave the room with the blood. "Shall we go speak to Mr. Sloan, then?"

Merryweather's eyes widened, and he darted a look at the detective.

Detective Graham frowned. "Absolutely not, Miss Bremerton."

She braced herself for a battle. "Detective, I am perfectly capable of visiting a tavern in the middle of the afternoon, I assure you. And I am not afraid of a disreputable neighborhood. Do not presume it is your place to shield me from—"

"Constable Merryweather will go," Detective Graham said in a hard voice that reminded her very much of his gruff temperament two evenings before.

"But, Detective, I—"

"Bring Sloan to the station for questioning." Detective Graham didn't acknowledge her protest but continued to speak to the constable.

"Yes, sir." Merryweather put on his hat, tugging the brim and inclining his head as he passed Sophie. "Good day, my lady."

"Constable," Sophie said in acknowledgment. Once she was left alone with Detective Graham, she scowled at the man, sat back down, and returned to her drawing.

Detective Graham gathered the soiled napkins, the paper with the bloody stripe, and the horse statue. "Is there anything else you should like to see before leaving, Miss Bremerton?"

She didn't look up from her work. "I don't believe so."

"You're angry." It wasn't a question.

"I grow weary of being told what I may or may not do," she replied, pressing too forcefully with her pencil and tearing through the paper. "But I do not suppose you could even begin to understand what I mean."

Detective Graham sat beside her on the settee. "You are right. Though I might try, I cannot understand. Not fully."

She gave him a flat stare, bothered that he hadn't even tried to argue. "You've never been ordered about?"

"Certainly. By my superiors, my rent collector, my employers—as a child, I was ordered about by the sweep I worked for." His lip curled. "But the difference is none of it was ever done out of care for me or concern for my safety."

Sophie saw a flash of something in his face, a vulnerability she was certain he'd not intended to reveal, and it tugged at her heart. She wondered what secrets his past held. Had nobody ever looked after him? Protected him? Loved him? And did he mean he was concerned for her? The idea gave her a pleasant wiggle in her tummy. But of course, policemen were concerned for everyone's safety.

He tucked the bundle of evidence under his arm and stood. "I am sorry to add to your distress."

"I am not so very fragile." She held her shred of pride tightly, afraid that if she let it go, he would see behind it the uncertain woman who was neither pretty nor interesting enough to entice a detective to attend a ball with her or keep from disappointing her own parents.

"I know," he said. "But still, I ask you to trust my judgment concerning your safety in working on this case."

She considered. Were his words a projection of his own pride when it came to his case? Or did he speak out of true concern for her? And why did it matter so much?

"I do, Detective," she said, wishing she didn't sound so naive. "I trust you."

CHAPTER 9

JONATHAN SQUINTED UP AT THE sky as he left the assembly hall with Miss Bremerton. The day was warm, but late-afternoon clouds gathered. An evening storm was likely within the hour.

Miss Bremerton pulled on crocheted gloves and then took his arm as they descended the stairs to the street.

Jonathan liked the feel of her hand on his arm. Walking with her was much different from walking with Sergeant Lester or another of the officers. He and Miss Bremerton were not simply walking side by side, headed in the same direction, but together. And the sensation was very agreeable.

He considered the afternoon they'd spent together. He'd initially dreaded the young lady's involvement with the case and had braced himself for a day of annoyance at her interfering. But in reality, he'd found himself pleasantly surprised with her company. And even more surprised that she'd turned out to be an asset to the investigation. Miss Bremerton was intelligent and insightful, both attributes he'd not expected when she'd barged onto the crime scene two nights before.

He'd certainly not expected Miss Bremerton to draw his emotions so close to the surface—twice within just a few hours. He blamed the reactions on a woman's influence—something he was very unaccustomed to, both as a man with no family and a police officer. To what else could he attribute his desire to confide secrets, parts of his past he'd never revealed to anyone, and his very nearly breaking into tears—twice? He smiled, thinking how Tom had always warned him to "beware of females and their crafty ways."

They arrived at the waiting police carriage, and Jonathan reached for the door handle.

"Where to now, Detective?" Miss Bremerton asked.

Her voice sounded tired. Jonathan glanced at her, then looked closer. Miss Bremerton's face was void of color. He released the carriage door. He had noticed her go pale when they'd discovered blood in the closet, and again when they'd discussed how the bodies might have been removed, but he hadn't mentioned it in front of the other constables, thinking the observation might embarrass her. He had assumed the shock would pass quickly, but apparently there was more to her reaction than mere aversion to the crime's details. "Miss, when did you eat last?"

She rubbed her forehead. "This morning. Breakfast. And peppermints."

"And you had only a small cup of tea before we left your house." That had been more than six hours earlier, Jonathan realized. He'd been so intent on solving the case that he hadn't paid attention to basic necessities—not uncommon when it concerned only himself, but he felt a responsibility for her. "You must be famished."

"I am a bit hungry," she admitted.

"Come along." He motioned for the carriage driver to wait and led her to a bench on the river promenade, helping her to sit. "I'll be back in just a moment." He left the bundle of evidence beside her and hurried back up the street, pausing to instruct the driver. It wouldn't do to leave the young woman alone, but he spoke quietly, thinking Miss Bremerton would not appreciate Jonathan assigning someone to keep watch over her.

As he left the man and crossed the road behind the carriage, he pondered the very complicated Miss Sophronia Bremerton. She was confusing but somehow not frustrating. More like a puzzle he was intent on solving. He took satisfaction in their easy conversation and how well they worked together. It was strange, but he reasoned he'd not had many friendships outside of the constabulary, and aside from his acquaintance with his landlady, none involved a female.

Jonathan had only to walk half a block to a street vendor selling meat pies. While he waited for the man to wrap the pies in paper, he glanced back toward the woman on the bench by the river. She faced away from him, looking down, perhaps writing in her notebook. As a breeze blew the feathers of her hat, Jonathan wondered what she was thinking.

He thanked the vendor and started back, remembering Miss Bremerton's earlier proposal that he accompany her to the ball. Guilt soured his mouth. His rejection of the idea—or rather, his lack of response altogether—had clearly hurt her feelings, but he'd had no choice. How could he attend such an event? Besides, it wasn't a rejection of her . . . but she'd understood it as such, and in his incompetence, he hadn't corrected her.

He tipped his hat to a group of women walking past, then crossed the street. The sporadic dance instruction he'd received at the orphan school would in no way disguise his ineptitude in that regard. And one sentence out of his uneducated mouth would give him away to the *haute ton* as an imposter. The bitterness grew stronger, and he swallowed, not wishing to admit that his own pride was getting in the way of what was, in actuality, a very clever plan—all of the potential witnesses together in one place and a noblewoman as a partner . . . But he would be foolish to think a formal coat and hat would convince anyone he belonged among high Society.

He sat on the bench, offering Miss Bremerton a meat pie. "I know it's not as fine a meal as you're accustomed to, but police rarely have the luxury of a fancy dinner while working a case."

"It smells wonderful. Thank you."

"You're quite welcome."

She turned over the wrapped parcel, her brow creasing as she pulled at the grease-stained paper. "How do I . . . ?"

Jonathan felt foolish. Lady Sophronia had certainly never been served anything as common as a street vendor's pie. "You'll want to remove your gloves," he said, holding the pie as she did so. He handed it back once her hands were bare. "Now, tear back the paper a bit at a time as you eat." He spread his handkerchief over her lap. "It can get rather messy."

She peeled back a corner of the paper and took a tentative bite. "It's very good."

"I'm sure it's not of the quality you're used to, but—"

"Detective," she interrupted with a gentle smile. "Stop apologizing. It's perfect."

He smiled, relieved.

They ate quietly for a moment, enjoying the cool evening breeze and watching the construction on the magnificent Albert Bridge. Jonathan wondered for a moment whether the increase in traffic across this part of the river would also increase crime.

"You don't really believe George Lewis's body was pushed through the window, do you?" she asked, taking him from his wandering thoughts.

He wiped gravy from his lip. "Perhaps both bodies."

"You think Jane Duffin was killed in the parlor closet as well?"

"We have no evidence to support it, but it stands to reason since the two were likely together."

"I don't see how it's possible." Miss Bremerton tore away more of the greasy wrapping and blew on the pastry and the gravy inside to cool it. "If Nick Sloan killed one, the other would have yelled or fought back. He could not have overpowered both at the same time. Surely someone would have heard."

He nodded. "It does add credence to the idea of a second person's involvement." He crumpled his empty paper into a ball and brushed crumbs from his trousers. "Not only to assist in the commission of the murders but in the disposal of the bodies as well."

"But who would do such a thing?" She swept a finger over her lip but missed a small crumb at the very corner of her mouth. "Who would be imposed upon to assist with something so horrible? Someone who owes Mr. Sloan money?"

He touched the corner of his own mouth in a demonstration of wiping away an imaginary crumb.

"Oh." She wiped her lip but on the wrong side.

"No. It's here." He brushed it away with his thumb.

Pink spots burst across Miss Bremerton's cheeks.

Jonathan pulled away, appalled at his action. "I apologize, my lady. I did not even think."

"So it is *my lady* again, is it?"

"I should not have behaved so familiarly."

She looked at her pastry. "Do not let it trouble you, Detective."

Her voice was low, and it sounded . . . well, he wasn't exactly certain how it sounded. Was she angry? Hurt? Offended? He looked around for something to defuse the awkwardness of the situation, and his gaze landed on her notebook. "May I?" He lifted it onto his lap.

"Of course."

He turned the pages, studying her artwork and notes. "George Lewis and Jane Duffin left the kitchen to find somewhere to be alone." He was glad to return to the comfort of discussing the case. "What is more private than a closet in an unoccupied room?"

"Yet Nick Sloan knew they were in there," she said. "But how? Did someone tell him? And once he knew, he convinced a partner to help him to sneak into the assembly hall, murder the pair, and move the bodies to Spitalfields?"

A thought occurred to Jonathan. "Or . . . there is another possibility . . ." He spoke slowly as the idea formed. "What if their presence was initially unknown to the murderer—or murderers?" He turned to the sketch of the parlor. "This room was on the other side of the assembly hall from the dinner and lecture—not only a perfect spot for a romantic meeting but for a secretive conversation. It is possible that Jane Duffin and George Lewis overheard something they weren't meant to . . ."

"And when they were discovered in the closet, they were killed for it," Miss Bremerton finished. She turned her knees to the side, glancing back over her shoulder at the assembly hall as she leaned toward him. Apparently her former discomfort was forgotten, and for that Jonathan was glad. "Detective, the murderer may not have been Nick Sloan at all."

Jonathan nodded, rubbing the lumpy pocket watch fob as he considered. The witness list and the suspect list had just become one and the same.

"But it couldn't have been a member of the Kingsclere Hunting Club," Miss Bremerton said as she turned back toward Jonathan.

"You think only servants capable of murder?" He could not keep the resentment from his tone.

"Of course I don't." She took a bite of her pie, chewing as she looked toward the Thames. "But I know those men." She spoke more softly, and now she looked afraid. "Some I've known my entire life. I cannot believe any of them capable of something so evil."

He nodded, understanding fully as his burst of anger faded. In his years as a police officer, he'd seen countless good people driven to abhorrent acts, and when revealed, their friends and family were nearly always unwilling to believe their guilt.

He turned a page in the notebook. Now that the idea of an overheard secret had taken root, it seemed the most logical. It provided motive, and unfortunately for Miss Bremerton, the most likely perpetrators in this scenario were the lecture attendees. Not only would two gentlemen have moved unnoticed through the assembly hall but they also would have been able to leave the party for an extended amount of time without drawing attention— something impossible for a servant. They'd also have had the means to transport the bodies. But this new theory brought its own batch of questions.

He turned another page, looking at the drawing of the alley behind the Porky Pie. "This really is remarkable," he said. "Your memory for details and the ability to render such a picture . . . I must admit some jealousy."

She glanced at him, her expression doubtful.

"You don't believe me?" he asked. "Surely you must know how rare your talent is."

"Unfortunately, drawing remembered details is not the talent my parents hoped for." She pressed together her lips and glanced up at a couple walking past.

Jonathan wondered what sort of people found such an amazing ability to be lacking. "And in what discipline would they rather see their daughter excel?"

"Beauty, I suppose." She shrugged, giving a sigh that somehow managed to sound resentful and resigned at the same time as she stared down at the last bits of her pastry. "And desirability. To my parents, the greatest accomplishment lies in making a fortunate match. And as you see, I am hardly equipped—"

"Beauty is not a talent," he said. "It is luck. But you do possess quite a bit of it." He thought it impossible that her parents didn't see what was to him blatantly obvious. Miss Bremerton was lovely and grew even more so the longer he spent in her company. Perhaps he hadn't noticed the first time they'd met, but now he wondered how he'd missed it.

Her blush returned. "I'm sorry. My intention was not to beg for a compliment." She folded the paper around the remains of her pie. "I . . . well, let's say my interests lie in another direction—in journalism—and that disappoints them greatly."

Then they are fools. Perhaps he'd begin his interviews of the hunting club members with Miss Bremerton's father, Lord Mather. And conduct it in the cells.

To keep from giving voice to the disgust he felt toward Miss Bremerton's parents, Jonathan looked back at the drawing, and this time something caught his eye. There appeared to be a shadow in the window above the alley. He turned the page toward her, tapping his finger on the window. "Miss, what is this here?"

She studied the spot he indicated. "Yes, I remember the curtains moved as if something . . . or someone . . . passed behind. I'd forgotten about it."

"That someone might be a witness," he said, feeling the charge of excitement that came with a new lead. He rose and pulled her to her feet, retrieving her bag, notebook, and the bundle holding the statue. Her face had regained its color, and for that he was glad. "I do hope your energy is restored, Miss

Bremerton." He offered his arm, walking with her to the waiting carriage. With any luck, this discovery could lead to a break in the case.

CHAPTER 10

SOPHIE FELT IMMENSELY BETTER AFTER eating the pie. She settled back in the seat of the police carriage and opened her notebook. Seeing the sketch of the parlor closet, the sight and smell of the blood returned. But this time the nausea didn't accompany the memories. Detective Graham had been right about her just needing food, and once she'd gotten the knack of eating a greasy pastry with her fingers, she'd thought a vendor's pie on a riverside bench to be one of the most pleasant meals she could remember. Perhaps a large part of her enjoyment could be attributed to the absence of her mother criticizing each bite that passed her lips, but that didn't account for all.

She added some details to the sketch, remembering the upholstery pattern on the chairs in the closet and the design of the window drapes.

In the fading light coming through the carriage window, Detective Graham studied the drawing of the alley. His brows were pulled tightly together, and he rubbed his forehead as he contemplated.

Sophie's mood was unexpectedly amiable. She was tired. The carriage was sturdy but hardly comfortable, and next to her was a man who'd had given her a tongue-lashing and sent her away only two days earlier. None of that explained her contentment. As she considered, she came to the conclusion that her weariness was caused by hard work, and that, along with the quest for justice, brought a fulfillment that was very satisfying.

Detective Graham leaned back his head against the seat and closed his eyes.

Sophie wondered if he was sleeping or thinking. She suspected the latter. The detective didn't seem to be a man to rest when there was work to be done. An admirable trait. And it brought to mind other aspects of Detective Graham's character.

He was blunt but refreshingly so. One didn't have to wonder what he was thinking or whether he had an ulterior motive.

The intrigues and games of high Society surrounded Sophie, spreading into nearly every aspect of her life, but she had little patience for the artifice. It felt very comfortable to be with a person whose intentions she didn't have to question. Detective Graham was strict, demanding of the constables who worked beneath him, but he was generous with compliments as well. The wiggle returned to her tummy when she remembered the compliment he'd paid her. Did he truly think her beautiful? Of course, he was likely just being polite, but the sensation remained. And Sophie didn't push it away.

The detective leaned forward and looked through the window. He glanced at Sophie, gave a nod, then went back to studying the drawings.

His eyes seemed always to be alert. And Sophie sensed that the awareness of his surroundings that served him so well as a police officer had been honed by a need for survival. From things he'd said, she'd deduced his childhood had been difficult. Though he spoke politely, beneath his words was a roughness that intrigued her. What had he overcome? He certainly wasn't refined, nor was he educated, but in Sophie's opinion, his intelligence and intuition more than compensated in that regard. He was fair, she thought, and not one to hold a grudge—evidenced by his treatment of her today compared to that of the day they'd met at the crime scene.

Sophie smiled, feeling a fondness for her friend. The thought brought her up short. She was being silly, allowing the man's praise and attentions to go to her head. Though she and the detective were friendly, she could hardly call him a friend. They'd been acquainted for only a few days. And fondness? That was hardly warranted. She felt admiration for him on a professional level. Nothing more.

The carriage stopped in front of the Porky Pie just as raindrops began to tap on the roof. Sophie and the detective exited onto the street and hurried past the mouth of the alley to the building across from the pub, standing beneath the shelter of a small overhang above the door. Perhaps it was because the crowds and police were absent or because a murder had been discovered here the day before, but Sophie's nerves were on edge. The street was dark, with the nearest lamp half a block away, and she could feel rather than see people watching from the shadows.

She moved closer to the detective, nearly falling back when he pulled open the door.

"After you, miss."

Sophie glanced back over her shoulder, then entered the dimly lit building. She knew from the outside that the building was two stories high, but she had not expected so many doors lining the narrow hallway. In the rooms beyond and above she could hear bumps and scrapes as people moved about, along with voices, dishes clinking, a dog barking, and a baby crying. The building was filled with the smells of supper, but instead of feeling warm and cozy, the smells blended with mildew and the odor of wet animals and unwashed bodies, turning her stomach.

Detective Graham touched the small of her back, urging her forward toward a darkened staircase.

Sophie took a few steps, then moved to the side of the hallway. "I'll follow you, Detective."

He went ahead.

The stairs creaked beneath them. Halfway up they came to a landing and turned to follow the staircase in the other direction. The sounds of something skittering on the wood made Sophie pull her skirts tightly against her legs, worried a rat would crawl up them. Detective Graham walked ahead steadily, and she followed as closely as she could without actually grabbing on to the detective's arm.

The door at the far end of the dark hallway corresponded with the window outside where she'd seen the shadow.

When they reached it, Detective Graham knocked.

A noise sounded in the room beyond.

"London Constabulary," he called. "Open the door."

The door opened a crack.

"Is that you, Constable Merryweather?" A woman's voice spoke through the gap.

"Detective Jonathan Graham." He pressed a hand against the door to keep it from closing. "And my associate, Miss Sophronia Bremerton. We have a few questions, if you please."

The woman pulled open the door, hinges creaking. She stepped back to allow them to enter, then looked into the hall quickly before closing the door behind them.

The room was hardly more than a closet. The only heat came from a coal stove in the corner. A small table with two chairs was pushed against the wall beneath the window and a bed against the opposite. Clothes hung on lines across the room, and a large washtub stood in the corner between a narrow wardrobe and a wooden-backed bench piled with laundry. There was barely space to walk, and two extra adults in the room made it impossibly crowded.

A boy jumped up from his seat at the table. He was young, no older than eight, Sophie thought, and very skinny. "Good evening, Detective."

Detective Graham smiled and shook the boy's hand. "Nice to see you again, Freddy." He removed his hat. "And this must be your mother."

"Martha Payne," the woman said.

Her expression went from suspicious to worried, her wide eyes making her look much younger than Sophie had originally estimated. Martha Payne couldn't be more than a few years older than Sophie's own age of twenty-two. She studied the woman. Her face was lovely and her figure small and slender. If her eyes were not so tired, and with a new gown, she could easily pass as a true beauty of high Society.

"Is Freddy in trouble, sir?" Martha asked.

"No, nothing like that." Detective Graham shook his head. "Very sorry to interrupt your supper." He glanced at the table, where two bowls of some sort of stew were partly eaten. A slice of bread sat beside each bowl.

Sophie couldn't help but feel a pang of guilt as she compared the meager servings to the enormous meal that was surely sitting at her family's dining table right now.

"We've just a few questions," the detective said.

Freddy nodded. "About the dead lady."

"Yes, I wondered if you"—Detective Graham looked between them—"either of you . . . saw anything unusual in the alley two nights ago . . . before the police arrived."

"I didn't see anything." Martha's gaze darted toward the window, then to her son. "Neither of us did." She licked her lips, her brows pulling together. The question had frightened her.

Detective Graham stepped close to the table. He moved the curtains and looked down through the window. "From here, you have an excellent view of the entire alley. Are you certain you saw nothing?"

"That's what I said." Martha folded her arms tightly.

"And where were you Monday night, madam?" Detective Graham asked.

"Here. Minding my own business." Martha picked up a blanket from the bed, folded it, and smoothed down the edge. She deliberately avoided looking at the detective. "Doing my washing and fixing supper for Freddy."

"If you please, Mrs. Payne," Sophie said. "Our intention is not to frighten you. The dead woman's name was Jane Duffin. We only wish to discover who did this to her. If you saw anything last night, anything at all, it might help."

"There was—" the boy began.

"Quiet, Freddy." Martha's voice was shrill. She set the blanket on the bed and opened the door. "I answered your questions. If that's all, I'll thank you to leave now."

Sophie's temperature rose. It was obvious the woman was keeping something from them. "If you please, madam—"

"Thank you for your time, Mrs. Payne." Detective Graham spoke over her. He put on his hat and inclined his head. "Sorry to have disturbed you."

Sophie couldn't believe that he wouldn't continue the interrogation. Martha was lying; Sophie was sure of it. She opened her mouth to say so, but Detective Graham caught her gaze. He narrowed his eyes and shook his head slightly, communicating that he understood her frustration, but further questioning would do no good.

Following his lead, Sophie bid the Paynes farewell and followed him through the hall and down the stairs.

Once they were outside beneath the porch overhang, Detective Graham turned to her. "What do you think?"

"The woman knows something, but she will not tell us." Sophie glanced toward the door, feeling the urge to go back inside and demand that Martha tell the truth. "She is scared."

"She has a child to protect." He looked up at the rainy sky and then offered his arm. "Come along."

She took his arm, but instead of leading her to the carriage, he led her toward the pub.

Detective Graham opened the door, letting out a cloud of odors and noise from the establishment.

"What are—?" Sophie recoiled at the boisterous laughter and the smell of alcohol and unwashed bodies coming from inside the Porky Pie. "What are we doing here?"

"Waiting," Detective Graham said. "May I buy you a drink?" They entered and sat at a table in a corner near the door.

Sophie kept her hands in her lap, not wanting to soil her gloves with whatever stained the tabletop.

"Come sit here by me, love!" a red-faced man called from a far table. He raised his glass and winked at Sophie.

His friends laughed.

Sophie darted a look at the door, measuring the distance toward the exit. "Detective, I really don't think—"

"Trust me," Detective Graham said, looking perfectly comfortable in the seedy pub.

A serving woman with her hair tied up in a scarf approached their table. She raised a brow when she saw Sophie, her gaze traveling over her gown. "What'll you have?"

The detective ordered their drinks.

The server returned a moment later, placing two smudged-looking glasses filled with amber-colored liquid on the table. She stared at Sophie's gown again, making Sophie wish she'd brought a shawl. "Anything else?"

He pulled aside his coat, showing his badge. "Might I have a moment of your time?"

She scowled, putting a hand on her hip. "Shoulda known you was a copper."

The detective sat back, spreading his hands wide. "Was it my dashing good looks?"

She rolled her eyes as if his suggestion was absurd, but her mouth pulled just a bit. Apparently she wasn't completely immune to his charm. "You look too nosy-like. Most folks come in here and keep their heads down. Coppers are always asking questions."

He grinned. "You must know what I'm planning to ask, then."

"Whether I seen anything strange two nights ago when that woman was killed." She lifted her chin in the direction of the alleyway.

"Did you?"

"Too busy working. Not a lot o' time to be gawking out the window, same as I told the coppers before."

He nodded. "Did anyone . . . strange come into the pub Monday evening?"

"Stranger than your fancy lady?" She jerked her head toward Sophie.

Sophie pulled back, not sure if the woman had just insulted her or not.

"Just the constables." The server shrugged and turned to leave.

Detective Graham chuckled and took a drink.

Sophie didn't touch the dirty glass.

The pub door opened, and Freddy Payne came inside. He looked around until he spotted them, then made his way toward their table.

"This is hardly the place for a child," she whispered.

"He's right on time," Detective Graham muttered back.

"You expected him?" Sophie asked.

"The lad knows something," Detective Graham said. "Flashed him a coin when his mum wasn't looking."

"But how could you have possibly known he'd come?" she asked.

"I suppose I recognize the sort of lad he is. Reminds me of myself at his age." He pushed out a chair with his foot, inviting the boy to sit. "Hello there, Freddy."

"Evening, sir. Ma'am." The boy pulled off his cap. He hunched down in his seat, glancing at the door as if worried he'd be seen. "I saw something Monday night." He spoke in a quiet voice, and Sophie had to lean forward to hear.

"What did you see, Freddy?" Detective Graham had lowered his voice as well.

The boy glanced behind him again, then turned back and folded his arms as if waiting for something.

Detective Graham slid a coin across the table.

Freddy snatched it up. "The lads and I were gathered down the street, sir, and I seen a wagon stop outside the alley. Thought it was a laundry delivery for my ma, so I hurried over to help her carry it inside. But it drove away quick. And that's when I saw the dead lady."

"You think the wagon brought the woman?" Sophie asked.

"Don't know, ma'am," Freddy said. "Ran for the police as soon as I saw her lyin' there."

"Must have been around seven thirty," Detective Graham muttered to Sophie. He turned to the boy. "Can you describe the wagon?"

Freddy pursed his lips to the side. "Like the laundry wagon . . . dark color, maybe black or brown with a door in the back. But the sign was different than normal."

"What did it say?" Sophie asked.

He shrugged. "Dunno, ma'am. Can't read."

Sophie blinked, surprised. The boy was certainly old enough to attend school.

"Do you remember anything about the sign?" Detective Graham said. "What made it different? What color was it?"

"The sign was white with black words." Freddy pursed his lips again, and then his eyes lit up. "And a blue bird."

"That is very helpful." Detective Graham tossed the boy another coin.

"Thank you, Detective. And please don't tell Ma I talked to you."

"Of course. And thank you for your information."

Freddy took a deep gulp of Sophie's drink and swept the back of his hand over his mouth as he plunked it back onto the table. He gave a cheeky bow, put on his hat with a grin, then hurried out of the pub.

Sophie stared after him, shocked at the boy's audacity.

Detective Graham leaned back in his chair and laughed.

CHAPTER 11

WHEN JONATHAN LEFT THE COURTHOUSE the next day, after giving testimony against a burglary gang, he was met by a constable with a report of another body discovered near Wentworth in Spitalfields.

An hour later Jonathan and Sergeant Lester crouched in the shadows, studying yet another murder victim in what was becoming an almost daily ritual. Today, however, the body hadn't been left in a public alley but at an abandoned worksite. The location was not one Jonathan had frequented, but it was known to him. They were in the burnt husk of an old workhouse. Fire had destroyed the building over a year earlier, and apparently city planners and parliament couldn't reach an agreement over what should become of the property. Months of disputes had resulted in a stalemate.

The owners wished to tear it down completely, as well as some of the surrounding buildings, to accommodate an inner-city railroad. The local council hoped to raise funds to rebuild the workhouse, and the latest party to join the fray was a group of philanthropists petitioning for a finishing school that catered to underprivileged young ladies.

Since no decision had been reached, the city had enclosed the area with a temporary wooden fence in a pathetic attempt to keep out vagrants and criminals. The remains of the massive stone building were blackened, one wall completely collapsed.

As they waited for a photographer and Dr. Peabody, Jonathan and Sergeant Lester were careful not to disturb the crime scene. Neither man touched the body—no need to check for a heartbeat. The man was clearly dead and had been for some time.

Jonathan sat back, pressing the back of his wrist to his nose in hopes of stifling the odor. Animals had found the corpse long before a constable had smelled it, and Jonathan feared there was little hope for identification. Thank goodness Miss Bremerton had not accompanied him today. The young woman did not possess a weak constitution, but this . . . The sight was disturbing, even to a seasoned police detective.

"A pity Lady Sophronia didn't come today," Sergeant Lester said, swatting away a slow-moving fly.

Jonathan's gaze snapped to the sergeant, and he wondered if the man had developed overnight the power to read minds. "Why do you say that?"

"She'd have already drawn the scene, and we could be finished here." Sergeant Lester shrugged. "Not the most pleasant body we've come across." He glanced around. "Nor do I fancy the location. Bit eerie, if you ask me. Lady Sophronia would at least provide the opportunity for pleasant conversation."

"And *I* don't?" Jonathan snorted. He rose, walking toward the gate to wait for the photographer there. He nodded to the constables posted at the crime scene entrance.

"No offense to you, Detective," Sergeant Lester said, catching up to walk with him. "Nice change of pace, having a lady around. That's all I meant."

"None taken." Jonathan looked up the road in both directions, then turned to face the sergeant. "Do you really consider this crime scene to be the place for a young lady of genteel breeding?"

Sergeant Lester frowned. "I suppose not." He motioned toward the corpse with a tip of his head. "Grisly one today, isn't it? But I did find a nice rat." He patted the lump in his jacket pocket. "Perhaps Lady Sophronia might come to the station house on occasion. Having an artist at hand could be advantageous. If a witness were to describe a criminal to her as she drew—"

"I'm certain Lady Sophronia has better things to do than to sit around H Division, sketching criminals," Jonathan said before the sergeant could finish. The man's words stirred up an uncomfortable combination of feelings. The mixture of enjoyment at Miss Bremerton's involvement in the Jane Duffin case and the resentment that his own station in life was so utterly inferior twisted inside him, warring against each other. He felt foolish at his ease in her company and the pleasure he took in sharing the case with her. He'd seen the way the young lady had looked around the tenement building the night before. If she'd any idea of his origins . . . the places he'd lived made the Paynes' small flat look like a palace in comparison.

He popped a peppermint into his mouth and offered one to the sergeant, hoping it would keep the man quiet as well as ease the discomfort in his own stomach brought on by the odor of the remains. Speaking about Miss Bremerton dredged up emotions that were . . . complicated. And Jonathan didn't appreciate complicated.

The photographer's carriage arrived at the same time as Dr. Peabody's, and the sergeant helped carry the photography equipment through the worksite of the burned building. Jonathan walked with the doctor, leaving the medical students behind at the hospital wagon.

When the photographer saw the body, he cursed and cringed away, holding his nose.

"Come on, then." Sergeant Lester spoke in an encouraging voice, patting the man on the shoulder. "'S not so bad, once you get used to the smell. Now, where do you want this tripod?"

As the sergeant and photographer arranged the photography equipment, Jonathan and Dr. Peabody stepped closer to the body.

"What do you think, Doctor?" Jonathan asked. "Can you estimate a time of death?"

Dr. Peabody leaned forward on his cane and squinted through his spectacles. "Hard to tell without examining the internal organs. But based on the bloating and the smell, I'd estimate he's been dead at least three days." He pointed to the muddy patches. "Moisture could have exacerbated the process, however." He tipped his head to the side and crouched down, leaning his cane against a pile of bricks as he looked closer. "Cause of death is likely a blow to the head." He pointed to a dent in the man's skull. "But you undoubtedly deduced that already."

"All right, sirs, if you please," the photographer called. "I'm ready."

Jonathan and Doctor Peabody stepped to the side.

Sergeant Lester held the flashgun and lit the powder when the photographer removed the cap from the photo box's lens.

Even through his closed eyes Jonathan saw the burst of white light as the powder ignited.

The photographer replaced the cap and informed them the photograph would be delivered to the station as soon as it was processed. He dismantled his tripod as he spoke, anxious to leave.

Jonathan thanked the man, and Sergeant Lester walked with the photographer back to his carriage.

"Anything else on the two in the morgue?" Jonathan asked the doctor as they returned to the body.

"I'm afraid not." Dr. Peabody shook his head. "Is that peppermint I smell?"

Jonathan gave the doctor a sweet, and the pair rolled the corpse onto its back.

Both turned away quickly, holding their hands over their noses; the putrefaction smell was now, if possible, even stronger.

Jonathan held his breath and poked fingers into the dead man's pockets, hoping for a clue to his identity. The man's clothing was ordinary. A wool jacket, trousers, a worn shirt, and a necktie. He appeared to be neither wealthy nor impoverished—a typical working-class chap. He had no hat, and his hair was brown with a bit of gray, giving a slight indication of his age. The waistcoat pocket contained a simple pocket watch. No engraving. Jonathan turned to the jacket pockets.

"The young woman from Monday night's crime scene—Miss Bremerton— called on me early this morning," Dr. Peabody said.

Jonathan paused, and in his surprise he accidentally breathed in through his nose. He coughed, stomach wrenching, and looked at the doctor through watering eyes. "What did she want?" That Miss Bremerton had continued investigating on her own annoyed him, especially after she'd given her word not to. "She didn't demand to see the bodies, did she?" He reached across to search the pockets on the other side.

"No, nothing of the sort," Dr. Peabody said, turning the dead man's head to the side and studying the damage. "Similar to Mr. Lewis's wound," he muttered.

"Doctor?" Jonathan prompted. "Miss Bremerton's visit . . ."

Dr. Peabody looked at him through his spectacles, then blinked, appearing to remember what he was saying. "Yes." He laid the head carefully back on the ground and lifted a hand to study the fingers. "As neither Miss Duffin nor Mr. Lewis has any family to speak of, Miss Bremerton made arrangements for the victim's burials."

Jonathan stared at the doctor, but this time he remembered to breathe through his mouth.

"Very considerate of her, don't you think?" Dr. Peabody set down the hand and wiped his palms on his trousers. "Have you any more peppermints?"

Jonathan gave the man another sweet, and his mind turned over what the doctor had said. The information touched his heart in a way that surprised him. Jane Duffin was just one of the penniless victims in a city that pretended its lower classes didn't exist. But Miss Bremerton was different. For some reason, she saw what others of her class didn't. And she cared.

As he contemplated, he continued through the motions of looking through the man's pockets and from inside the jacket pulled a leather billfold. He stood as Sergeant Lester joined him and the doctor.

"Identification?" the sergeant asked.

Jonathan opened the billfold, finding a few pounds in an inner pouch. The other pouch contained slips of paper. Delivery orders from Bluebird Furniture Emporium.

"May I take the body?" Dr. Peabody asked.

"Yes, thank you," Jonathan said.

Bluebird Furniture. That must be the source of the wagon Freddy had seen. Was this man the murderer of the other two victims? Was he an accomplice?

Once the doctor and his students had taken away the body and Jonathan had set the constables to searching the scene and looking for witnesses, he and Sergeant Lester started back to the station house.

They stopped at a vendor's cart for bloaters, and as they ate the herring, Jonathan filled the sergeant in on what he and Miss Bremerton had learned the day before.

The sergeant's interviews at the Greys' household had turned up nothing, though he did find a cabbie who'd transported a lady in a blue dress from Hyde Park to Chelsea Monday evening.

Sergeant Lester picked fish bones from his teeth. "You suppose this delivery driver was an accomplice and his partner turned on him?"

"Possibly." Jonathan looked through the delivery receipts and pulled one out. "The final delivery Monday night—a pair of velvet-upholstered armchairs—was made to a Mrs. Kettle of South Kensington at five thirty." He pointed to the company's address on the receipt. "Bluebird Furniture Emporium is located on the road directly behind the assembly hall. I'd wager the two share a service lane."

"The dead man made his final delivery of the night and returned in his wagon just as the killer was looking for a way to transport the other bodies." Sergeant Lester snapped his fingers. "His was a murder of opportunity."

"Or necessity, depending on how you look at it," Jonathan muttered, thinking through the scenario. The theory made sense.

"Poor bloke was in the wrong place at the wrong time." Sergeant Lester shook his head.

The pair crossed the road to the station house in silence, and Jonathan contemplated the latest developments. If their theory of the crime proved true, the killer—or killers—had murdered three innocent people. But why? What did they hope to conceal? And why move the other bodies to Spitalfields? He was missing something.

Sergeant Lester reached for the handle but paused before opening the door to the station. "I heard what the doctor said about Lady Sophronia, about her buryin' those poor souls."

Jonathan raised a brow, waiting for the sergeant to continue.

"Haven't met many noblewomen," Sergeant Lester went on. "Those I have were rude or dismissive or bothered to have to deal with the police at all. But not Lady Sophronia. I like her." He gave a sharp nod. "She's a good one." He pulled open the door. "Wonder how she'd like a stuffed mouse. Maybe with a wee sketchbook and pencil . . . "

Jonathan stepped past the sergeant without comment. He didn't think one was warranted. He picked up his mail from the desk sergeant, hung up his coat and hat, and sat in his chair, pulling a stack of files toward him.

He opened a folder and started to write but stopped as a thought occurred to him. One he'd never have expected. He liked Miss Bremerton too.

CHAPTER 12

THE GREEN IN HYDE PARK north of the Serpentine was filled with spectators when Sophie arrived with Elizabeth Miller and Dahlia Lancaster. The air balloon wasn't scheduled to ascend for at least another hour, weather permitting, but crowds had already gathered, eager to watch the spectacle. Vendors taking advantage of a waiting company on a warm day sold flavored ices and sweets. Some enterprising merchants sold miniature balloons, silken fans adorned with balloon paintings, and even brooches in balloon shapes. Ladies and gentlemen wore their finest clothing and strolled among the booths, greeting acquaintances and enjoying the sunny morning. Working-class folks gathered as well, their clothes less fancy but every bit as carefully groomed. Children laughed, running throughout the chatting groups. The mood was festive and had the feel of a fair or a holiday celebration. Sophie couldn't help but smile in anticipation, opening her parasol as she stepped from beneath the trees of the footpath, into the sunshine.

In the center of a treeless expanse of lawn, the main attraction, a silken mass, striped blue and yellow, was being filled with gas. Over the colorful bladder stretched a netting of rope, attaching the balloon to a large basket. Bags filled with sand surrounded the basket, anchoring it to the ground.

"Oh, there is Vivian." Dahlia pointed toward the balloon.

Sophie spotted Vivian Kirby right away. Her scientific-minded friend was bent over, peering at a contraption of gears and speaking to the men operating the large pumps that distributed the gas.

"I must say I'm hardly surprised," Sophie said.

Elizabeth squinted toward the men. "In a perfect world, *she* would be directing the operation, and *the men* would ask the questions. I'm sure she understands the workings of a hydrogen balloon much better than they do."

Sophie smiled, pleased with the way her friends spoke about one another, even when the object of their discussion wasn't near. The behavior was not something she had formerly been accustomed to. She had no doubts that the Blue Orchid Society would defend her name as well, and knowing it, being able to trust this group of women, filled her with a warm comfort.

"Do tell us more about your new story, Sophie," Dahlia said. "Are you really investigating a murder?"

"Two murders, actually," Sophie replied, still surprised to be speaking so comfortably with Dahlia Lancaster, the most sought-after debutante in high Society. After the words were out of Sophie's mouth, she winced. "But I shouldn't say any more. I promised Detective Graham I would not disclose details of the case—not yet anyway."

"So this man tells you to remain silent?" Elizabeth snorted. "Typical."

Sophie shook her head, a burst of defensiveness prickling under her skin, even though she knew her friend's words were spoken partially in jest. She'd come to realize over the past weeks that Elizabeth was not always as angry toward the opposite sex as she acted, though the young lady did not tolerate injustice in any form and did not hesitate to speak up in the face of discrimination. "No, it's not like that at all," Sophie said. "*He's* not like that. In fact, the detective often asks for my opinion about the case. And he listens when I give it."

Elizabeth didn't look completely convinced.

"He simply doesn't want any part of the investigation revealed while we still search for the killer," Sophie explained further. "Tipping the murderer off to the police's plans to apprehend him would hardly do."

"That seems wise," Dahlia said.

"Or controlling," Elizabeth muttered. She gave an impertinent smile as her gaze, holding a tease, darted to Sophie.

Sophie smirked and was about to tease back when they were interrupted by the approach of Lord Meredith, Lord Ruben's closest friend.

"Good morning, ladies." He pulled on his hat brim and inclined his head in a slight bow. The ruby pin in his necktie glinted in the sunlight.

The women greeted him in return.

Lord Meredith wore his tailored coat with an easy elegance that gave the impression that he hadn't given more than the briefest thought to his presentation, though Sophie did not think it likely. Not when the cut of his trousers and his waistcoat were the very height of style. Unlike the other members of the West End Casanovas, Lord Meredith wore no mustache but grew his side-whiskers down past his ears.

"How do you do today, Miss Lancaster?" he asked Dahlia.

"Very well, sir. Thank you."

Dahlia's voice was soft, and she appeared to be uncertain—a trait Sophie did not realize the young lady possessed. Her wound at the hands of Lord Ruben was still raw.

Lord Meredith cleared his throat, clasping his hands behind his back. "I thought to inquire . . . perhaps call on you sooner, but—"

"Meredith, there you are." Lord Ruben pushed through a group of people, emerging with Lady Lorene Stanhope on his arm. His eyes widened when he saw Dahlia, and his brows wrinkled. The expression was gone just as quickly, replaced by his typical bored arrogance.

Lady Lorene gave Dahlia a haughty sneer. She pulled on her fiancé's elbow. "Come along, Ruben, darling. Lord Everleigh has claimed an ideal viewing location for us on that hill."

Sophie and Elizabeth looked at Dahlia and then at each other.

Dahlia's cheeks were dark, and her chin quivered.

"It's a balloon, my lady," Elizabeth said in an irritated voice. "When it rises, anywhere in the city is an ideal viewing location."

Lady Lorene ignored Elizabeth. "You'll join us as well, Lord Meredith?"

Lord Meredith looked between the two groups, his gaze lingering on Dahlia with something very like concern in his eyes. "Ah yes. I'll be along in a moment."

Elizabeth watched Dahlia as well, but instead of concern, anger sparked in her eyes. "Please excuse us." She pulled her cousin away without waiting for acknowledgment from the others.

"How very rude," Lady Lorene said. She curled her lip, watching Dahlia's retreating form, and pulled Lord Ruben away, inclining her head to Sophie as she passed. "Lady Sophronia."

Lord Ruben touched his hat brim in the briefest acknowledgment.

Sophie muttered a farewell to the couple and turned to bid farewell to Lord Meredith as well but changed her mind when she realized she had the rare opportunity to speak with one of the Casanovas alone.

Lord Meredith glanced between the two departing pairs. "I suppose things must be . . . difficult between Miss Lancaster and myself now." He grimaced. "I wish it were not so."

"Perhaps," Sophie said, not exactly certain what answer to give.

He cleared his throat and looked down at Sophie as if surprised she were still there. He must have been speaking to himself.

"Lord Meredith, I wonder if I might ask you some questions," Sophie said before he could leave. "It will take just a moment."

"Writing a story, are you?"

"Yes." Sophie took the notebook from her bag. "Did you attend William Charles Baldwin's lecture on Monday evening?"

He gave a nod. "I did. Fascinating, to say the least."

Sophie considered what questions to ask. "And was it well attended?"

"Extremely. I reckon it was the most popular event the Kingsclere Hunting Club has hosted in years. The hall was very crowded."

"Can you tell me the names of some of the attendees?" She smiled in what she hoped looked like an interested and not interrogative manner. "Readers love that sort of detail. Just some of the people you remember."

Lord Meredith scratched his cheek. "People came late and left early all evening, but let me see if I can remember specifics . . . I sat on the second row beside Ruben, and your father was directly behind us. We spoke for a few moments before the lecture began."

Sophie nodded, writing the names in her notebook. That coincided with what her father had told her as well.

"Everleigh was there with his German friend. We had dinner together. And Benedict, though he left early, of course. Photographs of hunting trophies are not exactly to his liking."

Sophie wrote Lord Benedict's name down, noting that he left early. In this she wasn't surprised. Lord Benedict was, by reputation, unconventional. The future Duke of Ellingham was a great lover of nature and animals. Sophie had even heard he refused to eat meat. She didn't believe he'd be pleased to hear details about an African hunting expedition or see the evidence of the animal casualties that had resulted from it. Besides, she and the detective were looking for someone who had arrived late to the lecture or perhaps hadn't attended at all. If the murder had occurred between six and seven, she and Detective Graham had reasoned, it would have been during the dinner.

"And you must have heard Prince Alfred attended," Lord Meredith said.

"I did hear," Sophie said.

"Charles Stratford, Arthur Grey, Jack Rothschild, Chatsworth, of course . . ." He continued listing names, and finally Sophie stopped him.

"Lord Meredith, did you notice anything unusual that evening?" she asked.

"I'm not certain . . ." he began.

"Was anyone behaving strangely?"

He squinted, looking unsure of her meaning. "During the lecture, you mean?"

"No. Yes." She huffed out a breath through her nose and shook her head, frustrated that she'd not prepared better. She'd hoped to find some new information to share with Detective Graham, but she didn't know how to tactfully ask if any of Lord Meredith's friends had appeared murderous on Monday evening. "I'm sorry. I'm not being clear. I suppose I just wanted some interesting details for my story."

"If you'd like, I could introduce you to Mr. Baldwin. An interview with the man himself may provide the details you are looking for."

The offer's thoughtfulness surprised Sophie. She hadn't expected anything of the sort from one of the Casanovas. "Thank you, my lord. I would appreciate that very much."

Lord Meredith motioned toward the balloon with the head of his walking stick. "It appears the balloon is nearly ready to ascend."

Sophie hadn't even noticed the silk bladder was completely filled. The brightly striped sphere rising above the crowd was a spectacular site. The balloon looked as if it were pulling to lift off, and men in official uniforms surrounded the basket, holding fast to ropes to prevent it from doing just that.

"Oh yes." Sophie turned to a blank page in her notebook. "Thank you for your time. I must start my sketch before I miss the launch completely."

He tugged on his hat brim. "Very nice to see you, my lady. I'll leave you to enjoy your day."

Sophie bid Lord Meredith farewell. The crowd had swelled, with people pressing close together. A few scuffles broke out on the edges of the gathering, and she noticed constables moving among the throng, keeping order.

She found Elizabeth and Dahlia closer to the launch site. Vivian had joined them as well. A pity Hazel hadn't come, but a crowd this size would be more than their friend could manage. Sophie hoped she would at least watch the balloon from a window.

". . . the silk of the balloon is varnished with rubber dissolved in turpentine," Vivian was saying, "making it airtight to keep the gas from escaping." She glanced up and smiled. "Good morning, Sophie."

"Good morning." Sophie grinned at her friend.

"You are just in time. I was just about to explain how the hydrogen is created," Vivian said in her steady voice. "You see, a quarter ton of sulfuric acid is poured onto a half ton of scrap iron, then fed into the bladder through lead pipes . . ."

Sophie listened with half an ear as she sketched the balloon and the crowd surrounding it. Two men in top hats and coats had climbed into the basket and now waved at the spectators. Their waves were met with cheers.

"Monsieurs Charles and Roberts intend to take meteorological measurements of the atmosphere high above the earth's surface," Vivian said. "They carry a barometer and a thermometer to measure the pressure and temperature of the air. Won't the results be fascinating?"

Sophie wrote down the information for her balloon-launch story.

One of the men in the balloon basket raised his hands, and the crowd went silent. He called out a command in French. The workers released the ropes, and the balloon started to rise off the ground.

The crowd gave a collective gasp, followed by cheers and applause.

One of the men hadn't released his rope fast enough and was pulled off his feet. The balloon lifted him into the air.

Below, people screamed. Some yelled for him to let go his hold, but it seemed he was too panicked to do so.

Sophie held her breath.

Dahlia's hands were pressed to her mouth.

The men inside the basket leaned over the side, yelling commands to the man as they rose higher over the trees.

Finally, the worker let go and dropped, crashing down through a large birch tree as he fell.

Police officers ran to the rescue, and Sophie moved for a better view, sketching the balloon rope and the panicked man being pulled into the air as she took a step forward.

After a moment the circle of police moved away, and the man stood in the middle of them, holding his head. One of the police officers held on to his arm, supporting him.

Seeing the man unharmed, the crowd cheered again.

"Oh, thank heaven," Dahlia muttered.

Sophie continued to walk closer, wanting to get at least the man's name for her story. If he was in any condition to provide a comment, that would be even better.

By the time she was able to push through the crowd, she saw a nurse holding a cloth against the injured man's head. Police still stood around the scene of the accident.

An officer walked toward her, and Sophie smiled when she saw it was Constable Merryweather.

He pulled on the brim of his bucket hat. "Lady Sophronia."

"Constable Merryweather, what do you do here? This is a long way from Whitechapel. Are you on duty?"

"London City Police needed some extra security for the event." He hooked his thumbs in his belt. "Distracted crowd. All eyes looking upward. Perfect opportunity for dippers and the sort."

Sophie put a hand on her bag, glad for his warning against pickpockets.

"Suppose you're hoping for an interview?" He stabbed a thumb over his shoulder, motioning toward the injured man.

Sophie glanced behind the constable. The man who had fallen had been led to a spot in the shade, and the nurse attending him was inspecting his arm. He winced when she lifted it.

"An interview is not necessary. But perhaps a report on his status? And do you know his name?"

"Name's Clive Butler," Merryweather said, watching her write in her notebook. "Broken arm, I think. Knock on the head left him seeing stars, but doesn't seem the worse for wear."

"That is fortunate," Sophie said. She glanced upward. The balloon was very high now, and so small. "I am glad I found you today." She smiled at the constable. "Are there any new developments in our murder case? Were you able to interview Nick Sloan?"

Constable Merryweather frowned, apparently considering whether or not he should share details of the case with her when the detective wasn't present. "I did," he answered after a hesitation.

"And what did you find?"

"Sloan seemed genuinely distressed when he heard about the murders." The constable glanced around as if nervous he'd be overheard. "I didn't detain him. He appeared convincing to me. Detective Graham agreed with the decision, since we've no evidence to the contrary."

"I hope to call on Detective Graham tomorrow, with the list he needs."

Constable Merryweather nodded. "He'll be glad for the information." He pulled on his hat brim again. "Keep an eye on your valuables, my lady."

Sophie turned, her thoughts back on the murder investigation. She'd fetched the list from the Kingsclere Hunting Club this morning after calling on Dr. Peabody, and the sheer number of names on it had made her ill. At this rate, they'd never narrow down the suspects.

She did not pay attention to where she was walking and bumped into someone going the other direction. She looked up and winced when she saw it was Lord Everleigh. "I beg your pardon, my lord."

"Lady Sophronia." He gave a curt bow and continued on, most likely in search of her sister.

She returned to her friends. The other ladies had decided, in her absence, to visit Hazel, and Sophie was thrilled by the idea. An afternoon with the Blue Orchid Society was just the thing. Then, Saturday night, they'd meet again at the assembly hall for Lord Ruben and Lady Lorene's engagement ball.

The heat returned to her chest and neck when she remembered Detective Graham's rejection of her proposal to attend the ball as a means to finding the murderer.

Pushing away her embarrassment, she considered the man himself. She'd spent hours with him the day before but still did not know the first thing about Detective Graham. The man was private, and his past certainly held secrets. Was he more than he appeared? She remembered the bullet on his pocket watch fob and the small scrap of information he'd given about it. What was his friend's name again? Tom Stackhouse.

Sophie's curiosity was piqued, and she decided to send a note to the *Illustrated London News*'s research assistant, Mrs. Ingram, requesting some information. Perhaps the real mystery wasn't the murders but the man solving them.

CHAPTER 13

JONATHAN LEANED BACK AGAINST HIS desk, standing with one leg crossed over the other. He studied the board propped against the wall behind it. Miss Bremerton's drawing of Jane Duffin's body in the Porky Pie alley was stuck with a tack to one corner, and beneath it was George Lewis's name, written on a scrap of paper, along with the crime scene photograph of Alfred Burgess, the Bluebird Furniture delivery driver. The coroner's reports were on the board, as well as photographs taken by the doctor of the victims' injuries. Jonathan had attached a drawing of the horse statue and a map of the city with the Belcourt Assembly Hall and the locations where the bodies were found circled in red ink. Over the past days, he had written and crossed out various leads. The door to the pub had turned up nothing, and no physical evidence had been found at the scene, aside from the body. He'd pinned lines of thread identifying relationships and possible motives, but instead of making the case clearer, as laying it out in a practical manner was wont to do, the board only created confusion and more questions.

"Too many suspects," Sergeant Lester muttered from his chair in front of the desk. He tossed the list of assembly hall employees onto the desk and rubbed his eyes.

Jonathan stuck the paper to the board.

A sharp rap came at the office door, and Sir Peter Dennington, the chief inspector, entered the office.

Jonathan straightened, and Sergeant Lester jumped to attention, offering the chief inspector his chair.

Sir Dennington ignored the gesture. "*Three* bodies?" He waved at the board. "And all related? Tell me you have a suspect."

Jonathan shook his head. "We're following up every possible avenue, sir, but so far—"

"I've just had a visit from Assistant-Commissioner Pembroke. The borough council is calling for this case to be solved, immediately. Some are questioning my competence to manage the division." He placed both hands on Jonathan's desk and leaned forward, his face reddening. "I don't need to tell you your future here is on the line, Detective." He glanced to the side. "And yours, Sergeant."

"Yes, sir," Sergeant Lester said.

"I understand, sir." Jonathan kept his voice calm, knowing the chief inspector needed only to release his frustration. Once he yelled and blustered, he'd return to the rational, sharp-minded person Jonathan admired, leading the H Division station house with a firm hand and unwavering loyalty to his men.

Sir Dennington nodded and stood, straightening his coat. He let out a breath and relaxed his shoulders. "Now then, where are we in solving this? What do you need from me? Manpower? Warrants? The constabulary is at your disposal, Graham." He rounded the desk, taking a closer look at the board. "Who are our suspects?"

Jonathan moved to the side to give him space. "Sir, the case is . . . complicated. We proceed cautiously by design."

Dennington turned toward him, folding his arms. "And why is that?"

"The murder could very likely be a member of the Kingsclere Hunting Club," Jonathan said.

Sir Dennington cursed, rubbing his temples. "Tell me you jest."

"I wish I were, sir. To accuse a man of rank—possibly a nobleman— without sufficient evidence . . ." Jonathan left the remainder unspoken.

Sir Dennington nodded. He looked back at the board. "A false accusation in that case would be far worse for H Division than three unsolved murders."

"Agreed," Jonathan said.

"Your discretion is understandable," the chief inspector said. "But you must remember the delay could end all of our careers."

"And leave a murderer walking the streets, free to kill again," Sergeant Lester reminded him.

"Quite right." Sir Dennington gave a quick nod. "Use any resources you need; follow every lead. Solve this case, Detective. Promptly." He turned and left the office without another word.

Sergeant Lester sat back in his chair. "How do we proceed then, sir?"

Jonathan sank into his own chair, tossing the sergeant a peppermint and then putting one into his own mouth. He folded the empty sack, disappointed to have eaten the last sweet.

He could think of only one plan they'd not pursued, and the idea of doing it—of attending tomorrow's ball—left him with a pit in his stomach. There must be something else.

The hour was nearly ten when Sergeant Abner poked his head into Detective Graham's office. "Beg your pardon, Detective. A lady's here to speak with you, sir." He glanced over his shoulder.

Constable Hutchings appeared in the doorway behind the desk sergeant, looking excited. "An elegant lady, sir."

Sergeant Lester perked up. "Lady Sophronia?" He hurried from the office. Jonathan heard his voice echoing though the station as the sergeant gave an impromptu tour. He entered a few moments later with Miss Bremerton on his arm. "And here is Detective Graham's office. Desk's rather untidy at the moment." He swept an arm toward the chair he'd vacated.

Jonathan stood. "Good morning, Miss Bremerton." Abner was right; she did look elegant, making the room appear shabby by comparison.

"Nice to see you, Detective." She handed a piece of paper across the desk. "The list of Kingsclere Hunting Club members. As you see, it is quite extensive."

Jonathan glanced at the paper, and his insides dropped. He retook his seat, looking closer at the names. There were well over seventy. "Have we an idea which of these attended the event Monday?"

"I made a few discreet inquiries." She came around to his side of the desk and leaned over his shoulder, pointing. "A star beside the name means he attended for certain. An *X* indicates he did not attend. And this little circle means he arrived late. As you see, I managed to identify only a very few."

Jonathan was tempted to glance up at her but feared if he did, she'd move away. And he liked the feel of her so close.

Sergeant Lester leaned across the desk and peered at the list as well, viewing it upside down. "It is a good start, my lady."

She looked up, but instead of responding, Miss Bremerton gasped, looking past the detective. "Gracious, what on earth? What is this?" She pushed past the sergeant to the side of the room and moved a pile of papers away, revealing a pair of taxidermic rabbits in boxing clothes. The animals were enclosed in a miniature pugilist ring and posed in the act of fighting.

Jonathan had grown so used to the rabbits on the top of his cabinet that he'd completely forgotten about them. Aside from a photograph of Queen Victoria on his wall, the animals were the only adornment in his office.

Miss Bremerton touched one of the animal's ears. "Good heavens. I've never seen anything like this."

Jonathan rose. A burst of defensiveness flared inside him at the idea that the woman would be repulsed by the dead animals and that she would say as much within hearing of Sergeant Lester. "Miss Brem—"

"How utterly charming," she interrupted before he could distract her. "Look at the tiny gloves. And their fluffy little tails. Wherever did you find such a thing, Detective?"

Relief relaxed the tension in Jonathan's gut, and he sat down again in his chair. "The display was created by Sergeant Lester."

"No." She touched her breastbone and turned to the sergeant, who had gone completely red. "This is absolutely splendid, Sergeant. I didn't realize you possessed such a talent."

Sergeant Lester shrugged, looking as pleased as a stray cat that had come across a misplaced Christmas turkey. "I do enjoy my wee friends."

"And are you a pugilist, then, Detective Graham?" she asked.

Now it was Jonathan's turn to shrug and look modest. "I box now and then." He rose and stuck the hunting club list to the board beside the list of assembly hall employees, glad for an excuse to turn away.

"'e's just bein' humble. Scrappy one, Detective Graham is. A real bruiser. Learned to fight as a lad in—"

"That's enough small talk," Jonathan interrupted, not wanting the conversation to continue on its current course. "We've three murders to solve."

"Yes." Miss Bremerton moved back past the sergeant and took a seat in the other chair across the desk from Jonathan. "What new developments have we?" She looked up at the board behind him, her brow wrinkling. "Did you say *three* murders?"

"Aye," Sergeant Lester said. "Found another stiff just yesterday."

Miss Bremerton rose again and came around the desk to look closer at the photograph.

Jonathan stepped toward her, blocking her path.

Miss Bremerton nearly ran into him. She stopped, grabbing on to his arm to keep her balance, then took a step back, releasing her hold.

"It's not a pretty sight, miss," Jonathan said. "Perhaps you'll just take our word for it."

The corners of her eyes tightened in a look he recognized as stubbornness.

"'e's right, my lady. As gruesome a corpse as I've ever seen," Sergeant Lester said. "What with the rats gnawed on him and all the worms. Poor chap was so bloated—"

Jonathan cleared his throat, shooting the sergeant a look instructing him to desist in the description. He touched Miss Bremerton's arm with one hand and motioned with the other for her to return to her chair.

She looked as if she'd argue but returned and sat all the same, folding her arms. "You believe this new murder to be related to the others?"

"Unfortunately, yes." Jonathan nodded as he also resumed his seat. "The victim was Alfred Burgess, a delivery driver for the Bluebird Furniture Emporium."

"The wagon Freddy saw." Miss Bremerton's eyes lit up. She frowned. "But then, did Alfred Burgess murder Jane Duffin and George Lewis?"

"I think not," Jonathan said. "The Bluebird Furniture Emporium shares a service lane with the Belcourt Assembly Hall. Our theory is he was returning from a delivery precisely when the murderer—or murderers—needed a way to transport the bodies."

"He was killed for his wagon," Miss Bremerton said. "How terrible." She squinted up at the photograph, and Jonathan hoped it was far enough away that she could not make out the details. "Where was his body found?"

"A worksite in Spitalfields," Sergeant Lester said. "Within a block or so of the others."

"And how was he . . . ?" She winced.

"Bludgeoned like Lewis—maybe by the same weapon," the sergeant said.

Miss Bremerton took out her notebook. She studied the board for a long time, her gaze moving from pictures to lists to names, jotting down notes as she did. Finally she shook her head. "We are making no progress." She turned the page in her book with a slap of paper. She drew broad strokes with her pencil, sketching what Jonathan assumed was the board. "Our suspect list grows along with the murders," she continued. "If anything, we are further from solving the case than before."

Jonathan could not argue, even though her words were rather an insult to his police work and the constabulary. Her conclusion was spot on.

"What do you propose, Detective?" Miss Bremerton asked. "Shall we go back to the scenes? Interview everyone on these lists?" She gave a frustrated sigh.

Jonathan leaned forward, resting his arms on the desk and hoping to look confident in what he was about to say, even though he felt exactly the reverse. "The ball tomorrow night," he said, mouth going dry. "I . . . me . . ." He cleared his throat. "For me to attend the ball. And Sergeant Lester. It is the best plan." The words fell out of his mouth in a mess that made his face redden. He must sound like a simpleton. He glanced at the sergeant, seeing the man nod in agreement.

"But we cannot execute it without your help, my lady," Sergeant Lester said.

"I see." Miss Bremerton blinked and frowned, looking from the sergeant to Jonathan. Her look turned scrutinizing.

Was she seeing an uneducated and unsophisticated man who'd dared suggest that he could rise above his class and blend with the highest circles of Society? Jonathan shifted in his seat, feeling exposed and foolish.

She pulled her lips to the side, her gaze still on him, then glanced at the sergeant before turning back to Jonathan. "Obviously you will wish to intermingle with the Kingsclere Hunting Club members. But you do not wish for them to know you are police officers, or they will not speak freely in front of you." She chewed on her lip. "But how will they be convinced you belong among them . . . ?" Her voice was low, trailing off as she considered.

Jonathan squirmed under her scrutiny. "I know I am not well-spoken, and I have little experience dancing or—"

"You have much more worthy attributes, sir, and a far superior character than any two members of elite Society combined," she muttered, staring at a spot over his shoulder. "Do not trouble yourself on that account." She waved her hand in the air as if to flick the idea away. Another moment passed, and Miss Bremerton's gaze sharpened. She looked between the men and rose quickly to her feet, a grin growing on her face. "I believe I have an idea."

Jonathan still hadn't fully processed her words. Had she complimented him? He contemplated the words and realized she had indeed bestowed a compliment. And she'd given it as an afterthought, a distracted utterance, as if it were something obvious and she'd not said it merely to flatter him. A warm glow expanded inside his chest as he considered her words. *Much more worthy attributes and a far superior charact—*

"Detective Graham, are you listening to me?"

Jonathan realized Miss Bremerton and Sergeant Lester were both staring at him, as if waiting for him to speak. "I'm sorry," he said, pushing away the thoughts and bringing the moment back into focus. "My mind wandered."

Miss Bremerton gave a *humph* sound and put her hand on the desk as though to force him to focus. "Detective, I asked what do you know of Serbia."

He tipped his head to the side. "Serbia? The country?"

"Yes, the country." Her lips twitched.

"Very little, I'm afraid. I don't see what that has to do—"

"For this plan to work, we have much to prepare." Miss Bremerton's eyes were bright with excitement.

"What is the plan?" Jonathan asked.

She continued on as if she hadn't heard him. "It will require some deception." She grinned, showing her dimples. "But you must trust me."

"The plan, my lady?" Sergeant Lester prompted.

"No time to explain." She pushed her notebook into her bag. "I have too much to do. Come to my house this afternoon at three o' clock—yes that should be enough time while my family is away—and I will reveal all." She whirled and hurried from the room.

Jonathan and Sergeant Lester stared at one another, and Jonathan wondered to what he had just committed them.

CHAPTER 14

THE CARRIAGE CAME TO A stop, jolting Sophie from the spinning thoughts in her head. She looked through the window, recognizing the storefront of the *Illustrated London News*.

The balloon article! In all the excitement she'd completely forgotten the work was due. Thank goodness Jasper kept better track of her errands than she did. She couldn't ask for a better driver.

She hurried through the office door, hoping the errand would be quick and wondering how she could possibly get everything done in such a short time. There were lists to make and messages to send, and she needed to speak with Mimi.

Sophie walked straight through the maze of activity to the editor's desk, taking out her notebook from her bag as she greeted Mr. Leonard.

"There you are, Miss Propriety." He blew out a puff of smoke and glanced at the clock, his frown making his similarities to a walrus all the more apparent. "Just a few moments shy of deadline."

"I'm sorry, sir." She turned quickly through the pages, searching for the article and drawing, and as she did so, some of the other papers slid out onto the floor.

Mr. Leonard picked up the drawings from the murder investigation, his brows rising as he glanced at them. "What have we here?"

"I beg your pardon." Sophie snatched them from his hand, replacing them with her article and balloon drawing. "Here they are." She stuck the pictures back into her notebook. A drop of sweat dripped down her back. *Calm down, Sophie.*

Mr. Leonard took the article and sat back with his pen. He slashed lines through words, muttering to himself as he read.

As the editor worked, Sophie considered what exactly to do first. *I shall need to find a tailor who will work fast, and a cobbler . . .*

Mr. Leonard circled an entire paragraph, drawing an arrow showing where it should be moved. He made a few notes at the end of the story, then put the paper into his basket.

Oh, and a barber . . .

The editor glanced at the balloon drawing and handed it back to Sophie to take to the engravers.

She crossed the room to the engravers' corner. *I wonder if there is time for dance instruction. The waltz, at the very least. The steps are easy enough if he can just master the rhythm . . .*

Mr. Potts scowled when she approached.

"How do you do today, sir?" She smiled as she handed him the illustration.

"More lace." He grunted, tossing the paper onto the table.

Sophie opened her mouth to say something complimentary but was interrupted by a woman's voice calling to her.

"Lady Sophronia!" Mrs. Ingram waved and motioned her over.

"Please excuse me." Sophie was glad for an excuse to leave the crotchety man. She crossed through the crowded office. "Mrs. Ingram. How very nice to see you."

"I've the information you requested." The research assistant pushed aside a mess of wayward curls and dug through a stack of papers, sliding out a folder. She turned it, glancing at the name on the edge. "Tom Stackhouse. Tragic story."

Sophie had almost forgotten that she'd requested the information in the first place. "Thank you very much." She opened the folder and glanced inside, seeing articles and reports, then closed it, deciding to read it later. She had enough on her mind today. "I am much obliged," Sophie said. She opened her bag to put the folder with her notebook, but the notebook was gone.

She found it right where she'd left it, on Mr. Leonard's desk, and stuck it into her bag. "Good day to you, sir." She called the farewell as she rushed through the door and back into the carriage.

Once the carriage started moving, she sat back, heart beating, and sighed loudly. *I must calm myself, or I shall truly be fit for Bedlam.*

Holloway, the butler, announced Detective Graham, Sergeant Lester, and Constable Merryweather exactly at three o'clock, and he showed them to the first-floor sitting room.

When the men entered, their eyes went wide at the sight of the four young ladies and one elderly woman with her dog, waiting for them.

"My lady . . ." The detective hesitated in the doorway.

"Please, Detective, just hear me out." Sophie hurried over and took the detective's arm before he could change his mind and leave.

The other men joined them, nodding to the ladies.

"First, introductions must be made," Sophie said. "Grandmother, you remember Detective Graham and Sergeant Lester. Allow me to introduce Constable Merryweather." Sophie continued. "Constable, this is my grandmother, Lady Mather."

Constable Merryweather greeted Mimi, looking confused as he bowed.

"And, gentlemen, these are my dear friends," Sophie said. "Miss Vivian Kirby, Miss Hazel Thornton, Miss Elizabeth Miller, and Miss Dahlia Lancaster." She indicated each woman in turn.

The men and women exchanged the appropriate bows and greetings, and Sophie led Detective Graham farther into the room to a small sofa across from the hearth and sat beside him.

The large room was usually arranged with smaller seating areas throughout, where groups could visit more intimately. But Sophie and Mimi had moved the chairs and sofas into a *U* shape facing the hearth. More suitable for a meeting, they'd decided.

Since Detective Graham was the person in charge of the operation, Sophie had thought he should sit at the head of the group. Besides, from that spot it was more difficult to escape. The other men sat in chairs on either side of the sofa.

On either side, between the men and the fireplace, two women sat on a settee—Elizabeth and Vivian beside Sergeant Lester, and Hazel and Dahlia next to Constable Merryweather. Directly next to the fireplace, Mimi sat in her favorite chair beside Elizabeth.

In the center of the grouping was a low table with plates of biscuits, pastries, and sandwiches. Sophia had noticed how Sergeant Lester had enjoyed tea before, and she wanted the men to remain in a pleasant mood. She'd also added a bowl filled with peppermints, thinking Detective Graham would appreciate it.

Dorrit alternated positions between her pillow near the window and Mimi's lap.

A soft breeze blew the sheer curtains, stirring fresh flowers on the tables as Sophie poured the tea. But despite the comfortable setting, friendships, and good food, there was no conversation. The company waited for her to reveal the reason they'd all been gathered.

At Sophie's urging as she resumed her seat, Constable Merryweather and Sergeant Lester filled their plates, but Detective Graham held his cup and saucer in his lap and looked wary, sitting on the edge of the cushion as if ready to bolt at any moment.

Sophie was tempted to grab on to his arm again to keep him from doing just that. She needed to speak quickly and make her plan sound convincing. She cleared her throat. "I realize you didn't expect to encounter so many people, Detective. But as my grandmother and I spoke, we realized it would be advantageous to have additional allies involved with the plan. And you shall understand why presently."

"What exactly *is* the plan, my lady?" Detective Graham asked. His expression had not changed, and she knew the next few moments were crucial if she were to convince him.

"You shall attend the ball in disguise," Sophie said. "As a *Serbian count*." The declaration came out more dramatically than she'd intended.

The other Orchids shared surprised glances, and Sergeant Lester covered his mouth as if hiding a smile. Constable Merryweather stared, mouth filled with biscuit.

Detective Graham shook his head and moved to stand, but Sophie rose first, planting herself directly in front of him, her knees nearly touching his, so that if he stood, he'd knock her over or possibly spill his tea. "Please listen—it will only take a moment."

He sighed and settled back in the sofa, waving for her to continue. His gaze was flat, his expression clearly conveying that he believed this to be a waste of his time.

Sophie was not deterred. The plan she and Mimi had devised was a sound one. She had only to convince the detective of it. She stepped back to where she could address the entire group in front of the hearth, though she spoke to Detective Graham.

"Sir, it is not as ridiculous as it first seems. As you no doubt are aware, the guests who will be at the ball are all members of a very exclusive group.

Every single attendee is well acquainted with every other. And not only by name—they know each other's families, associates, business dealings, and even private relationships. To pretend you are a member of high Society whom nobody has happened to meet before would be an impossibility."

Some of the young ladies nodded their agreement.

"I considered claiming you as a distant relative," Sophie said. "But of course, my parents would know better." She raised a finger. "And that's when I realized that in order for nobody to wonder why they'd never met you before, we must be more distantly acquainted."

Sophie glanced at Mimi and, seeing her grandmother's nod, continued. "Foreign visitors are afforded a measure of forgiveness when their words, appearance, or actions are not precisely au courant. Of course people realize customs are different in various parts of the world. And not only are the faux pas overlooked, they are celebrated."

"People do love to pretend tolerance of foreigners," Elizabeth muttered.

Sophie smiled at her friend. She glanced around at the others in the room, glad that none seemed to be disagreeing—so far, so good. "To claim that you are Canadian or American presents equal difficulty as to why nobody has ever heard of you. Too many people have connections across the sea, and if you were asked about a person whom you should know, it would be difficult to maintain the ruse. Your mistakes would be discovered. And it is the same with France—not to mention, nearly every person at the ball will be fluent in French, and I did not know whether any of you—"

"I do not speak French." Detective Graham's expression had grown a bit less skeptical, but he was still far from convinced.

She nodded. "The rail line from Subotica has recently been completed, giving a perfectly reasonable reason for a Serbian dignitary to visit, and the country's borders are in such turmoil between the Austro-Hungarian dual monarchy, the Ottomans, the Belgrade revolution, the Hapsburg Empire, the Kingdom of Croatia-Slavonia . . ." She counted off the various problems facing Eastern Europe on her fingers. "Very few people outside the region have a full understanding of the politics. Nobility loses or gains land and titles, and the rulers, especially the local ones, change often enough that nobody—especially someone from as far away as England—can keep track. No questions would be asked you could not answer, and they would not know if you made a mistake, especially if you pretended limited understanding of the English language." She finished the explanation in a rush as she ran out of breath.

"Brilliant," Vivian said, holding up her index finger. "Royalty with a vague pedigree will be believed without question, and one would not wish to admit one's ignorance of the Serbian political climate."

Sophie smiled, clasping her hands together, feeling excited that her argument seemed to be convincing. "Mimi and I have devised an identity for you." Detective Graham's expression was thoughtful—an improvement from skepticism. "My grandmother has an old . . . ah, friend." A blush started on her neck. "Mimi, perhaps you should explain."

"Yes, dear." Mimi sat up straighter, looking around the group. "You see, after my husband died, I traveled quite extensively. During my stay in Venice, I made a very good friend, Count Jovan Branković. He had recently lost his wife as well, and we took to one another immediately." The older woman's eyes went soft, and she gave a gentle smile. "Jovan's eyes were the most striking green, and oh my, did he ever love to walk along a moonlit beach. He was so very attentive to me and quite passionate—"

"Mimi," Sophie interrupted. She could feel her blush spreading and did not dare to glance at the men. Their discomfort at the direction the conversation had taken was palpable. She glanced at her friends.

Hazel and Dahlia had both gone red as well. Elizabeth did a poor job of hiding her giggle behind a handkerchief. Vivian remained, of course, unflustered, watching Mimi thoughtfully.

"Perhaps you will tell how Count Branković was received in London," Sophie, prompted.

Mimi broke off a bit of a biscuit and fed it to Dorrit. "Oh yes, well, of course Society fawned over him, wished to know all about him, to be around him and be noticed by him. He spoke very little English, and his dancing was atrocious, but a more charming man you could not hope to meet."

"The point is," Sophie said. "The count was easily accepted by Society."

"He was," Mimi said. "And I was the envy of quite a few ladies, I'll tell you. He, with that seductive accent—"

"And it would not be strange for his son or grandson to call on you when he visited London," Sophie said quickly, steering the conversation back on track.

"It would be perfectly natural," Mimi said.

Sophie turned to Detective Graham. "You see, sir? It is a bit unconventional, but the plan is sound. At Lord Ruben's engagement ball, you shall be introduced as Count Nikola Branković. Mimi has already informed the hosts that we bring a guest."

Detective Graham looked at Sergeant Lester. "What do you think, Sergeant?"

The sergeant frowned and shrugged. "I see no fault with the plan. Lady Sophronia has considered all angles, it seems." He grinned, lifting his teacup in a salute. "And I should very much like to see you costumed in finery and mingling with the swells."

Constable Merryweather snorted but was silenced by a sharp glance from Detective Graham. The constable took a deep drink of his tea and turned to study the pattern in the carpet.

The detective glared at the sergeant as well, until Sergeant Lester shook off his grin and adopted a serious look. Detective Graham turned back toward Sophie. He tipped his head to the side, raising and lowering his brows once.

Sophie took the gesture as agreement—or at least resignation—and a thrill of excitement skittered down to her fingers. She moved back to sit on the sofa, bringing the bowl of peppermints with her.

Detective Graham put a sweet into his mouth and glanced at the others in the room. "And, if I may be blunt, what do these other young ladies have to do with the business?"

"Support," Elizabeth said, turning toward him. "Isn't that right, Sophie?" Sophie nodded, and she continued. "Between all of us, one can manage to be near you throughout the evening. We shall interrupt if a conversation seems to be near to revealing you or if someone acts suspicious."

"You shall need more than one dance partner," Vivian said.

"And we can help with the investigation as well," Dahlia said.

Sophie smiled at Dahlia, knowing how difficult this particular ball would be for her, grateful her friend had put aside her own discomfort to help.

Detective Graham raised a brow at Sophie.

"I told them about the case," she admitted, wincing as she realized she'd not yet broken that news to him. "Yesterday, when I didn't believe you would be at the ball, I asked for their assistance."

He pressed his lips together, and his brows drew close together.

Clearly the man wasn't pleased. "These women can be trusted," Sophie said. "I swear to it. And we need as many ears as possible to garner information about each of our suspects. There are simply too many for you and me to speak to all of them in merely a few hours."

Detective Graham's expression did not soften. "My lady, if you remember, you made a promise to me that you would not go off investigating on your own."

A prickle of resentment ran up Sophie's spine. "I did not intend to be alone, sir. And surely you must see that more help is to the benefit of the investigation."

From the corner of her eye Sophie saw Elizabeth fold her arms. She certainly had opinions about the detective's words. Thankfully she did not voice them.

"We will be discreet, sir," Hazel said in her quiet voice.

The other women added their agreement, assuring the officers that they would use the utmost caution in their questioning, and glancing at one another with excited smiles. They were delighted to be part of the investigation. It would certainly make the ball more interesting.

Sophie did not allow the detective's irritation to deter her. "I plan to take my notebook—it will not be unusual for me to be drawing at the event—and I will collect information. You will each report to me all that you learn as the evening proceeds."

Detective Graham nodded, a touch of resentment still evident in his pursed lips. "I will see that you have a copy of both suspect lists." He turned to Sergeant Lester. "Inform Mr. Smudgely at the Belcourt that you, Sergeant, are to be portrayed as an employee for the evening. You are to have access to the serving and kitchen staff."

Sergeant Lester nodded. "'Tisn't royalty, but I shall manage," he muttered in his gravelly voice, a smirk pulling at his mouth.

Detective Graham ignored him and turned to the constable. "Merryweather, you shall work in the stables. I'm certain Nick Sloan will be pleased to have your assistance, especially as it portends to clearing his name."

"Yes, sir." The constable gave a sharp nod, looking as if he took the duty very seriously.

Detective Graham let out a heavy breath. "Now, Lady Sophronia, I have but one day to be remade convincingly into Count Nikola Branković."

The thrill of excitement returned, and Sophie clapped her hands. "Then, let us get to work, Detective."

CHAPTER 15

JONATHAN LIFTED HIS CHIN, MOVING his head side to side as he studied the false mustache in the mirror. It was dark, thick, and curled upward on the ends in a style the women had told him was very much in line with the men of the Balkans. The patch of hair glued to his top lip changed his appearance slightly, but it was nothing at all compared to the rest of his costume.

He wore a military-style coat in dark blue, with epaulets on the shoulders and golden rope adornments on the cuffs, buttons, and collar. A red-and-white sash was tied around his waist and held a curved sword in its sheath. Instead of a necktie, a large pendant hung from a thick ribbon at his throat beneath his collar. Jonathan had no idea whether the pendant was truly a symbol related to the nation of Serbia, but he wouldn't put anything past Miss Bremerton or her grandmother. Somehow the women had managed to procure the entirety of his wardrobe, complete with medals on his chest and some sort of a fur cap, as well as shiny black boots, and have the entire thing tailored to fit him in only a day.

After giving her approval of his costume, the dowager countess had departed to prepare herself for the ball. The butler, Holloway, had left him only a few moments earlier, and Jonathan remained in the entry hall, waiting for Miss Bremerton.

He pressed between his fingers, making the stark white gloves tighter on his hands, and brushed a bit of lint from his sleeve, trying to focus on little tasks instead of the rush of nerves that nearly overcame him each time he contemplated everything that could go wrong tonight. Most scenarios involved Sergeant Lester and Constable Merryweather having a hearty laugh at Jonathan's expense when they laid eyes on him as Count Nikola Branković, and all involved him being exposed as an imposter.

But, in spite of its absurdity, Jonathan still could not think of a better plan. He clasped his hands behind his back and paced. The past day and a half had been a whirlwind. A dance master had spent the afternoon teaching him a few basic steps, and while Miss Bremerton was running around London in search of the finishing touches for Jonathan's costume, Miss Lancaster had volunteered—much to Jonathan's embarrassment—to partner him as he practiced.

Miss Thornton had given him instruction on his accent—apparently her father had a Russian friend—and practiced with him until satisfied that he had the proper cadence and pronounced his sounds correctly. "When in doubt, speak loudly and with clipped vowels," she'd instructed.

Miss Kirby and Miss Miller had quizzed him about basic facts concerning the struggles of the nation he was to claim as his homeland, and he was again embarrassed at his lack of formal education. But after a few hours studying a map and discussing the history, they declared him to know as much, if not more, than most people at the ball.

Contrary to his initial assumption, the young women had proved to be nothing like the arrogant debutantes he'd expected when he came into the sitting room the day before. He'd actually enjoyed the time they'd spent together planning the operation, something he'd never have believed possible when it was presented. Miss Bremerton's friends were intelligent and thoughtful and witty, much like the young lady herself, as evidenced in her detailed planning and the bowls of his favorite peppermints he'd noticed.

Hearing footsteps above him, he turned and looked up.

Miss Bremerton was walking across the landing above the entry hall. She stopped at the rail and bent down to fix her shoe. When she straightened, her gaze met Jonathan's, and she smiled.

Jonathan had a surprisingly strong reaction to the gesture. His breathing choked off, and a current jolted in his chest. It was, of course, not the first smile he'd seen on Miss Bremerton. He supposed he could blame the unexpected response on his nerves, but the truth was Miss Bremerton—no, she was Lady Sophronia tonight—looked utterly exquisite.

Her hair was fashioned in soft curls pinned around her head and falling over her shoulders. A sort of feathery arrangement held it in place. The style was so unlike the practical one she usually favored that the difference was startling. She wore a peach-colored gown with ruffles and lace and other details he did not know the names of—except for the tournure, but it was hardly appropriate to notice that. Her neck was bare, save for a simple string of pearls. Long white gloves were pulled up past her elbows, and her sleeves were gathered gracefully on her upper arms, revealing the tops of her shoulders. The dress flattered her both in shape and color, and for a moment, the romantic nature of attending a ball with a beautiful woman gave him a thrill—until he remembered that they were hunting for a murderer, not out for a night of pleasure.

She rested a hand on the rail, and her smile grew, showing the dimples that had so intrigued him the first time he'd seen them.

Jonathan realized she hadn't before now seen him fully attired in his costume and for a moment felt a self-conscious apprehension. He gave a stiff bow. *I look ridiculous.*

Lady Sophronia nodded her approval, and the action eased his worry, albeit slightly. She opened her mouth to speak, but before she did, a voice sounded from the stairs above her.

"Oh, Sophronia, really? The *peach* dress? You know it is all wrong on you. The color does nothing for your skin tone."

An elegantly attired woman in a burgundy gown, whom Jonathan could only assume was the countess, descended the stairs. She shook her head, making a tsking sound as she neared her daughter. "And see how the waist pulls here. Could not Sally make your corset any tighter?" The woman gave a dramatic sigh, tugging on the back of the bodice. "This is what you get for indulging so, Sophronia. How often have I told you to limit your pastries? And now, here we are, attending the most important event of the Season, and you looking so—"

"Mother, we have a guest," she interrupted in a calm voice that was at odds with the color in her cheeks.

The countess looked down into the entry hall for the first time, her mouth forming an *o*.

Lady Sophronia took her mother's arm, and the pair started down the stairs.

Heat spread up Jonathan's neck, a combination of embarrassment at overhearing the exchange and anger that her mother would treat her so. He studied Lady Sophronia's face for a clue as to how her mother's words affected her. Though she held a serene expression, he could see her lips were pulled tighter than usual.

"Mother, allow me to introduce you to Count Nikola Branković."

"Oh, of course," the countess said as they reached the lower floor. "I have heard of you, Count Branković. What a delight to meet you at last."

Lady Sophronia gestured to her mother. "My lord, may I present Lady Mather."

Jonathan gave a formal bow, just as Lady Sophronia had instructed. He took Lady Mather's hand and gave it an exaggerated kiss as Mimi had assured him was the custom in Serbia. "A pleasure, Lady Madder." He pronounced the words as he and Miss Thornton had practiced.

"And I am so pleased you will attend the ball tonight. You know, I have *two* daughters, and you will no doubt wish to meet Lady Priscilla as well."

Jonathan gave a sharp nod. "I veel hope to make her acquaintance."

Holloway informed them the carriage was waiting, and Lady Mather hurried away to locate her husband, muttering about him losing track of time, again.

Lady Sophronia put a thin wrap over her shoulders and attached a bag to her wrist, through which he could see the outline of her notebook.

Jonathan offered her his arm as they stepped outside, and the two took their places in the carriage to wait for her parents. He glanced through the open carriage door and, seeing they were alone, took the chance to speak in his regular voice. "I did not have the opportunity to tell you how beautiful you look, Lady Sophronia."

As she sat directly beside him in the darkened interior of the carriage, it was difficult to make out her expression. Jonathan felt her smirk and eye roll more than saw it.

"You do not need to compensate for my mother, Detective. My feelings are not delicate and do not require reassurance."

"I do not mean to sound pandering."

She shrugged, shifting in her seat to face him more directly. "As you said before, beauty isn't a talent. It is not the virtue I hope to be known for. A person's existence must be very bleak indeed if all he or she has to offer is a pleasant face."

"Yes. You are much more than that. And yet, I speak the truth when I say you are beautiful."

She looked down, and he wondered if she believed him.

Jonathan opened his mouth to reiterate his point but was interrupted by the carriage driver informing them Lord and Lady Mather would join them at the ball.

Lady Sophronia nodded, looking unsurprised by the news. "Father must be absorbed in his ledgers." She moved her skirts, scooted around to sit on the bench facing Jonathan, and gave the order to depart.

Jonathan was disappointed that they were no longer sitting close. He sat back in the seat as the carriage started away, shifting the sword so it didn't pull on his sash. His hand strayed to his chest out of habit, but his pocket watch fob wasn't there. Instead he fidgeted with the buttons on his sleeve as his thoughts moved over the plan. The young ladies were reliable, of that he had no doubt. Between all of them, they should manage to speak with most—if not all—of the suspects who had been guests at the lecture. Sergeant Lester and Constable Merryweather would be able to move and speak much more freely in their realms. After tonight Jonathan hoped to have the identity of the killer. But so much could go wrong—and nearly all of the risk of error lay with his ability to carry out his charade.

"You're nervous."

Jonathan smiled at the hint of teasing in her voice, the reminder that he'd said the same thing in their first carriage ride together.

"Anxious," he said.

"We'll find the killer."

He touched his fingers to the mustache, pressing down to make certain it was firmly affixed. "I worry I'll make a mistake—botch the entire operation with a misplaced word or gesture."

"Set yourself at ease, Detective. People will see what they wish. Once they hear your title, nothing you do will matter." A touch of bitterness had entered her voice.

"And that is why you do not use yours," Jonathan said.

"Yes. I wish to be known for more than just to whom I was born," Lady Sophronia said. "To be seen." She looked down, folding her hands together. "You will understand after tonight."

To be seen. Her words had been almost pleading, and Jonathan felt the pain behind them.

The carriage drew to a stop, and the door opened. She took in a deep breath and let it out slowly, eyes closed. "You and I both wear masks tonight," she said, leaning forward to move past him and leaving a flowery scent. She took the carriage driver's hand to descend.

Jonathan let out a breath as well. He stepped down from the carriage, offered his arm to Lady Sophronia, and joined the crowd ascending the assembly hall stairs. He couldn't help feeling like a soldier stepping into battle.

⤬

The Belcourt Assembly Hall was completely the reverse of the empty building Jonathan had visited three days earlier. The globe chandelier shone unbelievably brightly, music spilled from the ballroom, delicious aromas filled the air, and all around were the sounds of voices and laughter. The large entry was crowded with opulently attired guests. Men in dark jackets mixed with women in colorful gowns and glittering jewelry, top hats and feathered headdresses bobbing among them.

Lady Sophronia led him to the coat closet they'd inspected a few days earlier, and they left behind his furry hat and her wrap. He'd have liked to leave the sword since the thing banging into his leg was quite bothersome, but apparently presentation was more important than comfort.

Three couples stood near the ballroom's entrance, welcoming the guests: two older and one younger. The engaged couple and their parents, he assumed.

As they waited in line to be greeted, Lady Sophronia introduced him to the couple in front of them, Lord and Lady Hampton.

The elderly pair appeared to be nearing their eightieth year. Perhaps Lord Hampton was even older. The man was slender with a shock of white hair and thick white eyebrows. He wore thick spectacles and held an ear trumpet up with one hand and leaned on a cane with the other. Lady Hampton's hair was silver, and she was rounder than her husband. She wore a gown of deep purple and a necklace with so many diamonds it resembled a chandelier. Even with her wrinkles, she was a striking woman.

"Count Branković." Lady Hampton touched her fingertips to her breastbone as Jonathan bowed and kissed her hand. "How wonderful to meet you. You are quite like your grandfather."

"Dank you," Jonathan said, clipping the syllables like Miss Thornton had taught him. "Dis is indeed a compleement."

"Doesn't he look like his grandfather, my dear?" Lady Hampton spoke with a loud voice into her husband's ear trumpet.

"Eh?" Lord Hampton leaned closer to his wife.

"Count Branković." Lady Hampton spoke even louder and slower. "You remember, he was a friend of Lady Mather's."

"Oh yes, Lady Mather," Lord Hampton said, his face lighting up. "Splendid woman. Bit peculiar, I'd say, but never dull, that one." He tipped his head, looking closer at Jonathan. He squinted. "Had a paramour, you know. A count, I think he was. Looked a bit like this one." He nodded at Jonathan.

"Yes, my dear." Lady Hampton gave her husband an affectionate pat on the arm. She turned back to them. "Lady Sophronia, you were so missed at our ball. I do hope your headache is improved."

"It is," she said. "Thank you. I was sorry it prevented me from attending. Your ball is one of my favorite events of the year."

"Yes, well, you must take care of yourself. I know how taxing the Season can be, every day filled with visits and concerts and assemblies, and last Tuesday was no exception. My poor husband was very disappointed to have missed the hunting lecture. So many gentlemen going on and on all evening about this elephant tusk or the height of that giraffe. He was quite put out." She leaned closer, winking. "But, of course, he'd not have been able to hear a word of it."

Lady Sophronia smiled. "I believe he'd have appreciated it all the same."

"Your hasband—he is hunter?" Jonathan asked.

Lady Hampton glanced at her husband, then at Jonathan. She nodded. "He is not as active as he once was, but in his day, he was quite the outdoorsman. If he were thirty years younger, he'd have loved to accompany William Charles Baldwin on his African safari adventure."

"Africa?" Lord Hampton leaned his ear trumpet closer to his wife. "Did you say Africa?" He shook his head and leaned forward, whispering to Jonathan in a loud voice. "You know, I had to miss William Charles Baldwin's lecture." He pointed toward his wife, then leaned even closer to Jonathan, cupping his hand around his mouth. "She said it wouldn't do to be late to my own ball."

Jonathan hoped his mustache hid his smile.

"As for myself, I think it wouldn't do for a wife to order her husband about." The old man frowned like a child who'd been sent early to bed. "Do you know Mr. Baldwin was attacked by a lion? Killed his horse and a hunting dog, but the man kept his wits, loaded his musket, and shot the beast." Lord Hampton demonstrated with his cane exactly how one would dispatch a lion. He wobbled, and Jonathan caught his arm to keep him from falling.

Once the elderly man had his balance again, he continued. "I hear Mr. Baldwin began his lecture with a shocking drawing of the incident, made by an artist who read his memoir. Caught the crowd's attention right away, I imagine." He scowled toward his wife again. "Not that I'd know for myself."

One of the host couples greeted the Hamptons, taking their attention.

Jonathan and Lady Sophronia shared a glance, the side of her mouth bouncing in just a hint of a smile. She'd enjoyed the interaction as well.

Jonathan would have liked to ask Lord Hampton further about the guests who arrived late to his ball, but he wasn't entirely certain he could trust the man's memory to be accurate. At least they could scratch Lord Hampton's name off the list of suspects.

Jonathan was introduced to Lord and Lady Dorrington, the Marquess and Marchioness of Molyneaux, and the happy couple: Lord Ruben and Lady Lorene.

He greeted them briefly and gave nervous replies that were hopefully attributed to the language barrier. He began to relax once he realized that while people were interested and inquisitive, none appeared to know enough about the conflict in Serbia to ask anything he couldn't answer. The ladies had been right in that.

He and Lady Sophronia entered the ballroom, and more introductions were made. Jonathan attempted to keep track of all the names and titles but found himself distracted, fascinated at watching Lady Sophronia move among high Society. She knew instinctively whom to flatter, which questions to ask about which family members, and which conversations to keep short. Jonathan was surprised at how effortlessly she moved from one topic to the next, always saying the right thing—but he realized quickly enough that she didn't offer any opinions of her own or ask prying questions. She was nothing like the nosy journalist he knew. She kept the conversations moving smoothly, but the subject matter never strayed from polite small talk.

As he watched, Jonathan noticed she even carried herself differently. She spoke more softly, her smile lacked brightness, and her movements were controlled, as if she were merely a shadow of herself, hollow.

Aside from the Hamptons, Jonathan sensed no affection in her interactions with the other guests. Lady Sophronia was playing a part— one she performed with skill, but it was still disconcerting to see so much of what made her *her* missing.

A group of young women approached, and Jonathan recognized one of them immediately. Miss Charlotte Grey. His first instinct was to hurry away, but Lady Sophronia had already begun introductions.

"Count Branković, please allow me to introduce my sister, Lady Priscilla, and her friends, Miss Charlotte Grey and Miss Helen Rothschild."

"How do you do, ladies?" He spoke in his stilted manner, kissing each of their hands in turn. The action elicited giggles from the women.

"I hear you are from Serbia, my lord," Lady Priscilla said.

Jonathan appraised Lady Sophronia's sister in a glance. She was beautiful—stunning, really—but he sensed right away there was little more to her. And the same appeared to be true of her friends.

"Dat is correct. Near to Vojvodina."

"So exotic," Miss Rothschild whispered to her friends.

They giggled again, apparently believing his deficiency in English affected his hearing as well.

Lady Priscilla slid closer, touching his arm. "I wonder about your coat, my lord. Do you serve in the military?"

Lady Sophronia frowned, and Jonathan was not displeased at the sign of jealousy.

"*Da.* I am major in the Syrmian Hussar Regiment." He repeated the words he'd memorized.

"You must have such stories." Miss Rothschild moved closer to his other side, nearly boxing Lady Sophronia out from the conversation.

Jonathan took a step to the side and pressed his palm against the small of Lady Sophronia's back to maneuver her into the circle.

"I do hope you intend to dance tonight, Count Branković," Charlotte Grey said.

Is she actually fluttering her lashes? He couldn't believe this was the same woman who had been so dismissive in her parlor only a few days earlier.

Sophie had been right about being known only for her title, and he could feel her frustration. Although, of course, in his case, it was precisely the reaction he needed in order to maintain his disguise.

Before he had the chance to answer Miss Grey's question, two men approached. One wore a thick beard, and the other, a younger man, had curly hair and long side-whiskers. The younger man bowed to the ladies. "Lady Sophronia, Lady Priscilla, Miss Grey, Miss Rothschild."

"Lord Meredith," Lady Sophronia said. "Please, meet Count Nikola Branković."

"A pleasure, my lord. And this is William Charles Baldwin." He introduced the ladies, then turned to Sophronia. "My lady, Mr. Baldwin has agreed to be interviewed for your article."

"Oh, thank you, sir," Lady Sophronia said. "Mr. Baldwin, I understand your lecture the other night was very well received."

He offered his arm. "I'd be pleased to tell you all about it, my lady."

Sophie hesitated, glancing at Jonathan, before taking the man's arm.

Jonathan felt a stab of panic. Would she leave him alone? He scanned the room, hoping for a glance of Sergeant Lester or one of Sophie's friends, then chastised himself for the reaction. He was a detective for the London Metropolitan Police Force. He hunted and apprehended criminals and villains on a daily basis. Speaking with some fancy gentlemen at a ball was likely the easiest job he'd ever do.

"Don't fear for your friend, my lady," Lord Meredith said. "I'd be pleased to introduce him around."

Sophie's gaze met Jonathan's, holding a question. He gave a small nod to reassure her. After all, this was why they were here. And while it may be uncomfortable, he needed to interview as many of the suspects as possible. Besides, he thought Lord Meredith seemed sincere enough. And, as noblemen went, rather likeable.

Sophie's eyes lit on something behind Jonathan, and her shoulders relaxed the slightest bit. "Oh, Count Branković, you remember my friend, Miss Thornton?"

"Yes. A pleasure to see you again, Miss Thornton." He rolled the *r* in her name a bit longer than necessary. The skill had taken quite a bit of practice, and he was proud to show off for his teacher.

Miss Thornton gave a small smile, looking down quickly.

The other gentlemen greeted Miss Thornton as well, and she replied shyly. Sophie had told him her friend suffered from bouts of panic, and Jonathan wondered if it was truly painful for her to be out in company. If that was the case, he appreciated her willingness to assist with the case all the more.

Sophie pulled her friend away from the others and spoke quietly for a moment, giving Miss Thornton the bag with her notebook.

"I can see you are very popular with the ladies, my lord." Lord Meredith clapped Jonathan on the shoulder. "Allow me to rescue you. Come along to the cardroom. I'm sure you'll appreciate conversation with members of your own sex."

Jonathan clapped Lord Meredith back. "Dat I vould, my lord. Lead de vay."

CHAPTER 16

SOPHIE GLANCED TOWARD THE DOORWAY as Sergeant Lester—in his server's livery—passed by the small room again. She felt a swell of affection toward the man, thinking she'd never known anyone so steadfast in the performance of his duty. The sergeant kept an extremely, almost comically, close eye on her. She looked back at Mr. Baldwin, but the man hadn't noticed her attention stray. He was settled comfortably on the small sofa and kept up a running discourse, telling in detail of his various adventures in Africa and the different species of animals he'd hunted. He stroked his thick beard as he talked, moving from story to story, and didn't seem to be nearing a conclusion.

Sophie nodded here and there, but she was having a difficult time concentrating on the man's words. Her foot tapped, and she tried not to fidget as she cast around her thoughts for a way out. Not only was she trapped listening to hunting tales while her friends and Detective Graham investigated the murders, but in order to speak uninterrupted, Mr. Baldwin had found an empty room—leaving open the door for propriety's sake— which just happened to be the small parlor where Jane Duffin and George Lewis had been murdered. Sophie could not keep her gaze from wandering to the closet door or the window as her mind conjured the scene that must have occurred merely a few days earlier. She shivered and purposely avoided looking at the horse statue.

She'd tried to ask Mr. Baldwin a few times about the lecture, specifically the attendees, but the man was understandably more interested in describing the actual experiences, rather than simply his presentation.

How can I leave without causing offense? Sophie had tried to keep track of time by counting the songs the orchestra played. How many dances had passed since she'd left the ballroom? Six? It must have been nearly an hour since she'd left the detective's side. How was he getting on? His impersonation of Serbian nobility had been well received, as far as she'd seen, but what had happened since they'd been separated? Had he made any headway on the case? Had his charade been discovered? At least she'd managed to tell Hazel about the lion drawing before Mr. Baldwin had taken her away. It could prove an interesting way for the ladies to begin a conversation about the lecture as well as determine who was present for the beginning of the lecture.

Mr. Baldwin took a breath, and Sophie took the opportunity to interject. "This is all wonderful information, sir. Thank you so much for—"

"I have neglected to tell you of the bull elephant that charged us in Zulu country," Mr. Baldwin said. He pointed, as if the animal were even now running toward them. "Enormous animal he was. One swipe of his trunk snapped White's gun clean in half." He lifted his arms, holding an imaginary weapon, and tilted his head to the side, sighting down the barrel. "I got off a good shot, hitting the beast in the shoulder—"

"I beg pardon, my lady." Detective Graham's voice interrupted in stilted English.

The unfamiliar sight of him in his thick mustache and uniform jacket startled her for just an instant.

He bowed from the doorway, and she saw the familiar tease in his eyes. "But I vould ask you for to dance. Dey are soon to play valtz."

"Oh, I would love to, Count Branković." Sophie rose and extended a hand to her bearded and long-winded companion. "Thank you so very much for granting me an interview, Mr. Baldwin. If you will please excuse me now . . ."

The hunter stood as well and accepted her hand. "Of course, my lady. If you'd like, I will call on you sometime this week, and we can finish—"

"De valtz begins." Detective Graham took her other hand, giving it a tug and pulling her away from Mr. Baldwin mid-sentence.

Sophie hid her laugh as she allowed herself to be pulled from the room. His action was brilliant. Mr. Baldwin could never accuse a count of rudeness.

"Have you been talking to him this entire time?" The detective kept his voice low so as not to be overheard by anyone they might pass as they walked.

She nodded, giving an exaggerated sigh. "I fear if you hadn't rescued me, I'd be listening to his stories until morning."

He moved her hand underneath his elbow, resting it on his arm, and led her back through the entry toward the ballroom at a more sedate pace. "You had the sergeant quite worried," he said. "He didn't consider it all the thing for Miss Propriety to remain in a private room, alone, with a man for such a long time." He winked. "I'm afraid he is extremely concerned for your reputation."

Sophie smiled. "He is very thoughtful. So tell me, what have you learned? And has the sergeant discovered anything? What about the others?" She stopped abruptly outside the large doors, away from the crowd.

He turned, one foot still raised, momentarily off-balance, as if he'd not intended to stop. But he stopped fully then, facing her, and glanced over his shoulder to the ballroom, then back with a quizzical bend in his brow. "You want to discuss this now? The waltz . . ."

"Oh." Sophie blinked. "You really wish to dance with me? I thought it was merely an excuse to draw me away from Mr. Baldwin."

He shrugged. "Why can it not be both?"

"Detective, it isn't necessary. I don't expect . . . You don't have to . . ."

"I wish to waltz with you." He leaned close, holding her gaze, and spoke the words slowly. Each syllable sent a shiver over her skin.

Sophie felt heat explode in her face.

Detective Graham's mustache twitched, and though she couldn't see it beneath the glued-on whiskers, she knew he was smirking.

Though Sophie had been led onto a dance floor hundreds of times, she'd never felt the fluttering in her chest that she felt now. All around, the eyes of the *ton* watched her walk with the mysterious count to take their places on the dance floor. He faced her, taking her hand and slipping his other around her waist. She gathered her skirts, feeling as though the usual dance position was much more intimate in this situation and much less routine. Was it because the two were embroiled in a pretense? Sharing a secret certainly contributed to the confusing emotions. But that couldn't account for the entirety.

The waltz began, and Detective Graham drew her to the side, sweeping her along with the beat of the music. He moved confidently, his shoulders square and head held high. Nobody would believe he'd learned to dance only yesterday.

Sophie's breath felt strained, and the heat from her blush had increased. She followed along, her feet remembering the motions that her mind could not. Her head felt rather light. When had she last eaten? The lightheaded feeling threatened to make her dizzy. She looked up to tell her partner that she needed to stop. But when her gaze met Detective Graham's, the troubling feelings stilled. His eyes held a smile. His face was familiar, warm—the face of her friend.

Her concerns eased, and her stiffness melted away.

As if by reflex, his arm tightened, bringing her closer until their bodies were nearly touching. The air between them was hot and electric, and more than anything, Sophie wanted to lean in to him and rest her head on his shoulder as he held her in his embrace.

She jerked back, mortified at the turn her thoughts had taken. Her feet stumbled, and the detective slowed, then stopped, a look of concern creasing the corners of his eyes. "My lady?"

"I beg your pardon." She gave a sheepish smile and pressed her hands to her heated cheeks. "How very clumsy of me."

The other dancers moved around them, but she knew she was drawing attention. Would her blush ever leave?

Detective Graham put a hand on her arm. "Are you unwell?"

"I am well. I apologize. Just a bit warm."

"Do you wish to stop? Or shall we continue?" He tipped his head to the side.

Sophie could feel him studying her, and the idea that he might see her thoughts was humiliating. She retook his hand, gathered her skirts again, and pasted on a smile.

He waited for the correct beat of the music, and they started again, but this time Sophie was determined not to allow her emotions to be clouded by their proximity. "Tell me—what did you learn from the gentlemen?" She kept her voice low enough that the conversation remained private beneath the sound of the orchestra.

Detective Graham raised a brow and watched her for another moment before answering. "I was pleasantly surprised by Lord Meredith and his friends. We enjoyed a fine time—conversation and drinks in the cardroom until their mothers shooed us all out to socialize."

"That is not what I meant." She rolled her eyes. "Did you *question* any of them?"

His lips twitched. "I mentioned that I enjoyed hunting, and then I listened."

"As they discussed the lecture."

The detective nodded.

"Did you learn anything new?"

He shook his head. "Unfortunately, no. Much to the disappointment of Miss Thornton and Miss Kirby, who were trying to look inconspicuous as they listened behind the door outside the cardroom. Your friends might consider careers in espionage."

Sophie frowned, frustrated that her marvelous plan was producing no results.

"But we are able to cross more suspects off the list. That is something, at least," he said.

"I suppose," she muttered, scowling.

He squeezed her fingers and leaned close to her ear. "We will find the killer, Sophie. Every step brings us closer to his discovery."

Sophie's cheeks flared again. This time it was not only his closeness but his use of her Christian name that brought on the reaction. Aside from family and a few older gentlemen who still thought of her as a little girl, no man had ever called her by her name. She stumbled again.

Detective Graham caught her, his arm tightening around her. He stopped again, resting his other hand beneath her elbow to steady her.

"I am so sorry," Sophie said, pressing her palms to her heated cheeks. Her voice came out breathless.

"Come along." He tucked her hand beneath his elbow and led her from the ballroom. They crossed the entry beneath the globe chandelier and entered the dining room. The room was filled with round tables this evening, where groups of guests sat visiting as they took refreshment. "I do not know why young ladies insist upon skipping meals," he grumbled.

Sergeant Lester was at the far side of the room stacking dirty plates on a tray. When he saw them, he motioned with his chin to the side, indicating he wished to speak with them.

Detective Graham nodded to the sergeant and looked around the room. "There is your grandmother, Sophie." He spoke in a quiet voice, hiding his English. "Eat something while I meet with the sergeant."

Sophie was still heated, which she told herself had nothing to do with the man holding her arm and whispering into her ear. "I'll come with you," she said, halfheartedly, not wanting to miss anything and at the same time needing space to regain control of her emotions.

"I promise to tell you everything," he said. "And if *I* do not, rest assured those two young ladies hiding behind the potted plant will."

Sophie looked to where he indicated and saw Elizabeth and Dahlia peeking at them between palm fronds. She couldn't help but smile at the sight.

When Mimi saw Sophie and Detective Graham approach, she waved for them to join her and her friends. "Oh, Count Branković, there you are." She allowed the detective to kiss her fingers. When she turned to Sophie, her eyes narrowed in concern. "My dear, you look quite flushed."

"My lady need to eat." The detective spoke in his stilted English for the benefit of the other women sitting with Mimi.

"Yes, of course." Lady Chatsworth vacated the seat beside Mimi, motioned for Sophie to sit, and waved for a server to bring tea.

"Thank you," Sophie said, wishing she could curl up on a sofa with her head in her grandmother's lap. She vaguely heard Mimi introducing the detective to her friends before he took his leave, but her thoughts were scattered.

She took a sip of the tea and gave a grateful smile when Mimi set a tray of teacakes and wafers in front of her.

"Now, Sophronia, tell me what is the matter," Mimi said once Sophie had eaten a few wafers. "Perhaps the excitement of the past week has been too much for you."

"I don't know," Sophie said. "Everything was fine until Det—" She glanced at her grandmother's friends. "Until the count took my hand for the waltz. When we danced, I felt happy and sad and hot and dizzy . . . My thoughts were all in disarray." She shook her head as if she could jostle the wayward thoughts back into place.

"Ah, I see," Mimi said. She raised a brow, and her lips twitched as she glanced across the room in the direction Detective Graham had gone.

The other ladies smiled as well.

Sophie's stomach tightened in apprehension of what the knowing smiles meant. "Perhaps it was a spell of hysteria," she offered, but the explanation sounded weak, even to her. Could they be insinuating . . . ? No. Sophie refused to believe it.

"Well, dearest," Mimi said in a gentle voice. "You are certainly not the first woman to find herself enchanted by a handsome man or to blush in his arms on the dance floor."

"No." Sophie gave a disgusted snort. "I don't . . . I am not the type . . ." What was wrong with her? Was a waltz with a man who called her by her Christian name all it took to turn her into a lovesick girl?

The thought brought her up short. Love? This couldn't be that. She couldn't be *in love* with Detective Graham. He was brusque, sometimes to the point of rudeness, and he knew nothing of literature and art. He always wore the same ugly brown hat and ate far too many peppermints.

"He is all wrong," Sophie protested.

"Aren't they always?" Mrs. Griffin said, shaking her head.

"We would never suit," Sophie continued. "It must be something else. My corset may be too tight."

The ladies glanced at one another, their smiles making Sophie want to argue all the more. They didn't know. None of them could explain this away so simply. Besides, she wasn't like all the silly women who came to balls expecting to be swept off their feet by a handsome suitor. She didn't believe in romance.

"Dearest, your grandfather and I could not have been less suited for one another. He was classically conservative, traditional, and stuffy—from an old, established family." Mimi gave a wry smile, rolling her eyes. "While I . . ." She waved her hand as if no explanation were necessary. "We met at a suffragette protest—well, *met* is a strong word for yelling at one another on the green at St. James's Park about the inequality of women."

"Oh, I remember it fondly," Lady Chatsworth said. "You in your white dress and laurel wreath and he, late for his parliament session, in his wig and robes." She snickered. "You raved about that 'horrid man' for months."

Sophie smiled, imagining the pair in their youth.

"Until the two of you were invited to the same house party in Southampton," Mrs. Griffin chimed in. "All of us endured three long weeks of glares across the dining table and uncomfortable arguments in the parlor until"—she widened her eyes dramatically—"that fateful afternoon."

"When the pair of you were caught in the rain and forced to take shelter in the duke's gazebo." Lady Chatsworth touched her finger to her cheek and scrunched up her face in a contemplative expression that looked very exaggerated. "What ever happened there, Emmeline? You still haven't told us."

Mimi waggled a finger at her friends and gave a playful scowl. "Never you mind." She turned back to Sophie. "The point is love doesn't always take into account political positions or proximity or rank." She made a circular motion with her finger. "Dearest, most of the people at this ball have wed or will for status or money. But a very few of us"—she nodded to her friends—"will have the great privilege of falling in love, and that, Sophronia, is a gift. It does not come without obstacles, and it is never a guarantee against a broken heart."

"But you will never regret it," Lady Chatsworth said softly.

Sophie opened her mouth to argue, but she stopped, remembering the look in Detective Graham's eyes when he'd rescued her from Mr. Baldwin—teasing, warm, familiar . . . Somehow it had both calmed her worries and sent her heart tumbling. Was that love?

"But . . ." Sophie could think of nothing to say.

"One cannot control matters of the heart," Mimi said. "But there are some things we can do to take our minds off the worry." She winked at Sophie and motioned to one of the servers. "Iced sherbets for all, if you please."

CHAPTER 17

JONATHAN STOOD WITH SERGEANT LESTER inside the kitchen, glancing through the partially open door into the dining room as he listened to the man's report.

". . . said she would have noticed if any of the other staff had gone missing between six and seven—even for a short amount of time. It was the busy time of night." The sergeant also glanced through the doorway. "Sir, I believe the killer must have been one of the guests."

Jonathan nodded. The investigation was certainly moving in that direction. "But who?" he muttered and reached to his chest before once again remembering he didn't wear his pocket watch. He'd not brought any peppermints either. He fiddled with the braids on his sleeves.

A pair of gentlemen approached the table where Sophie sat. Jonathan knew the two men; he'd been introduced earlier by Lord Meredith in the cardroom.

Lord Everleigh, Jonathan thought, was the sort of man who folded his stockings and cut his food into neat, uniform bites. His hair and mustache were beyond tidy and trimmed in the sort of way that hinted at obsessive, and his clothing appeared to have been starched by someone who didn't want him to bend in any way. As Lord Everleigh's gaze traveled around the room, he looked perpetually unsatisfied with what he saw.

Lord Chatsworth, on the other hand, wore his hair purposely mussed, his curls falling over his forehead. His clothes were fine and fit him well, but they were not immaculately pressed, and he had an amused air about him. From what Jonathan had gathered in their short meeting, Lord Chatsworth had quite the reputation as a ladies' man.

Lord Chatsworth kissed one of the older women on the cheek. His grandmother, Jonathan guessed, remembering the woman's name. He said something to each of the other ladies, making them giggle or blush, then sat down beside Sophie.

Jonathan stiffened.

"Who's that, then?" Sergeant Lester muttered. "Seems like a gal-sneaker, if you ask me."

Jonathan glanced at the sergeant, smirking at his use of the cant, then looked back at the table.

The other gentleman sat as well, and the pair started up a conversation.

Lord Chatsworth rested his hand on the arm of Sophie's chair as they spoke.

The sight made Jonathan's mouth taste bitter, and his chest went hot.

"I don't like that at all," Sergeant Lester said. "What's he playing at, flirting with Lady Sophronia?"

"It is none of our concern, Sergeant," Jonathan said.

Sergeant Lester grunted. "I just don't think it's proper, that's all, him taking such liberties."

"One might wonder at your interest in the lady's welfare." He had meant the words to come out as a jest but couldn't keep the sharpness from his voice.

"Just looking out for a friend, that's all." He folded his arms and squinted at Jonathan. "As are you, judging by your glower. If you don't mind my saying so."

"I do mind your saying so." Jonathan turned his back on the scene in the dining room, not appreciating the sergeant's insinuation, especially as it touched so close to the thoughts Jonathan had fought against all night. "This is not the society pages, Sergeant. The young lady's associations are none of our concern. We are not part of Soph—Lady Sophronia's world, and we would do well to remember it." Jonathan's voice came out sharply, and he'd almost called her Sophie. When had he started thinking of her in that familiar way? He went back over their interactions this evening. Had he spoken the name aloud to her? He believed he had. How had he dared to presume such intimacy? "We are poor policemen, and she is a lady. Just because she is polite doesn't mean she considers us to be her equals." He was saying the words more in reprimand to himself than to the sergeant, he knew, but this familiarity had gone too far. For both of them.

"Well, sir, I believe you're wrong. I don't think that sort of thing bothers Lady Sophronia."

"It bothers me," he muttered, pushing the door open and walking back into the room. As he did he nearly knocked over another server, who was bringing a tray of drinks.

"May I help you, my lord?" the man asked.

"I look for vodka," Jonathan said, using the excuse he and Miss Thornton had come up with should he be discovered somewhere he was not supposed to be.

"Yes, of course. I will bring your drink directly, if you'd care to be seated." He stepped out of Jonathan's way and gave a small bow.

"Dank you."

As Jonathan crossed the room and saw Sophie—*Lady Sophronia*— laughing with the gentlemen, he felt his chest grow even hotter. Sergeant Lester's affection for the young lady must be rubbing off on him. And the man's protectiveness. But Jonathan knew the feelings were all wrong, and fighting against them just made them grow into heat and bile in his throat.

He didn't know what had happened between himself and Lady Sophronia on the dance floor tonight. And he didn't fool himself for a moment that her reactions had been a result of overheating or hunger. He clenched his fists, frustrated.

What had he done wrong? Had he upset her? He thought all young ladies liked to dance, but perhaps he was mistaken. Sophie was not exactly a typical young lady. But for a moment, as he held her, he'd thought . . . His ears burned, and a mixture of bitterness and shame churned in his gut—he had presumed too much.

She was Lady Sophronia, daughter of a peer of the realm, and he an orphan from the rookery. A fancy costume and an evening among high Society didn't change the bare facts. They were working a case together, nothing more. Their relationship was mutually beneficial for each of their careers, and once the case was solved, it would end.

He neared the table and slowed, listening to the conversation.

". . . still in the dining room when the lecture began—quite a few of us. Lost track of time, I suppose," Lord Chatsworth was saying. "We were quite disappointed to miss the tale of the lion attack, and once the lecture ended, we remained behind to see the picture."

"I don't blame you," Sophie said. "It was, from what I hear, the most exciting part of the evening." She turned to Lord Everleigh. "Did you attend the lecture as well?"

Lord Everleigh sniffed, flicking a crumb from the tablecloth. "I did. Though, I hardly see how my attendance is relevant to your article."

"It is the society column," Sophie said. Her voice sounded tight, as if she were covering irritation at the man's rudeness. "Readers are interested in who does what." She turned back to Lord Chatsworth. "Who stayed behind with you after the lecture?"

Lord Everleigh glanced up, and seeing Jonathan, he stood. "Count Branković, do join us."

Jonathan gave a sharp nod. As he walked to an empty seat, he paused behind Sophie's chair. "Pardon, but my lady is feel better?"

"Much better. Thank you, my lord," Sophie said. She glanced up at him, but her gaze did not meet his.

"Count Branković, you are acquainted with these gentlemen, I believe?" Lady Mather asked.

"Da. I meet them in cardroom."

"Lord Chatsworth is my grandson." Lady Chatsworth gave a proud smile.

Jonathan nodded again. He sat on the other side of Lord Everleigh, leaving only one empty seat at the table, between himself and Mrs. Griffin. He motioned between Lord Chatsworth and Sophie with a wave. "I have interrupted. Please, continue to speaking."

"I hear you are a great hunter, my lord," Lord Chatsworth said to Jonathan. "And do tell us what game there is to be had in Serbia."

"I love hant, yes," Jonathan said. "Bear, wolf, deer . . ." He thanked the server who set his glass on the table.

"If you are still in Britain this August, my father hosts the hunting club on his estate in Scotland. You would be very welcome to join, sir, though you would find our grouse and fox to be tame prey compared to a bear."

"Dank you." Jonathan raised the glass. "I would like very much."

Lord Everleigh waved to a man in the doorway, motioning for him to join them. The newcomer's face was wide with a square jaw and stoic expression. His hair and mustache were fair, almost white, and he walked with surprisingly straight posture toward the table to join them.

Lord Everleigh greeted him, introducing him as Hans Hofman, a business associate from Germany.

Hans spoke with a thick German accent. He bowed stiffly when introduced to the ladies. And gave a familiar nod to Lord Chatsworth.

"Please, meet Count Nikola Braković, from Serbia," Lord Everleigh said. Mr. Hofman bowed. *"Vy daleko ot doma."*

Jonathan blinked, and his heart stuttered. The man spoke Serbian or Russian . . . or was it another language? One the count could reasonably not understand?

Blast. How do I respond? From the corner of his eye, Jonathan saw Sophie and her grandmother jolt. Hoping to disguise his shock at the unexpected circumstance as well as give himself time to think, he stood, then lifted his glass in a toast, giving a wide grin and breaking into loud laughter. He clapped Hans Hofman on the shoulder. "Ah, is good hear familiar tongue. But if you don't mind, I prefer practice Engleesh."

The German tipped his head to the side and opened his mouth as if he'd say something else, but he was interrupted by the arrival of Miss Miller.

Seeing her, the other gentlemen stood.

"Count Branković, there you are," Miss Miller said. "The two-step is about to begin, and you did promise to partner me." She wagged her finger, giving a teasing reprimand.

"Oh," Jonathan said. "I beg pardon, miss." He set down his drink, excusing himself to the rest of the table, then offered his arm, leading the young lady from the room.

When they reached the entry, he let out a breath, glancing around to make certain they were alone. "That was quick thinking, Miss Miller. Another moment and I believe I'd have been exposed."

She shrugged, looking pleased with herself. "A gentleman needs to be rescued by a lady every now and then."

Jonathan laughed, feeling giddy with the relief that coursed through him. He glanced back over his shoulder, making certain they'd not been followed. When he turned back, a new worry occurred to him. He winced. "I beg your pardon, miss. I hope you don't expect me to actually dance the two-step—not that I oppose your partnership—but I don't . . ."

"Of course not, sir." She curled her lip, scoffing as if the idea were preposterous.

Jonathan didn't know whether her words were meant as an insult, but his gratitude to the young lady overrode any offense. "Then, perhaps a walk in the gardens?"

"If you'd like." She nodded but didn't take his arm again. Instead she clasped her hands behind her back, preceding him as they walked along the edge of the ballroom and out through the doors onto the assembly hall's patio.

The evening breeze felt pleasant after being in the crowded room. They stepped down to the manicured gardens, following one of the pathways between borders of shrubs and flowers. Wrought-iron gas lamps stood at intervals between the trees and benches, giving patches of light.

Once certain they would not be overheard, Jonathan turned to his companion. "What have you discovered, Miss Miller? Anything new? Or have you already found and arrested the murderer?"

She smiled dryly at his attempted humor. "My friends and I have spoken to nearly every person on the suspect list. Only a few remain, and I would not be surprised if the others are even now interviewing them." She glanced back at the assembly hall, then continued walking. "Miss Thornton has the list, and you will see the pool of hunting club members unaccounted for between six and seven on Monday night is quite small. I think we may be very near to finding the killer."

Jonathan was surprised at how efficient the young ladies were. Of course, the results would not be entirely accurate. People forgot details or purposely left them out when questioned. But the amount of work this saved the police force was phenomenal. "I can't thank you enough for your help," he said. He swept his arm down, motioning at his jacket, then touching the mustache. "I had my reservations about the plan tonight, but it was well-thought-out and is likely to result in an arrest." He clasped his hands behind his back as well, giving a satisfied nod. "If Lady Sophronia hadn't stumbled upon the crime scene Monday evening and recognized the faults in Jane Duffin's gown, these deaths would likely have never been solved."

Miss Miller studied him with one raised brow. "I don't think many men would admit that."

"You don't have a high opinion of many men, do you, Miss Miller?" He kept his voice light, not wanting his words to sound like an accusation.

She frowned. "If you were ignored your entire life and treated as though your opinion didn't matter, you would feel the same."

The young woman obviously had no idea what life was like for a homeless orphan in a slum, but Jonathan didn't argue. Though he did not know much about women, he knew when to remain quiet.

"You see firsthand how valuable women are in this investigation, and yet, would the police force ever allow a female constable?" Miss Miller's voice grew demanding. "A female detective?"

"The Pinkertons in America employ lady detectives," he said. "And I hear they have been very successful. But police work is dangerous, miss," Jonathan couldn't help adding. "I would not wish you or any woman to encounter the things I see on a daily basis in Whitechapel." He knew without looking that his answer had angered her.

"Because we are fragile little flowers," she said in a sarcastic voice.

Jonathan stopped walking and turned to face her directly. "Miss Miller, three years ago the constabulary was sent to apprehend a violent street gang. We found their headquarters at the dockside, and half of our number circled behind to cut off any escape." He reached for his fob before again remembering he didn't wear it. "I was with those at the front entrance. We hoped to take them by surprise, but they were ready for us."

Jonathan clasped the hilt of his sword, needing something for his hands to do. "I was at the very front of the battering brigade, and we breached the door—I, the first inside. But the force of breaking through the door caused me to stumble. The first round of enemy bullets flew over my head."

He shook his head, breathing heavily through his nose as he tried to get through the story with no emotion.

"My closest friend was directly behind me." He swallowed, trying to push down the lump growing in his throat. "The man as dear to me as any brother. I watched him die. And it should have been me." Jonathan crossed his arms. "I would never wish that experience on anyone—especially not a young lady."

"And only men are capable of enduring pain?" She scowled, but he could see that his story had affected her. "A woman's strength would surprise you, Detective, if she were only permitted the opportunity to prove herself."

"I—" He cleared his throat, knowing that whatever he said next would be the wrong thing, wondering how he'd come so close to tears again, and cursing the fact that they'd ever gotten onto the subject at all.

"Sir!" Sergeant Lester came up the path behind them at a quick pace.

Jonathan didn't think he'd ever been so happy to hear the man's voice. He spun. "What is it?"

"Merryweather found a witness. He waits to speak with you in the stables."

At last.

"Shall I send Lady Sophronia to the stables as well, Detective?" Miss Miller said. "Or would you rather I bundle her in cotton and set a nanny to watch over her?"

"Yes, if you please." Jonathan ignored her sarcasm. "She'll want to hear as well."

He inclined his head in a farewell and started with Sergeant Lester toward the stables as the lady walked back toward the ballroom entrance.

Sergeant Lester motioned toward the departing woman with a thrust of his chin. "Best watch yourself with that one."

"Too right," Jonathan agreed. He slowed, not wishing to risk Sophie's displeasure should they question the witness without her.

They crossed the gardens, following the intersecting pathways, and neared the stables on the far side of the assembly hall. The area was darkened, lacking the gaslights that lit the rest of the property.

Footsteps approached, and both men turned quickly.

"What is it?" Sophie asked, her voice breathless. "Did you find the killer?"

"Not yet, my lady," Sergeant Lester replied. "Merryweather found someone willing to talk."

They followed the long wooden building, and as they drew closer, they saw Merryweather waiting with another man. The two were dressed in working clothes and stood beside a doorway, backlit by lanterns.

The stables were set far enough away from the assembly hall that the noise and smells of the animals wouldn't disturb the guests. Most of the horses and carriages were in the large yard beyond where the drivers and stable staff tended to the animals, and Jonathan could hear the sounds of the men socializing as they waited to return the guests home. He glanced back at the assembly hall. The ballroom windows glowed in the darkness, and a few others showed light behind their curtains. Music drifted out through the ballroom doors.

He didn't think his and Sergeant Lester's departures had been noticed, but he wasn't certain about Sophie's. Beckoning with a flick of his hand, he motioned the group toward a shadowed area. In the moonlight the group could still see one another but would be inconspicuous at a distance from the assembly hall.

"Now, what have you, Constable?" Jonathan didn't bother with introductions or niceties.

"Sir, this is Ned Tucker—works here in the stables." Merryweather stood straighter, holding himself at attention in spite of his lack of uniform. "Claims he saw something Monday night." He tipped his head. "Tell 'em what you told me, Ned."

The stable hand shuffled his feet, looking nervous. Not unusual for a person dealing with the police. He glanced at Sophie, as if uncertain whether he should speak in front of her.

"Go on, then," Sergeant Lester prompted.

"Didn't think much of it at the time, you see—not until Mr. Merryweather started asking questions."

Jonathan cleared his throat, giving a nod to urge the man to continue but not allowing himself to look too eager and risk putting the man on his guard.

"Monday night we were on our toes, sir. Gentlemen coming and going at random. Some carriages were hardly here for an hour before we were sent to retrieve them. Others stayed longer. But one . . ." He looked over his shoulder as if he could see the carriage through the building. "One remained long after the others were gone. We reckoned the gentlemen had gone along to another event with a friend. But the driver had no orders to leave, so he stayed." Ned shrugged. "Stablemaster had sent the other lads home but kept me here to muck out the stalls while we waited for the owner to return or send word."

"And did he return?" Sophie asked.

"Aye, and that's the strange part, my lady." He looked back again. "The two gentlemen didn't arrive by cab. Returned on foot. Came by way of the river."

Two men. Jonathan's mind worked through different scenarios. Had they abandoned the furniture wagon and walked back to the stable yard to prevent a cabby from identifying them? Or was this merely a coincidence? Or could they even trust Ned Tucker's story? He seemed even more nervous than was usual during inquiries.

"Did you recognize the gentlemen?" Sergeant Lester asked. "Or remember the name of their driver?"

"Driver kept to himself." Ned shook his head. "Don't know the gentlemen's names, but I saw the pair again tonight. Arrived together, same as before."

"Can you describe them?" Jonathan asked.

"Fancy-like, sir. And the carriage had a crest on the door." He gave a meaningful look at that bit of information. Jonathan nodded. If the man was correct, the suspects were noblemen—or at least, rode in a nobleman's carriage.

"The one in particular stood out," Ned said. "He—"

A whistling sounded by Jonathan's ear.

Ned Tucker dropped.

Jonathan grabbed Sophie, pulling her to the ground just as another whistling sounded overhead.

Merryweather cried out.

"We're under fire!" Jonathan called as another shot hit the stable behind him. "Get down!"

Sergeant Lester pressed against the wall next to him. They were exposed, sitting out here in the open, with no idea of the shooter's location.

"Inside," Jonathan said, not sure who could hear or who was able to follow the order. Ned was most certainly hit, and perhaps Merryweather as well.

At a crouch, he pulled Sophie along the side of the building and pushed her through the doorway, pressing her against an inside wall. He covered her with his body, chest against her back and chin on her head. More shots hit the doorframe.

Sophie trembled, and he put his arms around her. "Sergeant!" he yelled. "Are you hit?"

"No, sir." Sergeant Lester's voice came from the other side of the doorway. "But Merryweather's down. And Mr. Tucker."

Jonathan was impressed at the steadiness in the man's voice.

"Shooter's inside the assembly hall." The sergeant risked a peek through the doorway. "He's stopped, I think."

"Or he's just waiting for us to go after the others," Jonathan said.

"Can't leave them there." Sergeant Lester peeked out again. "And someone must have heard the shots."

"Agreed," Jonathan said. The sergeant was right. The shooter wouldn't continue to fire, not from his current location anyway. The noise would have drawn attention from the others in the building. Most likely, he was already on the run.

Jonathan started to move, but Sophie grabbed one of his arms. "No! You can't go out there!" Her voice was high, and he could hear the panic in it.

She twisted around, clutching him with both hands now. Tears glimmered on her cheeks in the moonlight, and her breathing came in bursts.

Inside Jonathan's chest something cracked. In light of what he'd told Miss Miller only half an hour earlier, why had he permitted Sophie to come? Why had he allowed her to be part of the case at all? He cupped her cheek. "The shooter's gone now, Sophie. I must help the others."

She nodded and leaned her face in to his hand. "Please be careful. I couldn't bear it if—" Her voice caught, and another tear spilled from her eye.

"Stay here." Jonathan pressed a kiss to her forehead and pulled away. He motioned for the sergeant to follow. Keeping low, they made their way back to the others.

When he reached Merryweather, Jonathan pushed the man onto his back. Merryweather's chest was wet, but no wound was visible in the darkness. Jonathan pulled off his gloves and touched his neck, relieved to feel a heartbeat.

"Tucker's dead," Sergeant Lester said.

Jonathan nodded. "Help me move Merryweather."

They dragged the constable through the door to where Sophie waited with a wide-eyed stablemaster and a younger boy.

She retrieved a lantern and brought it close, gasping when she saw the blood on Constable Merryweather's chest, but she didn't draw away. She set down the lantern and knelt beside the constable, brushing damp hair from the injured man's forehead.

Sergeant Lester pulled open the man's shirt, revealing the wound.

Jonathan forced away the painful flashes of memory at seeing a friend lying unresponsive and bleeding. The stablemaster brought some cloth, and Jonathan instructed Sophie to hold it against the wound. She looked much calmer already, and he knew having a task would help keep her panic at bay.

"Send for Miss Thornton," Sophie said to the stablemaster, her voice still shaky. "Inside the assembly hall. She is a nurse."

The man nodded and motioned for the boy to do so.

Sergeant Lester stood and used a knife to dig a bullet from the doorframe. He held the bit of metal close to the lantern. "Thirty-eight caliber," he muttered.

"A pistol," Jonathan said. "Easy to hide."

"Good aim," Sergeant Lester said, pocketing the bullet.

A hunter. Jonathan stood, feeling anger rise inside him. One of his men was down and their best witness dead. He ripped off the mustache and removed his jacket. "Enough games. Sergeant, call for Dr. Peabody. And

I want every available officer. Close the stable yard gates. Block the exits. Nobody leaves this blasted party until we've spoken to each and every last guest."

CHAPTER 18

THE NEXT MORNING SOPHIE LEFT her bedchamber much later than usual. She could already hear her mother and Prissy in the dining room and paused on the upstairs landing, wanting a few more moments to herself before joining them.

She turned away from the rail, leaning back and allowing all the emotions from the night before to rush over her. The utter terror at being under fire and watching a man die before her eyes squeezed her heart, constricting it in a vice. Her mind had gone completely blank as panic froze her body and thoughts, but Jonathan had known exactly what to do. He'd pulled her to safety, held her, comforted her . . . The vice loosened, and a warmth filled her as she remembered the feel of being held.

Sophie hadn't told anyone aside from Mimi and her grandmother's friends about the dance and her reaction. And though she'd initially balked at the women's explanation, chalking it up to teasing or the elderly ladies' misunderstanding the situation, now . . . now she believed they might be right in their assumption.

Even as he'd directed the questioning of guests and the search of the assembly hall, Jonathan had remained in close contact as she and Hazel tended to the constable and waited for the doctor. Sophie would never have believed herself to be one of those women who wished to be mollycoddled, but she found it a very pleasant sensation to know that Jonathan's thoughts had often turned to her through the course of his work. He'd been worried for her but had also kept her appraised on the status of the investigation, likely knowing she'd pester him with questions if he didn't.

A set of pistols had been found in a storage closet, but they had no identifying marks. Their owner was still unknown. Sergeant Lester believed the shooter, or shooters, had fled. "Wouldn't linger, waiting to be caught, would they?" he'd asked.

Once the doctor had taken Merryweather and Mr. Tucker's body away, Jonathan had insisted Hazel and Elizabeth accompany Sophie home. He'd held her hand as the carriage was sent for, and when the other women had climbed inside, he'd pulled her into a tight embrace. Though he'd said nothing, she'd understood completely. The terror they'd experienced and the relief that they had both come away unharmed—the feelings were impossible to express in words. But they couldn't go unshared. She'd held him tightly as well.

A sigh escaped, and Sophie pressed her hands to her pounding heart as she walked down the stairs, savoring the memory of that moment.

The bliss fled, however, once she entered the dining room.

"There you are!" Prissy's glare was so filled with vitriol that Sophie stopped mid-step. "I do hope you're happy, Miss Propriety." She spat the name as if it were a curse word.

"You have *ruined* us, Sophronia." Lady Mather dabbed a handkerchief to her red eyes. She held smelling salts in her other hand. "This is what comes from allowing you such freedoms. I told your grandmother no good would come from you writing for the paper, and now our reputations are utterly ruined." She waved around the handkerchief.

"We are not ruined, Mother." Sophie kept her voice calm. Her mother was prone to exaggeration, and Sophie's work at the newspaper was one of the many upsetting topics that usually sent her on one of her tirades.

"Oh no?" Lady Mather tapped her finger on a stack of letters on the table. "Three—*three* cancellations for our dinner party next week. And I am sure more are to come."

"And what of Everleigh? He will never have me now!" Prissy wailed, taking out her own handkerchief.

"How dare you bring such shame on our household." Her mother pointed her finger at Sophie. "You and that . . . detective, deceiving high Society—our friends—with your little charade and destroying the future Marquess of Molyneaux's engagement ball. This disgrace will be remembered in our circles forever. It is beyond the pale."

"Mother." Sophie slipped into her chair, feeling badly for the footman who was holding it ready. The poor man was doing his best to pretend not to notice the hysterics happening around him. "I did not destroy anything.

A man was murdered. Another shot. The *killer* ruined the party, not I. And certainly not Detective Graham."

"It was the most important ball of the Season." Prissy's anger had turned her face splotchy. "And Everleigh did not even see me home last night."

Lady Mather patted her younger daughter's arm in an attempt to console her. She turned back to frown at Sophie. "To be . . . *interrogated* . . . like a common criminal. And all because my daughter thinks she is above the rules of decorum. Well, I will have no more of it. You are never to write another word for any newspaper. Never! Do you understand? You may not step one toe inside a newspaper office for as long as you live, and do not dare to reach for that pastry, Sophronia."

Sophie pulled back her hand. She spooned fruit onto her plate instead and poured a cup of tea. She wanted to calm her voice before speaking. Letting out her own anger would only intensify the situation. "Mother." She spoke in a quiet voice. "People were murdered. It was a murder investigation. Surely you can see that is more important than a ball."

"*Servants* were murdered, Sophronia." Her mother shook her head as if she were dealing with an imbecile. She rubbed her temples. "A lady's maid—"

"And Charlotte said she wasn't even a very good lady's maid," Prissy interjected.

Her mother nodded her agreement with Prissy. "You have no idea how this has . . . how it will continue to affect our family, Sophronia. You care only for—"

"Sophronia! Come here at once."

All three ladies jumped as Sophie's father's voice boomed through the entry hall.

In spite of their disagreement, the women looked at one another with confused expressions. Her father rarely took an interest in his daughters' affairs. In her entire life Sophie had only been summoned into his office a very few times—and never with an angry bellow.

Sophie ignored Prissy's smug smirk as she left the dining room and crossed the entry hall to her father's office. The door was ajar, and she pushed it open, stepping inside.

None of the ladies in the household were permitted in Lord Mather's office, except on very rare occasions—and only if invited. Sophie glanced around, taking in the heavy dark furniture and the rows of bookshelves as she walked deeper into the room.

Her father sat at his desk, reading a newspaper behind a green-shaded lamp.

"Good mor—" Sophie began.

"Do you know what this is, Sophronia?" He cut off her words. He held up a parchment-colored envelope between two fingers. "A letter from the hunting club," he said before she could answer. "How do you explain this?" He flicked his wrist, flinging the letter onto the desk.

Sophie wasn't certain how to answer. "I don't know what the letter—"

"One of our members, suspected of murder?" He cut her off again, his voice becoming louder and his face turning redder. "This club has a glorious tradition, Sophronia. It is a pillar of Society." He gripped the arms of his chair. "Your father, grandfather, great-grandfather—eight generations." He pinched the bridge of his nose. "For nearly four hundred years, knights and nobility have graced the Kingsclere's noble halls, and today—" His cheeks puffed out, and he waved around his hands as if it were simply too much effort to put together a sentence in this situation. "My own daughter. You would slander its glorious name for a story?" He folded his arms, waiting for a response.

An uneasy feeling joined Sophie's frustration and bewilderment at her family's reactions. How had her mother known Jane Duffin was a victim in this case? And who told her father the Kingsclere Club members were part of the suspect pool? Had the police given out the information when they'd questioned the ball guests? She didn't believe they would. "What story, Father?"

Lord Mather slammed the newspaper down on the desk in front of her, and Sophie's heart stopped. She was too shocked to even draw enough breath for a gasp. There, beneath the headline "Kingsclere Rookery Murders," her drawing of the crime scene in the alley behind the Porky Pie covered half a page.

"No, no, no. It can't be." Sophie pulled away the paper from beneath his hand, reading the story. Her stomach twisted with every word. It was all there. The victim's names, the manner of their deaths, the smear on the windowsill, the investigators' theories.

"The hunting club is convening a special session today. Very likely, they'll ask for my resignation," Lord Mather said.

Sophie could hardly hear him as she tried to make sense of what she was seeing. She turned the page, and her heart stopped again when she recognized her drawing of the assembly hall parlor. Jonathan was crouched down in the closet, examining the floorboards. Sophie put a hand over her mouth, glad she'd not eaten that pastry, or she'd likely not be able to keep it in her stomach.

"How . . .?" She looked up at her father, blinking as she tried to process how this could have happened. "I didn't write—"

A memory popped into her mind. That day at the news office, she'd dropped her notebook and Mr. Leonard had asked about the drawings. But she'd taken the notebook away. *No. That's not what happened.* She'd noticed it missing when she'd gone to put Tom Stackhouse's folder into her bag, and she'd found she'd left the notebook on the editor's desk.

"He stole my story." Anger sharpened her scattered thoughts into a blade. "I must go, Father." She rushed from the room.

"I'm not finished—" Her father's voice came from behind, but she was already on the stairs.

When she reached her room, she flipped through her notebook, and fury made her hands shake. The pages of her investigation had been removed.

⌐⟨⫞⟩¬

In the carriage on the way to the newspaper office, Sophie read through the news story again. Not only had the *Illustrated London News* published the police department's information and the steps of the investigation, they'd also included witness names and testimonies from her notes. Were Martha Payne and Miss Primm in danger?

There, in black and white, was a picture of the murder weapon. Every advantage the police had over the murderers was gone. The enormity of what Sophie had inadvertently done threatened to crush her, and she wished more than anything she'd brought Mimi along for support.

She took the folder from her bag, feeling a bitter guilt as she held it. If she hadn't been so inquisitive about Jonathan's friendship with Tom Stackhouse, none of this would have happened. She began flipping through the pages with nervous energy, and she started reading.

Twenty minutes later Sophie threw open the door to the newspaper office and stormed inside. She marched past Mrs. Ingram, through the staring news reporters, and straight to the editor's desk.

Mr. Leonard looked up, cigarette hanging from his lips, but did not have a chance to speak.

Sophie shook the paper in his face. "Explain this, sir."

He gave a wide, walrusy grin and blew out a puff of smoke. "Miss Propriety, that is our best-selling paper, ever. It's still morning, and we're running another printing already. You should be congratulating yourself, my dear."

She pushed the paper closer to his face, pointing at the drawing. "I am not your dear. You *stole* this information from me. I did *not* give you permission to print it."

He folded his hands across his wide belly, and his eyes took on a shrewd look. "You left the article—however unfinished—on my desk, as you do every week." He lifted his chin the slightest bit, as if daring her to argue.

"But you know I didn't intend you to print this," Sophie said.

His expression changed into something more calculating, and he set the cigarette in a tray. "My lady, you did marvelous work—far better than I'd have expected. You've proven yourself to be as competent a news reporter as any I've known." He took the paper from her, spreading it out on his desk and smoothing it with his hands. "If you're willing to accept a position as a senior news reporter, I'd be pleased to have you."

Sophie snatched back the paper, crumpled it into a ball, and resisted the compulsion to throw it into his face or light it on fire with his smoldering cigarette. "I shall not, sir. Not now, not ever. Your selfishness has caused more damage than you could ever know." She dropped the paper onto the ground and spun, needing to leave as quickly as possible. Jonathan would know how to fix this, but she had to make one stop before going to the station house.

She stepped outside and slammed the door behind her, saying goodbye forever to "Miss Propriety's People and Prattle" and the *Illustrated London News*.

CHAPTER 19

JONATHAN STARED AT THE NEWS story. *She couldn't have . . . she wouldn't.* He didn't know whether his head or his heart hurt worse. Sophie had betrayed him. She'd used him for her news story. And he was the fool who had allowed her to do it. Who had allowed himself think that just maybe—

Sir Dennington pounded on the desk, shaking the portrait of his family hanging on the wall behind him. ". . . a visit from the commissioner himself!" the inspector said. "Says you infiltrated the marquess's son's engagement ball with the help of a disguise and a group of young ladies— that you accused the Kingsclere Hunting Club of concealing murderers!" He crossed his arms, staring across his desk at Jonathan and Sergeant Lester, awaiting their answer.

"I—yes, sir. But it was myself, and not the sergeant, who involved civilians."

"What were you thinking, man?" Sir Dennington held up his hands, using them to chop the air and punctuate his words. He shook his head. "Impersonating nobility? I've had visits and letters all morning. The marquess is threatening to involve the prime minister." He pounded the desk once more, and his voice echoed through the station house.

Jonathan wished the man would just hit him or throw him into prison— anything would be better than this ache in his heart. How had he let himself be so utterly deceived? It was just as Tom had always said: *Never trust a pretty face.* "We hoped to gain information we would otherwise not have access to. Most of the nobility won't speak candidly to a police officer, sir."

"And now a constable is wounded." Sir Dennington sank into his chair, apparently done with his yelling—for now. "So tell me—what happened, Detective?"

Jonathan reported everything that had transpired since Sir Dennington had left his office two days earlier, explaining his reasoning for assuming a disguise and for recruiting the young ladies to assist in gathering information. He spoke in an emotionless voice, giving no personal details. Apparently they had all been imagined anyway.

He especially downplayed Sophie's involvement in the planning. Part of him still wished to protect her from any repercussions, and the other was too ashamed to admit he'd been so taken in.

The inspector listened, nodding here and there and leaning close when Jonathan described the shooting.

"Did you see from whence the shots came?"

Jonathan looked at the sergeant, giving him the chance to answer.

"From the assembly hall, sir. Based on the angle of the bullets we pulled from the stable walls, I'm sure of it."

"Your suspicions about the hunting club are not unfounded." Sir Dennington nodded, scratching his chin. "And you detained everyone in attendance last night?"

Jonathan shook his head. "Some resisted, sir." He gritted his teeth, frustrated that so many members of high Society were above the law. "Others left before reinforcements came to guard the exits."

"But we talked to most," Sergeant Lester said. "Apparently nobody saw or heard anything unusual."

"Not even gunshots?" Sir Dennington asked in disbelief. "And no one saw a shooter fleeing the scene?"

Jonathan shrugged. "Most were just put out at having their party ruined."

Sir Dennington nodded. He sighed. "I'm sorry to do this, but I'll ask you to turn in your badge and warrant card now." He stood back up, clasping his hands behind his back. "You'll be on leave without pay until this situation either runs its course or I'm ordered to ask for your resignation."

Jonathan set his badge and card on the table. "Yes, sir."

"And you as well, Sergeant."

Sergeant Lester swallowed. He took the card from his pocket and unpinned his badge.

Jonathan winced with the guilt of seeing his loyal friend punished for following his orders.

"That will be all for now, gentlemen," Sir Dennington said as a dismissal. His voice was not unkind, but it left no room for argument.

The two crossed the station to Jonathan's office.

Jonathan took a bag of peppermints from the coat hanging on his chair, offering one to the sergeant, then putting one into his own mouth. "I'm sorry, Sergeant. I should never have allowed this." He put on his coat, then slipped the peppermints back into the pocket.

A copy of the *London Illustrated News* sat on his desk, open to Sophie's— Lady Sophronia's—article.

Sergeant Lester stared at the paper, looking utterly devastated. "What do we do now, sir?"

Jonathan rounded the desk. He clapped the sergeant on the shoulder. "If you'd care to join me, I intend to visit the hospital. Let us see if Constable Merryweather has awoken."

Sergeant Lester nodded. He brushed the paper from the desk into the rubbish bin and stood.

Jonathan put on his hat. He picked up the papers Miss Thornton had given him the night before with the list and the ladies' notes on each suspect they'd spoken to. He was tempted to toss them, but he held on to them.

The other detectives and constables avoided eye contact as Jonathan and Sergeant Lester walked back through the station house.

Jonathan didn't blame them. He had made the most enormous mistake of his career, and H Division's reputation and the other policemen would suffer for it.

Sergeant Lester opened the door, but before Jonathan stepped through, Sergeant Abner came around the reception desk. "Sir, I've the information you asked for."

Jonathan took the file. "What is this?"

"The property history of the workhouse construction site. You asked me to uncover the records . . ." He raised his thick red brows. "Surely you remember, sir?"

"Yes, of course. Thank you, Sergeant Abner." Not wishing to appear ungrateful, Jonathan slid Miss Thornton's papers into the file from Abner and tucked it under his arm.

When they arrived at the hospital, they entered through the main entrance and continued on to the ward. On a typical visit to Dr. Peabody, Jonathan descended the stairs to the morgue. And, truthfully, he preferred that route. The hospital smelled of medicine and illness. People waited outside rooms, looking up with faces that contained a horrible combination of fear and hope whenever a doctor approached. And in the rooms beyond he heard moans and cries of pain. At least in the morgue, no one suffered anymore.

They entered the ward where Merryweather was being tended and found Lady Sophronia standing at his bedside, speaking with Dr. Peabody.

Jonathan wasn't prepared for the jolt of shock at seeing her. Anger and hurt warred within him, making his insides shake. His first impulse was to run; then he wanted to yell. But he did neither, only continued forward and assumed an aloof expression.

When she saw them, her face lit up, and she hurried toward them. "I'm glad you're here." She spoke to Jonathan, then turned and gave a smile and a nod to his companion. "And you as well, Sergeant Lester."

The sergeant inclined his head, but he didn't smile. "My lady."

Lady Sophronia's brow furrowed at his cold response, but she did not comment on it. "Detective, we need to talk. Something terrible has happened. The newspaper—"

"I've seen the newspaper, my lady." Jonathan kept all inflection from his voice, worried he'd betray his anger—or his hurt.

Her brow furrowed again. "Yes, well, we must figure out what to do. I have already—"

"I have come to inquire after the constable." Jonathan pushed past her. "Please excuse me."

"Detective?" She sounded confused. She spoke softer and much slower now. "I—would like to talk with you. Please."

He spun, his hands in fists at his sides. "You lied to me, my lady—betrayed my trust, manipulated me—to get your story. Well, now you have it, and I have nothing else to say to you."

Her eyes were wide, and he pushed aside his guilt at seeing the hurt in them. "But I didn't know." Her lips shook as she spoke. "The story was published without my permission. I promise I—"

"Sergeant, if you please, will you escort the lady out?" Jonathan motioned to Sergeant Lester. "We've police business to discuss."

Sophie stood her ground, putting her hands on her hips, her bag hanging from her elbow. "Will you not listen to me? Not even after—"

"I shall not make that mistake again." Jonathan's voice was low as he tried to hold back his anger but was not fully successful.

Sophie spun and started away, shaking off Sergeant Lester's outstretched hand as he tried to escort her. He followed behind instead.

Dr. Peabody raised a brow, but that was the only indication that he had overheard the conversation or might disagree with Jonathan's treatment of the young lady.

Jonathan continued on as if nothing had happened. He pointed with his chin toward the injured man in the bed. "How is he?"

"As I was telling the lady," Dr. Peabody said, "the constable's wound is clean. We removed the bullet without any problems, and very little damage was done internally."

"Has he woken?"

The doctor nodded. "For short periods. But staying awake for an extended time seems difficult for now."

"Is that typical? Will he heal?"

"If his wound doesn't develop an infection, he should be back on his beat in a few weeks."

Well, that was one good thing to come out of this day.

Sergeant Lester returned, his expression still glum. He offered a file to Jonathan. "Lady Sophronia asked me to give you this. Said she's sorry for being nosy." He shrugged.

Jonathan took the folder, glancing at the name on it. *Tom Stackhouse?* What was she playing at? And why did everything inside him want to run after her and beg her forgiveness?

"And this, sir." Sergeant Lester gave him Sophie's notebook.

Jonathan pulled a chair close to the bed, resting his head in his hands. Anger was the easier emotion, and he concentrated on that, feeding it until it obliterated the hurt—but as hard as he tried, he couldn't rid himself of it completely.

CHAPTER 20

SOPHIE FORCED HERSELF TO KEEP her head up and walk with dignity down the hospital steps, not wanting to make a scene. She could cry later. She held herself tightly, lest she break down. How could Jonathan believe she was capable of such manipulation? Why hadn't he listened to her? Her heart was shattered, and she was alone. Her family, Society, and now the man she trusted—the man she thought she might love—were all against her. And she'd never be a news reporter now.

Everything hurt, and she felt wrung-out. She wanted nothing more than to climb into bed after a decent breakfast and sleep for hours. Perhaps she'd wake and discover this was all a terrible nightmare. She tightened the clasp on her bag, glad she'd thought to give the file to Sergeant Lester. At least Jonathan might find some comfort in that regard.

"Miss Bremerton?" A woman wearing an apron over her worn dress and a kerchief around her hair stopped in front of Sophie, giving a curtsy.

Sophie studied her, for a moment unable to think how the woman might know her name.

"Oh, you don't remember me." Her face went red. "Beg your pardon, miss. I'm Martha Payne."

"Of course. You are Freddy's mother." Sophie smiled. "I am sorry I did not recognize you right away; my mind was elsewhere. How nice to see you." She was relieved to see that the woman was safe.

Martha glanced up at the hospital. "I heard Ernest—Constable Merryweather—was injured." She clasped her hands together. They were red and rough, with cracks on her knuckles. "Do you know if he is all right?"

Sophie looked up quickly, not wishing for the woman to see her staring at her fingers. "I just spoke to the doctor. He expects the constable to recover fully within a few weeks."

Martha's shoulders relaxed. She gave a smile, and Sophie noticed again how very lovely she was. Martha glanced again at the hospital. "Do you suppose I might see him?"

"The police are with him now—I don't know for how long." Sophie felt a pang at the reminder. "I don't believe they would mind if you paid a visit."

Martha shook her head. "I wouldn't want to bother them. I'll wait until later. Good day, Miss Bremerton." She curtsied and started away.

"Wait," Sophie said. She caught up to the woman. "Mrs. Payne, do you have somewhere you and Freddy might go for a few days? Perhaps a relative or a friend you could stay with? I believe you may be in danger."

Martha's face paled. "Why? What has happened?"

Sophie dreaded the explanation she must give and felt heat spreading up her neck as she considered exactly how she was going to explain that she'd accidentally published Martha's name and her son's in a news article the killer might read and discover they were potentially witnesses to his crime. After this, how would anyone ever trust her again? She sighed. "Would you join me for tea, Mrs. Payne?"

⚜

Three hours later Jasper carried the last of Martha's things into the boarding-house on Wilkes Street. The carriage driver's help finding lodgings near the laundry where Martha worked had been invaluable.

Sophie glanced around the room. Though it was furnished, it still seemed bare, and the Payne's few possessions did little to fill the place. But as sparse as it was, it was infinitely better than the room off Wentworth, and there was even a separate room for Freddy and space to hang the wash.

Martha hung a gown in the wardrobe.

"Now, the landlady has already been paid for three months," Sophie said. "That should give the police plenty of time to locate the killer and send him away for good."

Jasper tipped his hat to the women as he left the room. He had entrusted Freddy with the carriage and no doubt wished to return before the boy took a ride through the city.

"I cannot thank you enough for your kindness," Martha said. She took Sophie's hand. "I wish I could somehow repay you."

Sophie squeezed her fingers. "You can do that by staying hidden. Don't tell your old neighbors where you've gone, and keep Freddy close." She wondered how likely it was that Freddy wouldn't return to his friends. If only the boy were in school. That would keep him too occupied for mischief. Perhaps she would discuss it with Elizabeth, see what the child's options were.

Martha didn't release Sophie's hand. She held herself tightly and chewed on her lip.

Sophie sensed she had something more to say.

"Miss Bremerton," she began hesitantly.

"Yes? What is it?" Sophie prompted.

Martha glanced around the room, then looked down at her hands. She released her hold on Sophie and folded her arms. "This is all my fault."

Sophie's first thought was to brush aside the statement, to reassure the woman that of course this wasn't her fault. She was an innocent victim of circumstance. But something in the woman's voice made her pause. There was more.

"What is it, Martha?"

"I should have told you when you and the detective first came." She rubbed her arms. "But I was frightened, you see? I have Freddy to worry about, and . . ."

"I understand completely," Sophie said. "You can tell me now."

Martha's fingers tightened on her arms.

"Did you see something in the alley that night, Martha?" Sophie prompted.

Martha nodded. "Not so much saw. The alley was shadowed, you see, and I ducked away, not wanting them to see me. But I heard them. Two men." Her voice was a whisper.

"What did they say?"

"They argued," Martha spoke in a soft voice, glancing toward the open door. "About where to leave her, the dead lady. One wanted her to be found, and the other—he just wanted to hurry and leave. I didn't understand most of what they were saying."

Sophie's heart beat faster. "Anything else? How did they sound?"

"The one spoke proper—like an aristocrat. But the other—he was difficult to understand. He spoke slow and strange . . ." She pursed her lips. "I didn't hear him well enough to describe it."

Sophie nodded, feeling disappointed that Martha's information wasn't more helpful. "Thank you for telling me."

"Should have told you when you came before. But now Ernest is hurt, and it's all because of me."

"It's not your fault at all," Sophie said. "A villain is responsible for Constable Merryweather's injury, not you. You've been very helpful." She considered whether she should go to the police with this new piece of information. But it was hardly any more than they already knew. Perhaps she should just send a note. But if she did that, would Jonathan think she was trying to uncover more details about the case for a story? Losing his trust hurt more than anything else.

When Sophie arrived home to Park Lane, Lord Everleigh's carriage stood before the house, its polished crest gleaming in the sunlight. He must be paying a call to Prissy. Well, at least her sister's favorite suitor hadn't been put off by last night's scandal. That should make Sophie's family happy.

She climbed out of the carriage and thanked Jasper for his help. With any luck, Prissy and Lord Everleigh would be in the upstairs sitting room, and she could avoid them altogether.

Upon entering the house, however, she found that luck was not on her side. Lord Everleigh and Prissy were in the entry hall, donning hats and gloves.

Prissy smiled brightly when Sophie entered. "Sophie! Isn't this a treat? Lord Everleigh is taking me for a carriage ride in the park."

"Good afternoon, Lady Sophronia," Lord Everleigh said.

How he managed such condescension in the few words, she'd never know.

"Lord Everleigh."

"I do hope you'll join us," he said.

Prissy's head snapped around so quickly that her hat fell almost completely off. She straightened it and gave Sophie a scowl, clearly telling her sister to not even consider it.

Sophie started to pull out her hatpin, ready to decline the invitation. But she paused. Had anyone interviewed Lord Everleigh? She supposed so, but what if he'd been overlooked? He was definitely a member of the hunting club. He was at the ball last night. And she knew—from her sister's incessant bragging—that he was an excellent marksman.

"Thank you, my lord. I would like that very much."

Prissy shook her head frantically behind Lord Everleigh's back.

Sophie ignored her sister. Now that the idea had taken hold, she knew she'd not be able to put it out of her mind until she was certain Lord Everleigh could be eliminated as a suspect.

Hearing Dorrit's bark, Lord Everleigh glanced up the stairs. "I wonder"—
he pulled on his gloves—"should we invite your grandmother as well?"

Prissy's glare could have melted steel.

⤲⤳

A few moments later the four were situated in Lord Everleigh's open carriage
as it started toward Hyde Park.

Prissy kept her head turned away from the other women, watching the
houses as they passed, her arms folded like a child throwing a tantrum.

Mimi fussed over Dorrit, giving the dog a bite of biscuit.

Sophie studied Lord Everleigh.

The gentleman sat across from her, beside her sister. His posture was
perfect, his hat tipped exactly the right amount, and his clothing could
not have been more immaculate if it were hanging in a tailor's window. He
touched his waxed mustache with the tips of his gloved fingers.

Could it be him? He hardly seemed the type. What motive could he
possibly have for murder? She could think of nothing that might drive him
to kill, aside from someone scuffing his boots.

"Lady Sophronia," he said after a moment, hardly hiding a smirk. "How
goes your case? Have you found the murderer? Do you plan any more clandes-
tine operations?"

"No, the murderer has not been found." She answered the least patronizing of his questions. "*Yet.* But the police continue their search."

"And they still suspect a member of the hunting club?" he asked.

"You think it unlikely?" Sophie responded.

He curled his lip and snorted—in the most gentlemanly way possible.
"As a member myself, I am inclined to disbelieve the theory."

If one could kill with a pretentious tone, then he was the murderer for
certain.

"Of course it is not a gentleman," Prissy said. She fluttered her lashes at
Lord Everleigh. "Such an accusation is completely preposterous."

Mimi watched the conversation in silence. But Sophie knew her
grandmother was listening closely to the man's answers.

"And did you attend the hunting club's lecture last Monday, my lord?"
Sophie asked.

"I?" He blinked and gave a patronizing smile, as if indulging her game
of detective. "I did indeed, as I believe I mentioned to you at the ball."

"Do you remember how the lecture began?" Sophie asked, remembering their earlier conversation had been interrupted. "What picture did Mr. Baldwin show?"

"Oh, really, Sophie," Prissy said. "Are you interrogating Lord Everleigh now?"

His smile remained, but his eyes seemed sharper, almost challenging. "Lord Baldwin's picture was of an enormous lion attacking his horse."

Sophie nodded and could think of no further questions. His answer was correct, but the longer she spoke with him, the less she trusted Lord Everleigh. Arrogance did not make one a murderer, however. And she had to admit it was because of her injured pride that she hoped to find fault in him. Sophie scratched Dorrit's ears, looking away as if enjoying the view of the park.

Lord Everleigh, on the other hand, was not finished with the conversation. "It was fascinating, really, reading about it all in the paper. That detective and his wild theories." He smirked. "They seem very farfetched, don't you agree?"

Sophie's defensiveness rose in a spike. She sat forward.

"Detective Graham strikes me as a very intelligent man," Mimi said, her tone meant not only to censure Lord Everleigh but to placate her granddaughter's temper as well. She patted Sophie's hand.

"Wearing a costume, a fake mustache, and pretending to be Serbian nobility?" The odious man snorted again, this time sounding much less gentlemanly. "Hardly signs of an intelligent person."

Prissy giggled. "You are so right, my lord."

Sophie could not remain silent. "A police investigation is more difficult than one might assume from reading a newspaper article, Lord Everleigh. Detective Graham's theories about the case are extremely well-founded. But then, I did watch how he arrived at them."

"You really think two people were killed in a crowded building with no one noticing?" He shook his head. "And then that the bodies were dropped through a window in broad daylight and taken to Spitalfields in a Bluebird Furniture wagon?" Lord Everleigh laughed. "Ridiculous."

"Utterly ridiculous," Prissy agreed. She laughed as well.

"It is not the most . . ." Sophie's words trailed off. She'd not written about the Bluebird Furniture wagon in her notebook, nor had she drawn it because she hadn't seen it. She knew for certain it had not been in the article. There was only one way Lord Everleigh could know that detail.

She could feel the blood drain from her face as the realization came. Lord Everleigh was the murderer. Another piece of the puzzle moved into place—his accomplice. Martha had said the man had spoken strangely, slowly. Sophie had assumed she was describing a speech impediment, but why not a foreign accent? Hans Hofman could be his partner.

Sophie sat completely still. Now that she knew the truth, she must get word to the police. But how could she do so without alerting Lord Everleigh to her suspicion?

"It is not only preposterous but shows a sort of unhinged mind. I believe I'll recommend to the commissioner that Detective Jonathan Graham's suitability as a representative of the Crown be evaluated," Lord Everleigh said.

Sophie realized after a moment that he was studying her, waiting for a reaction. "It is very warm today." She attempted a smile. "I think perhaps we should return home."

Lord Everleigh held her gaze, and his eyes hardened. "Warm? I believe it likely to rain." He spoke over his shoulder without taking his eyes off her. "Duncan, stop the carriage, and close the top."

The coachman climbed down and closed the roof of the carriage, avoiding any glance at the ladies.

"Rain, I hardly think so," Prissy said. "The sky is clear."

"Exquisitely so," Mimi agreed, frowning at the closed roof.

"Lady Priscilla, you may be right after all," Lord Everleigh said. He leaned through the window as the driver fastened the last latch. "Duncan, let us take the longer route today."

"Yes, my lord." The carriage driver climbed back into his seat and urged the horses forward.

Lord Everleigh sat back and gave Sophie another smile, but instead of lazy arrogance, his look was pure evil. *He knows.*

Terror spiked through Sophie. She darted a look at the carriage door, then along the road for someone to call out to.

He cleared his throat and pulled back his jacket just the slightest bit so only she could see the pistol holstered beneath his arm. He looked pointedly at her sister and grandmother, then leaned back casually in his seat, his smile growing.

The driver pulled at the reins, veering the carriage off onto a side lane.

CHAPTER 21

JONATHAN CEASED HIS PACING AROUND the hospital and returned to the ward where Constable Merryweather lay.

In the hours since they'd arrived, Sergeant Lester had not left the younger man's side, but he had certainly made himself comfortable. His chair leaned back on two legs, and his head rested against the wall, his mouth open and snoring. His feet were stretched out, ankles crossed and propped on the bed next to the patient.

Jonathan sat in the wooden chair on the other side of the bed and pulled out the folder Lady Sophronia had given the sergeant. He brushed his fingers over Tom Stackhouse's name, written in precise letters, and vaguely wondered who had written them. Possibly the same person who'd compiled all the information inside. Whoever had done it was almost as skilled as Sergeant Abner at finding documents others had no idea existed.

Inside the folder was a copy of Tom's police force application, along with various articles in which he was mentioned as an investigator on a particular case or that documented hearings he'd testified in. One report listed his different addresses over the years, another his birthplace and parents' names. A letter recommending Tom's promotion to detective was signed by Warren Pembroke, the man who was now the assistant commissioner of the London Metropolitan Police force. Apparently Pembroke and Tom had worked cases together in the early days of the Force.

All of it was interesting—documentation of a successful police career—but Jonathan shuffled those pages to the back and looked over the paper he'd read dozens of times since he'd come across it in the folder.

From what Jonathan could tell, it was a collection of notes made by a news reporter who had conducted an interview with Tom. For what purpose the reporter had decided to interview a police detective Jonathan had no idea. Perhaps that would have been made clear when the article was published. But seeing the date on the notes, he knew why it never was. The notes were taken two days before Tom had died.

One particular passage stood out above the others. In the reporter's scrawling writing, he'd scribbled down a quote from Tom.

> *The police force is in good hands with the younger generation of men rising through the ranks. Those lads are braver and more intelligent than we ever were. One in particular I've known since he was a scrawny orphan scraping out a living, gathering cigar butts and rewrapping the bits of tobacco to sell. Used to give him peppermints. Taught himself to read, he did. And when he joined the force—must have been the proudest day of my life. We're a family, you see, the police. Look out for each other.*

Jonathan closed the folder, hearing Tom's voice in his head. *"We're a family."* Reading the quote was like opening an old wound and pouring healing balm inside. Each time, it hurt. But the pain lessened with every reading, and the peace it brought was a feeling Jonathan would never tire of.

Guilt and anger had burned inside him for so long, but Tom's words softened them into something warm. Jonathan had considered himself alone in the world and thought he always would be. He'd kept people at a distance, fearing their rejection or pain at inevitably losing them. But when he considered Tom, Sergeant Lester, Merryweather, the officers at H Division . . . Sophie . . . they had all cared about him in spite of his resistance. Was that family?

Merryweather groaned, shifting beneath the sheet.

Jonathan set the folder back on the floor and slapped the sergeant's feet off the bed, making the chair slam down.

The sergeant woke with a confused grunt, sticking his hands out to the side to regain his balance.

"He's awake," Jonathan said.

Merryweather blinked his eyelids slowly, as if they were heavier than he could manage.

Jonathan scooted his chair closer. "How do you feel, Constable?"

"Martha?" Merryweather muttered.

"It's us," the sergeant said. "Detective Graham and Sergeant Lester."

Merryweather's blinks sped up and his eyes peeked open. He squinted in the light before closing his eyes again. "I remember . . . I was shot, wasn't I?"

"Aye," Sergeant Lester said. "But Doctor Peabody said you'll heal."

"And Ned Tucker?"

"He didn't survive," Jonathan said.

Merryweather frowned. "I'm sorry to hear it." He shifted and gritted his teeth, stifling a groan.

Sergeant Lester stood. His face was worried. "I'll send for the doctor." He rushed to open the door and hailed a nurse.

Jonathan worried the constable would fall back to sleep. "Constable, the doctor can give you something for the pain. But before you go back to sleep, think back. Do you remember what Mr. Tucker was going to tell us? About the men he saw?"

Sergeant Lester returned to his seat. "Doctor's coming."

Merryweather tried to open his eyes again. "Something about a necktie. One of the men wore a large pin—a ruby, I think." He grimaced.

Jonathan could see it was painful for the man to speak, but this could be their only chance to learn anything new for hours. "Anything else?"

Merryweather grimaced again. "No. I'm sorry, sir."

"Lie back, Constable," Jonathan said. He couldn't help but feel disappointed that the clue they'd hoped for had turned out to be worthless. He rubbed his eyes, discouragement making him tired.

"Sir," Sergeant Lester said. His eyes were bright, and he leaned forward, looking excited. "The killer is a Casanova."

Jonathan stared at the constable, having no idea what his words meant. "What did you say?"

"The West End Casanovas." Sergeant Lester snapped his fingers. "Miss Propriety writes about them in her society column. The Casanovas always wear a ruby tiepin. It's a sort of status symbol." He touched his own necktie and gave a wise nod. "They are a very exclusive group, sir."

"How many are there? And who are they?" Jonathan asked. A small flame of hope lit. If the suspect list could be narrowed further . . .

"There are only five: Lord Ruben, Lord Meredith, Lord Everleigh, Lord Chatsworth, and Lord Benedict."

Jonathan raised a brow. All were peers—one an heir to a dukedom. Something tickled at the back of his mind, a thought he couldn't quite grasp. One of the names reminded him of something—but what? "And they are the only men in this entire city who wear a ruby tiepin?"

"I rather think so, sir. The accoutrement is quite well-known, and custom made. If another were to imitate it, they would seem to be pretenders, if you get my meaning."

Jonathan would never understand the thinking of the upper class. To claim ownership of a particular adornment seemed beyond conceited. But if it identified a suspect, he was all for it.

He rubbed the pocket watch fob between his fingers as he considered. If what the sergeant said was true—and Jonathan had no reason to believe otherwise—the murderer was one, or perhaps two, of five men. Five of the most powerful men in the country. Over the course of the ball, he'd been introduced to each of them, but what had he learned? Unfortunately, not much. Though they'd spoken, their conversation had been mainly about hunting, women, or the drudgery of balls in general. A few had discussed business ventures. Had any of them given a clue that could identify him as a killer?

Dr. Peabody came to check on Merryweather, and the men gathered their things to leave him to his patient.

Jonathan picked up the notebook and the folders, considering their next course of action as they left the hospital. He couldn't very well arrest the five men without cause. And a dead stable hand's testimony about a necktie bauble was hardly evidence.

The pair sat on a bench outside the hospital. He handed Sophie's notebook to the sergeant. "See what you can find in here," he said.

An idea occurred to him, and he flipped open the file from Sergeant Abner. He'd gone through the file a few hours ago, finding nothing of interest aside from city records and proposals for the building site.

Jonathan turned a page and found what he'd been looking for. *I knew I'd seen one of the names recently.* He poked the sergeant with his elbow. "See here. The Brookline Group made a proposal to Parliament two months ago, requesting a permit to build a railroad line through Spitalfields"—he studied the drawing, following the line—"and down to Wapping. They plan to reopen the Marylebone Tunnel beneath the Thames."

"A train beneath the river?" Sergeant Lester scoffed. "Impossible."

Jonathan stared at the map, running his finger along the rail line. "The proposed line would go through the workhouse building site and the Porky

Pie." He looked up as a thought occurred to him. "What if the sites where the bodies were discovered weren't random? If a neighborhood or a worksite is deemed too dangerous . . ."

"The government is more likely to agree to tearing it down," Sergeant Lester finished.

Jonathan flipped through the pages more quickly this time. He pulled out the document he was looking for, turning it for the sergeant to read. "The Brookline Group is a partnership with two owners: Hans Hofman and Lord Everleigh."

Jonathan tapped his foot against the floor of the police cab as he and Sergeant Lester rode toward Grosvenor Square. He felt the familiar weight of the badge on his chest and the warrant card in his pocket. Sir Dennington had been skeptical about the tiepin as evidence, but when he was presented with the timeline and the city records, he'd agreed there were just too many coincidences to overlook and that the suspects should at least be brought to the station to answer some questions.

The sergeant was going through Sophie's notebook. "Not one mention of Lord Everleigh at the lecture," he muttered, turning a page. He closed the book and twisted toward Jonathan, drumming his fingers on the cover. "Sir, do you think Lady Sophronia might have been telling the truth?" He grimaced.

Jonathan took the book, more for something to keep him from having to meet the sergeant's gaze than to do any actual reading. He opened it, recognizing Sophie's handwriting. She'd written each name neatly in a list down one side of the page, leaving room for notes in between.

"Maybe she *didn't* give permission for the article to be published," the sergeant continued.

Jonathan shrugged as if he'd not given Sophie's claim much thought—which could not be any further from the truth. At least his anger had dissipated, but the ache that had taken its place was so much worse. "That article nearly cost our jobs, Constable. It gave crucial police information to a murderer."

"Yes, but if she didn't mean to . . . shouldn't we at least give her the chance to explain?"

Jonathan offered the sergeant a peppermint and popped one into his own mouth. Of course the sergeant was right. But going back, apologizing, opening himself up to be hurt again . . . It was easier to be angry. He had to protect his heart.

The butler at Lord Everleigh's house told them his master was out paying calls for the afternoon. When pressed, he admitted he'd heard the gentleman directing the carriage driver to take him to Lady Priscilla's.

"I don't like that," Sergeant Lester said as they rode to Park Lane. "Don't want that man with Lady Sophronia."

Jonathan agreed fully, urging the driver to hurry. With Sophie's name on the article, he didn't trust any of the Casanovas with her.

When they arrived at Sophie's house and inquired after Lord Everleigh, Holloway gave an angry huff.

The reaction was more emotion than Jonathan had ever seen in the proper servant.

"Lord Everleigh took the ladies away two hours ago, Detective." His eyes tightened. "Said they were just going for a drive through the park." He shook his head. "Very rude to keep the dowager Lady Mather out so long in all this heat, if you ask me."

Lord Everleigh had taken Sophie's sister and grandmother in his carriage? In spite of his feelings of hurt, Jonathan could not leave without warning Sophie.

"Is Lady Sophronia at home, Holloway?"

The butler blinked and folded his hands together. "I beg your pardon, Detective. I was not entirely clear. Lady Sophronia is with Lord Everleigh as well."

A stone dropped in Jonathan's gut as cold spread through him. "You say they've been gone for two hours?"

"If you can believe it. A ride in the park indeed." Holloway frowned. "They should have returned an hour ago."

"She knows," Sergeant Lester said, his voice low and frightened.

Jonathan's heartbeat banged in his ears. He rubbed his eyes. "And *he* knows that she knows." Sophie must have figured it out. Of course she did. Why must that young woman be so blasted curious?

Sophie must have asked the wrong question, angered Lord Everleigh— angered *the murderer*—and now he had her. And based on his record, he wasn't likely to send her home with a stern talking-to. Everleigh had no reason to keep her alive and every reason to want her dead.

Jonathan clutched Sergeant Lester's arm as panic stole his thoughts. "Sergeant, where is she?" A murderer had Sophie—his Sophie—and he was helpless to save her.

Sergeant Lester winced. "We'll find her, sir."

"What's this?" Holloway asked. "What's happened to Lady Sophronia?"

"We can't search the whole city," Jonathan said, ignoring the butler. She'd already been gone for hours. Scenarios flashed through his mind, each more terrible than the one before. He darted a look at the door as if the answer would present itself. "Where would he take her?"

"Somewhere he wouldn't be seen," the sergeant said.

The men looked at one another, realizing at once where Sophie was.

"Quick, man!" Jonathan rushed for the door.

When they reached the police carriage, Sergeant Lester directed the driver to the station house.

"We haven't the time," Jonathan protested. The helpless feeling seizing his insides made him want to grab the reins himself and push the horses at a gallop. "Every moment she is with him—"

"Aye, sir." Sergeant Lester pulled open the carriage door, standing aside. "But if you've taught me anything, it's to follow procedure. We can't barge in there without support—not with Lady Sophronia's life on the line."

Jonathan scrambled into the carriage, his jaw so tight it ached. "Sergeant—" His voice cracked, and he pushed away his panicked thoughts, knowing he needed a clear mind if he was to help Sophie, and knowing they could already be too late.

CHAPTER 22

SOPHIE LOOKED AROUND THE BURNED-OUT room in the old workhouse. Long tables had once stretched across the space, but now most were broken or burned. Some were overturned, and others were stacked haphazardly against the wall, leaving a wide aisle down the center of the room between the two doors. A few chairs were spread around as well, but Mimi sat in the only one that was still functional. She held Dorrit on her lap, stroking the dog's fur to soothe the animal.

Light came from the gaping hole in the collapsed roof, filtering through dust particles and East London soot. The room was cast in an eerie gloom. Sophie had no way of judging the time, but she figured they had been at the worksite for over an hour.

Prissy stood in the center of the room, holding her skirts away from the burned furniture and walls and keeping her shoes away from the dirty puddles. She screeched whenever a rodent scampered past.

Lord Everleigh paced back and forth across one end of the room.

"Everleigh, how much longer must we stay here?" Prissy's voice was a whine. "It is so damp, and ash is on my skirts. I don't like it here at all."

"Just a bit longer." Lord Everleigh didn't look at her when he spoke. He glanced through the door, looking both ways, and went back to pacing.

Sophie focused on the exits, one at either end of the room, weighing their chances of escape. She believed she could make it alone, but she'd not leave her grandmother and sister behind with this madman. And that was something he obviously counted on. He was hardly bothering to watch them.

She considered calling out for help but would not while her sister and grandmother were within range of the man's gun. And besides, she thought that was exactly why Lord Everleigh had chosen this place. If she were to scream, her cries would likely go unheard. She leaned back against a dirty table, not caring about her dress, and considered another plan.

If the three rushed to the exit all at once, there was a likelihood that at least one would make it outside safely. She was certain one of them would be shot. And once the others were out, what would they do? They were directly in the center of the most dangerous area of the city. It wasn't worth the risk.

"But I want to go home." Prissy continued to whine. She crossed her arms and pouted. "Charlotte is hosting a card party this evening, and I must attend. And why are we in this horrible place anyway? You said we would stop for only a moment, and we've been here for—"

"Enough," Lord Everleigh snapped.

Prissy closed her mouth, her eyes wide in surprise at the typically composed man's show of temper.

"Do we wait for Hans Hofman?" Sophie asked, taking the attention away from her sister. She'd heard the carriage leave and suspected Everleigh must have a plan. Her fear had left her numb, and the calmness of her voice felt at odds with the shaking in her legs. She held tightly to the lip of the table on either side of her hips to keep her hands from trembling.

Lord Everleigh turned toward her, giving a sneer. "You're too clever for your own good, my lady."

"And what then?" Sophie decided to keep the man talking. Perhaps he would reveal something or let down his guard. "You plan to kill us? Leave our bodies around Spitalfields so nobody suspects a nobleman to be the culprit?"

Lord Everleigh took a few steps toward her, his mouth widening into a taunting smile. "Perhaps." He shrugged, fingering the pistol beneath his coat. "Or perhaps the discovery of three fine ladies, murdered in the streets of this blasted rookery, will be just the push parliament needs to grant permission for a railroad through this vile pit of filth."

"Everleigh!" Prissy gasped.

Mimi sniffed. "Really, sir. That is quite enough."

"Come, Sophie," Prissy said. "Let us wait in the carriage."

"Sit down, Lady Priscilla," Lord Everleigh said.

She looked around. "But it is filthy. I will not—"

He pointed the pistol. "You will sit down."

Prissy obediently slid back onto a table. She glanced at the others with an uneasy expression. "Everleigh, what are you playing at? I don't like it."

He stroked a finger along the gun's barrel. "Oh, my dear, it will only get worse from here."

Prissy's brows pulled together, and she held her lips tightly as if she were going to break into tears. She looked at Mimi and Sophie, wanting an explanation. "I don't . . ." She blinked, not knowing what to say.

"Do you want to tell her, my lady, or shall I?" Lord Everleigh said to Sophie.

"Prissy, Lord Everleigh is a murderer." Sophie spoke in a matter-of-fact voice, not wanting to give the man the satisfaction of glorifying his actions or give her sister fuel for the hysterics that were surely near to spilling out.

Mimi drew in a breath.

Lord Everleigh gave an extravagant bow.

"But . . ." Prissy looked at Sophie as if waiting for her to confirm this was all a joke. Seeing that her sister was serious, she looked at Mimi. "No. I can't believe it."

"You will," Lord Everleigh said. He gave a sneer, stalking toward her. "Very soon."

Prissy cowered back.

"Stop it," Sophie said.

He turned the pistol toward Sophie, moving in her direction. "Shall I? Shall I stop? Have I gone too far, my lady?"

Sophie knew he wished to frighten her, that he derived a twisted sort of pleasure from the power he held over them. She held her head up and didn't allow her fear to show.

"Sophie . . . ," Prissy said.

"Just do what he says, and remain quiet," Sophie told her. She didn't take her eyes from Lord Everleigh's pistol, staring at it in frozen fascination. She couldn't have moved if she wanted to.

Footsteps sounded, and Hans Hofman entered the room.

Lord Everleigh turned away, and Sophie's insides clenched. Her shaking started in earnest now.

Hans looked around the room with a horrified expression, his eyes growing wider as he took in the situation. "Vat is this, Everleigh? Vat have you done?"

"They know, Hans," Everleigh said in a calm voice, shrugging a shoulder and smoothing down his mustache with the tips of his fingers. "It can't be helped."

Sophie looked back to the other exit. Maybe while the two men were distracted, speaking to each other . . . She caught Prissy's gaze, motioning to the doorway with her eyes.

Prissy looked behind at the exit, then back to the men, shaking her head.

Mimi sat quietly on the other side of the room, petting Dorrit, but her face was ashen. Her composure was an act to keep her granddaughters calm. She was nearer to the exit than any of them.

Perhaps Mimi could make an escape. Sophie caught her grandmother's eye, tipping her head toward the doorway.

Mimi gave a small shake of her head. She'd not leave her grandchildren behind.

Hans scrubbed his palms over his cheeks. "Everleigh, it must stop. We cannot keep . . . I cannot." He motioned to the structure overhead. "I agreed only to burning the building. Nobody vould get hurt; ve vould have our railroad." He lowered his hands and looked at the women. "But this. This has gone too far."

"Do you want to hang, Hans?" Lord Everleigh spun the revolver in a slow rotation on his finger, watching it with a casual air. "I hear the long drop snaps a man's neck almost immediately, but not always. Then, of course, you must slowly suffocate as your brain is deprived of blood and oxygen."

Hans's already pale face looked even whiter. "No. Of course not."

Sophie caught Prissy's gaze and darted her eyes to the exit again. *Run!* She tried to will the word from her thoughts to her sister's. *Go now!*

"They are the only ones who know." Lord Everleigh waved the pistol toward the women. "The police will never figure it out. This is the last of it, Hans. It ends today."

Hans glanced at the ladies and back to his friend. After a moment he gave a reluctant nod.

Sophie's blood went cold.

Everleigh smiled, patting Hans on the shoulder. He turned to face them. "Now, where to begin . . ." He glanced at his companion, spreading his hand as if being generous. "Would you care for the honors?"

Hans still looked sickened, but he clenched his jaw and nodded, looking resolved to what he must do.

Sophie tensed, ready to fight or run.

Hans looked between the women, and his gaze settled on Prissy. He started toward her.

Prissy scrambled back over the table, falling in her haste to escape. She fought against her skirts, struggling to her feet, and ran toward the door.

Hans chased after her, grabbing her by the arms.

Dorrit started barking.

Lord Everleigh started toward Sophie, but hearing the dog, he changed direction, veering toward Mimi and raising the pistol.

Mimi pulled the dog close against her chest.

Energy surged through Sophie. "Do not touch my grandmother!" She ran at Lord Everleigh, grabbing on to his extended arm.

She'd hoped to pull off his aim or disarm him, but he was much stronger than she'd believed. He twisted and gave a shove that sent Sophie backward. She crashed into a broken chair and hit her head. Something sharp dug into her ribs, and for an instant, she couldn't draw a breath. She shook her head at the haziness and tried to get to her feet, the instinct to protect her family stronger than the pain. But her movements were sluggish.

"Sophie, stay down!"

She must be imagining Jonathan's voice. He couldn't really . . . She shook her head again, feeling dizzy as she pushed herself up to a sitting position to lean back against the wall. The room was blurry, but she could still make out the details.

At least half a dozen blue uniforms of police officers filled the doorway. Sergeant Lester jerked Hans away from Prissy, and Jonathan crossed the room toward Sophie at a run.

She let her eyes close as relief made her limp. *We are saved.* She breathed out a heavy breath.

Hearing a shout, her eyes flew open in time to see Lord Everleigh spin, his pistol aimed at Jonathan.

The constables drew back.

Jonathan stepped to the side, blocking Sophie.

Lord Everleigh grabbed Prissy, holding an arm around her waist and pulling her toward the exit. He turned the gun toward Sophie's sister. "You will let me through."

The constables moved aside, leaving the exit clear.

Lord Everleigh frowned, apparently not liking his chances of walking through the police, even with a hostage. He backed up, instead moving toward the other exit.

Prissy stumbled backward.

"Don't even think about moving." He jerked the pistol up in a demonstration that made the entire room flinch.

He's getting away! Sophie looked frantically around the room, but nobody dared charge the man while he held a gun to Prissy's head.

Lord Everleigh backed up farther, a conceited curl on his lip.

Prissy was utterly terrified. Her face had flushed, and tears rolled down her cheeks. She made a whimpering noise.

From the far side of the room, Dorrit barked.

And just like that, Sophie knew what to do. Her heartbeat sped up, and she focused. The timing must be just right.

Lord Everleigh took another step back.

Now. Sophie whistled. "Biscuit, Dorrit," she called in a sing-song voice.

Dorrit leaped from Mimi's lap and ran toward her, moving behind Lord Everleigh's feet just as the man stepped backward.

The small dog was just near enough to make him lose his footing. Lord Everleigh stumbled, spreading out his arm to keep his balance.

The instant the gun was no longer aimed at Prissy, Jonathan pounced, tackling the man to the floor. He wrestled the pistol from his hand.

Sergeant Lester handed off his prisoner to another officer and sprang forward to catch a swooning Prissy before she hit the ground.

Mimi snatched up Dorrit, cooing over the confused animal as the police shackled the criminals.

An instant later Jonathan's arms were around Sophie.

She wept against his shoulder, shaking and clinging to him as tightly as she could.

"You're safe now, Sophie. It's over."

"He . . . Lord Everleigh . . ."

"He can't hurt you now." He shifted, sitting on the ground and pulling away to examine her head. His eyes tightened as he moved the hair from her forehead. "This should be treated by a doctor." He drew out a handkerchief from his jacket and pressed it to her head.

"Mimi? Prissy?"

"They are unharmed."

Sophie felt supremely foolish, but she could not stop weeping. Her eyes and nose were dribbling, and she was making a hiccupping sound.

Jonathan pulled her against him, his arm tightening around her. "That was brilliant, you know," he said. "Calling the dog."

His voice rumbled in his chest beneath her ear. She nestled closer, wincing at the pain in her side but not wanting to pull away and see what caused it.

"Sir, the suspects are on their way to H Division. And the other ladies wait in the carriage." Sergeant Lester's voice sounded above Sophie's head. "I thought perhaps Dr. Peabody should have a look at 'em before they return home."

"Very good, Sergeant," Jonathan said.

"And Lady Sophronia?" the sergeant said. "She is well?"

"She will be," Jonathan said. "Tend to the other women, Sergeant."

The sergeant's footsteps grew fainter as he moved away.

"Come along, Sophie. It's time to leave now," Jonathan's voice rumbled again.

Her weeping had finally stopped, but she did not feel fully settled. "Will you hold me just a bit longer?" she asked, feeling silly at the request.

Jonathan laid his head on hers, careful to avoid her wound, and drew her closer against him. "As long as you'd like."

CHAPTER 23

SIR DENNINGTON SAT BACK IN his chair, a pleased smile on his face. Jonathan, Sophie, and Sergeant Lester had just finished delivering their report. The three sat across from the chief inspector, Sophie between the two men.

Two days had passed since they'd apprehended Lord Everleigh, Hans Hofman, and Duncan the carriage driver and charged them with the murders, but the business was far from finished.

The men would be granted a trial, and they would naturally hire the best barristers in the country to defend them. Jonathan didn't believe it would do any good. Not when three members of Lord Mather's household would give testimony. He frowned, not liking the idea of the ladies having to recount their experience in front of a magistrate. But all three of them had insisted, and if there was one thing he'd learned, it was that arguing with Sophie, Lady Priscilla, or the Dowager Lady Mather was a futile endeavor.

Jonathan glanced at Sophie. Though she claimed to be perfectly recovered, he knew her wounds still pained her. The puncture in her side from the broken corset bone in particular caused her to wince when she shifted, and her eyes still seemed a bit unfocused. Doctor Peabody had told her to expect headaches for at least a few weeks.

Seeing her in pain, Jonathan couldn't help but feel glad the H Division holding cells had been so crowded the past days as they'd welcomed their newest occupants. The other prisoners hadn't been impressed in the least with the men's credentials, and Jonathan imagined sleepless nights as Lord Everleigh and Hans Hofman worried what might happen should they fall asleep. He hoped the pair of murderers, especially Lord Everleigh, had found his new cell at Newgate equally unforgiving.

"The commissioner was very pleased with your strategy," Sir Dennington said. "Flushing out the killers through a newspaper article. He thought the idea ingenious."

"And I hope you did not correct him," Jonathan said.

"I did not." Sir Dennington smiled. "I expect you'll be promoted, Detective. And you as well, Sergeant." He folded his hands across his belly, looking extremely pleased. "After my own advancement, of course."

"That is wonderful," Sophie said. She patted Sergeant Lester's hand. "You are both very deserving of the recognition." She turned to Jonathan, wincing when she twisted, and reached to pat his hand as well but pulled back, her cheeks going pink.

"And you, Lady Sophronia," Sir Dennington continued. "Your help in this case was invaluable. And apprehending the murderers—"

"As I said, sir, my assistance was very minimal. You have an excellent police force."

He nodded. "That we do, my lady."

Once the interview was finished and Sophie had bid a fond farewell to Sergeant Lester, Jonathan accompanied her outside to the waiting carriage.

The two hadn't spoken since he'd brought her to the hospital two days earlier, and the air between them felt heavy with words unsaid. Words he didn't know how to say. Feelings he couldn't acknowledge. He felt a sick ache and a frustration at his own fears. Better just to let it end than risk being hurt. The investigation was over, and he had no reason to contact Lady Sophronia again. Was this goodbye?

Standing back as the carriage driver opened the door, Jonathan took Sophie's hand to help her climb inside.

But Sophie paused before getting in. She turned, holding her other hand against her side as she did. "Detective, I wonder if we might walk for a moment."

"In Whitechapel?" He glanced along the narrow street, at the crowds moving between vendors. Horse leavings and garbage piled in the gutters, and the smell of bodies and animals in close quarters hardly created the atmosphere for a pleasant afternoon constitutional.

"Perhaps we might find a cart with meat pies?"

Jonathan spread his hand in the direction of the food vendors.

Sophie gave instructions for her driver to wait.

As they made their way through the crowds, Jonathan kept a hand at the small of her back and an eye on the bag hanging from her elbow. Though it was still day, the area was not safe for a young woman in a costly gown.

They purchased meat pies and continued on, walking in silence as they ate. He didn't have a route in mind, but after a few moments, Jonathan realized they were walking toward Spitalfields and steered her in the direction of the Porky Pie. At least there, they could speak in relative privacy. He sensed she had something to say, and perhaps he did as well. If he could only find the courage.

Finishing his meat pie, he crumpled the greasy paper into a ball. His hands were sweaty as he tried to put words in his mind to the things he wanted to tell her. They arrived on Wentworth Street, and Sophie glanced up the road. "Oh, I know where we are."

"Perhaps a drink?" he suggested.

Sophie nodded, breaking off a piece of her pie's pastry and biting into it.

Luckily the pub was quiet before the evening rush. Jonathan and Sophie sat at the same table they had the first time they'd come. That night seemed an eternity ago, when in reality it had been only a week. The server with the scarf around her hair brought their drinks, and once she left them alone, Sophie set down the last of her pie.

Jonathan handed her a handkerchief for the grease.

"Detective, I promise I did not authorize that article to be published." She rubbed the handkerchief on her fingertips.

"You do not need—"

"Please, let me explain."

He nodded.

"I left my notebook unattended. I should have been more vigilant with the information you entrusted me with. The newspaper editor found the pictures and my notes and printed them without my permission. I would never have done that to you, Jonathan."

The sound of his Christian name on her lips made him pause, his heart catching.

"The investigation means more to me than just information for an article." She folded the handkerchief on the table. "*You* mean more to me."

She didn't look up, but her cheeks darkened at the last sentence, turning her words into cannonballs, smashing holes in the barricades around Jonathan's heart.

"I should have known it was something like this," he said. He looked into his glass as he spoke. "I should have given you the chance to defend yourself instead of forming a conclusion and—treating you as I did."

"You felt betrayed," she said. "I do not blame you for your anger."

"I should not have lost my temper. It was inexcusable." *You mean more to me as well.* He thought the words but could not make himself say them.

They sat in silence for a moment. Jonathan took a long drink and set the glass back on the table. "Sophie, that folder you gave me—"

"I should not have been so presumptuous," she said. "It was no business of mine; I just wanted to know . . . to understand you better." Her cheeks were aflame.

"I thank you for it," Jonathan said. He reached for her hand. "It was . . . it meant . . ." He shook his head, frustrated that the words didn't sound right. "I needed it."

She smiled, squeezing his hand. "I'm glad."

He finished his drink and glanced at the window, not wanting to be in Spitalfields after dark. "We should go."

As they walked back, Sophie slipped her hand through his arm.

"Will Miss Propriety find a home at a different newspaper?" Jonathan asked.

"I think, unfortunately, she has written her last column."

"A pity. Sergeant Lester will be devastated to be deprived of his society news." They crossed to the other side of the road, away from the heavier traffic. "What will you do now?"

Sophie moved closer to him as they walked past a crowded cart. "I thought I might start my own newspaper—one that works *with* the police. Mimi has offered the funding, and I—I am considering it."

She sounded nervous and excited, and Jonathan was pleased that she wasn't giving up on her dream. "If anyone can do it, Lady Sophronia Bremerton can."

"And perhaps we will work together on another case."

"Out of the question. I will not even consider it for a moment." Jonathan shook his head, moving her between two stopped hackneys.

"I thought we were a good team, Detective Graham," she protested. "But perhaps next time you will let me wear the disguise."

"There will not be a next time." He spoke in a firm voice but had the distinct impression that she would somehow talk him into it.

"Well . . ." She stepped away from a noisy fish vendor waving a herring. "Either way, I do think we should work closely together in the future."

"My lady, you are not a detective. What will it take for you to realize how dangerous this work—"

She let out a sigh. "Jonathan?"

He turned, wondering what had made her stop, and was not prepared in the slightest when she grasped his face, rose up on her toes, and kissed him.

He recovered quickly, wrapping his arms around her, careful not to press against her injured side, and kissing her in return. Sophie's lips were warm and her body soft against his.

"We should work *closely* together," she whispered as the crowd jostled around them like a stream flowing around a rock.

He smiled against her lips. His last bit of resistance fell away, and he kissed her again. His heart was filled with promise and hope. Jonathan knew he was no longer alone. He had a family; he was cared for. Sophie loved him, and he could trust her with his heart.

EPILOGUE

Two months later

"To Sophie." Elizabeth raised her champagne flute.

"Hear, hear!" Vivian said.

"Yes, to Sophie," Dahlia said.

Hazel smiled, raising her flute as well.

Sophie grinned. "To the *Illustrated Police News*." She clinked her own flute against each of her friends' and took a sip. The bubbles blended with the excitement bursting inside as Sophie looked around the newspaper office.

Stacks of fresh paper sat on the reporters' desks, ready to be filled with delicious stories, beginning first thing tomorrow morning. The engravers' workspace was set at the front of the office with big windows and equipment handpicked by Mr. Potts, her chief illustration engraver. A desk in the far corner surrounded by filing drawers would be occupied by Mrs. Ingram, giving the paper the advantage of her quality researching skills.

Sophie's own desk, around which her friends were gathered, was in the back corner, where she could watch over everything, separated by a wall from the presses. The smell of machines and oil and ink and paper made her giddy.

"To think you did all this yourself," Dahlia said. "We are all so impressed, Sophie."

"We are indeed," Hazel said. "It is wonderful."

"I did have help," Sophie said. "All of this was funded by Mimi. And Vivian helped choose and supervised the assembly of the presses. And of course my connection with the police department . . ." She could feel the blush spreading over her cheeks.

"Connection," Mimi said, entering the room. "Is that what you young people call it nowadays?"

"You most certainly could have established a news office without a man," Elizabeth said, handing Mimi a glass. "But Inspector Graham isn't so bad. He does at least admire your mind and encourages you to reach your potential. In that he is miles ahead of most of his gender." She gave a sigh with an impertinent smile. "If you must be engaged, I suppose you could do worse."

"I believe there are other attributes he also admires about Sophronia," Mimi said. She winked. "And she about him. Or that is the impression I get from all the stolen kisses."

"Oh, stop it," Sophie said, blushing. She gave her grandmother a teasing swat. She wished all of her family were as delighted about the engagement as Mimi, but her parents were at least tolerant of the alliance. Jonathan had saved their family members from murder, after all. And it did help that her father had been fully reinstated into the hunting club. "Now, tell me, Elizabeth, how goes your search for a school?"

"The proposal still requires government sanction," she said. "And now it is all even more complicated with Everleigh's trial and the property disputes. I may have to look elsewhere." She frowned.

"I am sorry," Hazel said. She looked down. "Nursing school has been difficult as well, with my . . . attacks. And on top of it, Father has requested that I join him for Christmas in Spain."

"Oh my," Dahlia said. "How exciting."

Hazel gave a small smile, looking anything but excited.

Dahlia did not report on her progress at the steamship company, and Sophie was nervous to ask. With her father's health failing, her friend had taken on more of the business responsibilities, and the evidence of late hours and hard work showed in dark bags beneath her eyes.

Sophie wished more than anything that her friends could be as happy as she was. She set down her glass, held out her arms, and waved her fingers, asking for her friends and Mimi to come closer. Once they had all joined hands, she looked around the circle of women, and a rush of tears pushed at her eyes. "We can do this," she said. "The Blue Orchid Society is comprised of extraordinary women, and we will reach our goals together."

"Without a man's help," Elizabeth said, giving a wink.

"Unless absolutely necessary," Vivian said in a voice so quiet that Sophie thought she might have been the only one to hear.

"We are so delighted for you, Sophie," Hazel said, squeezing Sophie's hand. "Don't let our complaining ruin this happy occasion."

"We are friends," Sophie said, releasing the other ladies' hands. "And friends have the right to complain whenever needed." She held up her champagne glass. "To friendship, and to the Blue Orchid Society."

The others raised their glasses and repeated the toast.

Sophie could not stop her grin. If someone had told her three months earlier that she'd be a member of a cherished sisterhood and have her own newspaper office and a fiancé, she'd never have believed it.

Hazel turned to Vivian. "You haven't yet told us about the science exhibition. How goes your entry?"

The door opened before Vivian could answer. Sophie thought Vivian looked relieved at the interruption, and she made a note to inquire about it once they could speak alone.

Jonathan entered the news office with Merryweather, Martha Payne, Freddy, and Detective Lester.

Sophie's heart tumbled over as it always did when she saw him, and she hoped the reaction never ceased. She brought the tray of drinks to greet her friends. "Martha, Freddy, I am so glad to see you." Merryweather and Martha both took a glass, and Sophie didn't miss the way their hands touched or the glances between the pair.

She looked away, reminding herself to respect their privacy, although she and Jonathan often secretly speculated how long it would be before the pair of them finally married. "How goes school, Freddy?"

"Well enough." The boy reached for a glass, frowning when Sophie lifted the tray out of his reach.

"Freddy is one of the brightest lads in his class." Merryweather ruffled the boy's hair and put his hand on Freddy's shoulder, giving a proud smile. "His teacher said she's rarely seen a child learn to read so quickly."

Freddy gave a pleased smile at the praise but hid it away quickly.

Sophie smiled. "And I am happy to see you as well, Sergeant Merryweather. Congratulations on your promotion."

Detective Lester stepped forward and handed Sophie a box wrapped in colored paper. It was close to the size of a gentleman's hat, and a piece of twine wound around it, tied at the top.

"Oh." Sophie handed the tray to Mimi and took the box. "What is this?"

Detective Lester scratched the back of his head, looking extremely uncomfortable. "Just a little somethin'."

"A gift," Jonathan clarified. One side of his lips jumped like he was suppressing a smile.

"How very thoughtful," Mimi said, handing Detective Lester and Jonathan each a champagne flute.

Sophie set the box on her desk and untied the twine. She pulled away the paper and lifted off the lid.

When she looked inside, she let out a squeal, but realizing what she was seeing, she turned the sound into an excited cry. "Oh my—it is perfect!" She reached inside and pulled out a wooden platform that held a stuffed mouse sitting at a desk. The mouse wore a gown and flowery hat and held a notebook. A miniature pencil sat on the desk next to a pile of papers.

"It's *you*, my lady!" Freddy said. "If you was a mouse."

Sophie set the display carefully on her desk and embraced Detective Lester, kissing his scruffy cheek. "I cannot imagine a more thoughtful gift."

The man's face went beet red.

Mimi's friends arrived, and while the older women and the younger fussed over Detective Lester and his creation and toured the office, Jonathan pulled Sophie away from the others.

He took the champagne flute from her hand and set both of their glasses on a filing cabinet, then pulled her to him. He cupped her chin, lifting her face and kissing her. "I could not be prouder of what you've done, Sophie."

"I haven't done anything yet." She nestled against him, resting her head on his shoulder. "We haven't even put out one paper."

His arms went around her. "But you will. And before long, the *Illustrated Police News* will be a must-have for every morning breakfast table."

"Right between the crumpets and butter balls," she proclaimed.

"And many a butler will burn his fingers ironing flat your pages."

Sophie laughed. She pulled back, putting her arms around his neck. "That will be the true sign of success. Here's to marmalade stains and burned butlers."

He kissed her, his lips warm and tasting of peppermint. "And to my Sophie. The nosiest, loveliest, most confusing woman in all of London."

Sophie kissed him back until her heart felt like it would burst. The sounds of her friends and family talking and laughing surrounded her. And Jonathan—held in his arms, she felt whole and safe and endlessly loved.

AUTHOR'S NOTE

BEFORE I BEGAN THIS PROJECT, I spent some time considering what exactly I wanted to say. What is important enough to me that I'm willing to spend an entire series exploring it? What have I learned, or what do I want people to know or to reexamine in their own perceptions?

Still looking for a direction, I read quite a few books and watched some movies, and after a while, I began to notice a trend that was so contrary to my own experience that I was surprised I'd never realized it before. It involves how women's relationships with one another are portrayed in fiction, especially in romantic stories, and it's something I'm guilty of in my own writing. Women are often represented as rivals, either to provide competition for the main character in vying for the same man's affection or simply to give the main character someone to compare herself to. Other times, they are underdeveloped secondary characters the heroine confides in when she wants to talk about the hero.

Neither scenario quite reflects my own experiences. From the moment I was born, my mother, sisters, grandmothers, aunts, cousins, friends, and teachers cheered for me, encouraged me, and offered advice as I grew up. And now I still find myself surrounded by strong, intelligent, supportive women in every area of my life. Women are my friends, my mentors, and my heroes. I turn to them when I'm hurting or unsure or happy, and time and again, I've been bolstered and comforted and inspired by my own Blue Orchid Society. The women I know are complex and interesting and filled with wisdom. And that is what I hope to represent in this series—the sisterhood that's often overlooked in stories but so prominent in the lives of real women.

I love the time period of this story. The industrial revolution was changing the way people worked and lived. Florence Nightingale was instructing nurses, and women were being admitted to colleges and inheriting property. Colonies were pushing back against English expansion. The suffrage movement was growing in both England and America. Women were working as detectives in the Pinkerton Agency and starting to get credit as writers and teachers.

It feels like such an exciting time, and such a turning point in history, and I wanted my characters to be smack in the middle of it, navigating these modern developments and adjusting to a changing world.

So this book is meant as a tribute to them—the women who came before—and to us, the women who follow in their footsteps. And to the sisterhood that has marched along throughout history, often silently and unnoticed, and shaped our world.

ABOUT THE AUTHOR

JENNIFER MOORE LIVES WITH ONE husband and four sons, who produce heaps of laundry and laughter. She earned a BA from the University of Utah in linguistics, which she uses mostly for answering *Jeopardy* questions. A reader of history and romance, she loves traveling, tall ships, scented candles, and watching cake-decorating videos. When she's not driving carpool, writing, or helping with homework, she'll usually be found playing tennis. Learn more at authorjmoore.com and on Jennifer's social media.

Facebook: Author Jennifer Moore
Instagram: jennythebrave